POSSESSION

NOVELS BY

Kamala Markandaya

POSSESSION

A SILENCE OF DESIRE

SOME INNER FURY

NECTAR IN A SIEVE

POSSESSION

A NOVEL BY

Kamala Markandaya *Psued*

Kamala Taylor

The John Day Company
New York

© 1963 BY KAMALA MARKANDAYA

All characters in this novel are fictitious. Any resemblance to actual
people, living or dead, is purely coincidental.

Library of Congress Catalogue Card Number: 63–10224

IN MEMORY OF MY FATHER

Book I

1

$\mathcal{I}$ FIRST met Caroline Bell at a party in Madras given by an old friend of mine, an ex-ruler of one of the smaller states of India who now cheerfully eked out his existence on parties and a pension of seventy-five thousand rupees a year.

She was the first person I saw as I entered the room, partly because she was magnolia-white and stood out in a company that was divided between brown and brick-red, partly because of the attention she was already attracting with her English good looks which, a rarity in India, passed here for a transcendent loveliness. But perhaps she was beautiful in her own right as well.

She was one of the few women in evening dress: a full-skirted gown of some sort of cloudy material in a dark gray that was almost the color of her eyes, against which her skin was a dazzling white; and spun-silk hair, between silver and pale gold, hung down to her bare shoulders. In one hand she held a fruit cocktail, from which now and then she selected, with great care like a child, the bits she liked best to pop into her mouth—daring behavior which delighted the crowd by which, needless to say, she was surrounded.

I wondered who she was, feeling that I would quite like to meet her, though without any great urgency, in the vague way one woman feels about another, and thinking that probably I wouldn't because of the crush about her. A little later, however, I saw her looking at me, and then, even more to my surprise, she slid off the bar stool on which she had been elegantly perched, brushed off her admirers with great competence, crossed the floor—hardly noticing the dancing couples in her way—and came straight up to me.

"I hear you've written a book about a village," she said. "I'd like you to take me there sometime."

She spoke directly, with that clear forthrightness just this side of insolence which the English upper middle class use in speaking to anyone who is not English upper middle class, and which would be insolence but for their serene unconsciousness of it. It is not always endearing.

"Surely it isn't necessary," I said, "for me to take you. Anyone can go. It is merely a question of buying a ticket and getting on a train."

She stared at me in pure puzzlement, as hard to offend as (in all fairness) to realize she was offending.

"But of course," she said. "Of course you could do that. But you'd never get to know the right people that way, would you?"

It took my breath away. Who on earth were the "right" people in a peasant village whom one ought to get to know, and what could this English milady's interest in them possibly be?

"An Indian village isn't like an English one," I said carefully. "I've no idea who the right people might be."

"I'm sure you have," she interrupted me. "The people who make arak. It is made in the villages, isn't it? Or is that another piece of wrong information?"

4

I understood now. Madras was dry, held fast in the puritan grip of Prohibition. But the grip could be relaxed: the law was not barbarous, it took heed of foreign essentials for living and made due provision. Perhaps she didn't know, although this was usually the first point on which Europeans sought enlightenment.

"Your information is quite correct," I said. "But there is no need to brave an Indian village. You can get your liquor easily enough here in town, after a few formalities."

"Oh that farce, yes," she said impatiently. "I know all about that. I'm not interested. I can get all the liquor I want any day. It's the arak that's unique."

Just then our host bustled up, beaming, thoroughly and rather endearingly enjoying his own party although God knows there must have been thousands like it before, with a spate of saucy, witty small talk, and belated introductions.

Lady Caroline Bell. So that was who it was. I had heard about her a dozen times in the week I had been in Madras. She was rich, divorced, wellborn, said fashionable Indian society, concentrating upon essentials: really rich, in the English way, with landed estates and money in sterling; really wellborn, descended from a long line of men who had ruled India in the days of the British Raj, not loosely linked to a little-known lord by marriage to an umpteenth cousin—which was the more usual cause for awe in India; and very boldly and publicly divorced, with headlines in the papers. She had also been reputed to be beautiful, though no great stress had been laid upon this as far as I could recall, probably because even her astonishing good looks lost impact compared to her other spectacular qualities.

And this darling of the gods, blessed by fairy godmothers, wanted of all things arak. Well, I suppose if you've got most of the things anyone could possibly want, you've got to roam farther and farther, like an animal in search of the salt-lick that gives savor to living.

But to me arak wasn't exotic. It was a cheap, crude liquor, made without any refinements whatever by the poor for consumption by the poor, and I had seen it bring so much wretchedness to human beings that I had come to think of it as evil in itself, which of course it was not. I certainly was not going to encourage its manufacture. I was about to say as much when I realized that we weren't alone: our host was still there, bubbling genially away. I shut my mouth and waited, and then Caroline said in that clear, high voice of hers, "Jumbo, be an angel and run away, will you? There's something we want to discuss."

And Jumbo obediently flapped his wings and was off, his short, dapper little figure soon lost among the dancers, for he was called Jumbo not because of his size, but because it was the custom for people of his class to be given nicknames partly because of the English upper-class predilection for them, partly for the convenience of their tongues, so that Bingos, Beppos, Binkies and Roys abounded in the luminous upper strata of erstwhile British India. A variation of this process had filtered down to me too: in Jumbo circles instead of my given name of Anasuya I was always called Suya, and a further diminution to nice sensible Sue was only avoided by the most strenuous resistance on my part.

"He is a pet, isn't he?" said Caroline with brisk affection, and to me: "Well?"

"Well," I repeated, "I'm not going to help you to your arak. It's foul stuff, it's illegal to get hold of, and I don't want to feel responsible for what it does to you."

"Why," she said, gray eyes wide with interest, "what does

it do to you? Blind you? I thought only methylated did that."

It came to me then that the havoc wrought was on under-nourished bellies, on the bare-bone living of impoverished peasants. On the wealthy well-fed like this woman—like any of us in the room, for that matter—it would result in no more than a rather rich hangover. Moreover, I couldn't help warming to the idea of helping some industrious peasant, laboring over his illicit stills, to a larger return for his efforts than he could ever hope to wrest from his own meager fellows. So I said, "Arak doesn't blind you, as far as I know. And I've changed my mind. I'll take you where you can get some if you're still interested."

She didn't seem surprised that I should suddenly change my mind; perhaps people invariably did, for her.

"Good, that's settled," she said. "When shall we go—tomorrow?"

"Yes, if you've no engagements."

"I'll put those off," she said cursorily. "Shall we meet at the Club?"

"I'd prefer the station. At nine o'clock."

"Nine o'clock Indian time?"

"Nine o'clock standard, anybody's time."

And so I made superhuman efforts and got to the station at nine, and there she was, the living English legend, punctual to the minute, wearing jodhpurs tailored in Jodhpur for all I know, so beautifully cut and finished were they, and a wild-silk shirt, and carrying an elegant pigskin case in which, presumably, to haul away the arak. And three hours later, hot and dusty from train ride and two-mile walk, we were seated in the hut of the village headman, on whom I had thought it politic to call, drinking his tea.

After the courtesies were over—and this took some time—I ex-

plained why we had come, and what the English lady wanted;
and the headman, who had the same beautiful directness of
approach as Caroline, said, "She is bizarre."

"What does he say?" asked Caroline.

"That you're very welcome," I said.

"I expect he said I'm dotty," said Caroline.

"I hope she's got a good head," said the headman.

"I'm sure she has," I said.

"Don't want any trouble," said the headman.

"What did he say?" asked Caroline.

"That he'll be delighted to help you," I said.

"I'm sure he's wondering if I'll pass out," said Caroline. "Tell
him not to worry, I won't."

I translated, it seemed unnecessarily, for the headman was
grinning away as if he understood. Quite possibly he did: when
people don't understand each other's language some sort of
sixth sense begins to work, making speech superfluous.

After this, and the courtesies of leave-taking, we made for
the arak huts—unaccompanied of course, for the virtuous headman would have no hand in illicit deals, but supplied with
explicit instructions on how to get there, and provided with the
open sesame. Presently we spotted the huts, nestled in a salu-
brious and concealing grove, and jogging along the path a solitary
toddy-tapper, across his shoulders a flexible lath from which
hung the open foaming toddy pots, toddy-froth and toddy
slopping over their rounded earthenware bellies at every step.
The smell of fermentation hung in the air—pungent, faintly
sick and sweet. Caroline turned to me: "We're there, aren't
we?"

Her whole face was alight, that well-bred, casually charming
and unexceptionable mask, which was all I had seen in the three

or four hours I had known her, broken down at last into something that was real.

"Yes," I said. "I hope you won't be disappointed."

And indeed, for the first time, I really did care a little, now that she was more human than masked dummy, whether she was disappointed or not.

We went inside the first of the huts, and there, after some preliminary ice-breaking, I left her, for women and liquor are international, their purchase and sale get along well enough in sign language; and moreover I knew she was safe, for the headman's powerful if invisible mantle very adequately covered both of us. Then I went off to look at some paddy fields, whose melting green I find extremely restful after the tar and macadam of cities, and looked at them until a scraggy villager appeared, prodding before him a still more scraggy bullock, which depressed me and hopelessly altered the view, so that I remembered I had promised Caroline to return in an hour and now it was getting on for two. I hurried back, but she was gone from the arak huts. I went out and to the village and asked if anyone had seen her, and the trouble was not that no one had seen her: everyone had, but she had chased them all away and nobody knew where she now was. With imperious efficiency Caroline had ensured her own privacy.

I hung about for an hour, fretting but not unduly worried—you can scour the world and not find anything as mild as a South Indian village; and presently up came a diminutive child, panting, to say he knew where the English lady was and he would lead me to her for a consideration. Here the headman intervened to box the child's ears. "What do you think she is— a tourist?" he cried. "Now take her to the lady and don't let me hear any more about baksheesh unless you want to feel the flat of my hand again." And the good deed well done he turned shining to me, one cupped palm edging forward to indicate that payment of baksheesh to urchins was one thing, a recognition of services rendered by elders quite another. What it meant, of course, was that I paid twice: once to the elder and once to the youngster (when we were on our way and out of sight); but the youngster gave value for money.

2

"NOW how much farther is it?" I asked him tartly. "You said ten minutes' walk and we've been walking ten minutes."

"We are already there," said the brazen child. "You see that hill? Your friend is there, a little way round it."

He pointed to a broken line of hills—more humps in the land than a true hill ridge—their outlines blurred by distance.

"Impudent jackal," I said. "I shall not stir another step. I shall sit here and you shall bring my friend to me—always supposing she is there, which I doubt."

"She is certainly there," said the child, with assurance. "I took her there myself."

"Then you can bring her back."

"If I go near again she will thrash me," he answered. "She has a stick. I will not go."

And I could not budge him.

"What did you take her into that wilderness for?" I asked irritably. "Are you mad? What is there to see in that pile of rocks?"

"I was leading her to the next village," he answered sullenly.

"It lies just beyond those hills. They make rice wine there, and she wished to taste it. . . . But on the way she sees this simpleton and sits down with him and that is the end of it, she will neither go forward nor come back with me."

"A simpleton? A man?" I could feel my scalp prickling, I castigated my earlier sanguinity.

"No, no, a boy from the village. A goatherd. He is always there."

He said no more and we walked on, and so I was wholly unprepared for the tableau Caroline presented. She was sitting in a mud-walled shelter precariously erected on the lower slopes of the hill my guide had indicated. Her head was bent, her hair spilling forward so that I could not see her face, in an attitude of concentration as deep as that of the goatherd next to her. He was in rags, smelling a little of his goats, which grazed unheeded farther up the hill slope, as oblivious of them and of us as was Caroline. Both of them were poring over the welter of color at their feet—saffron, vermilion and carmine, indigo, madder, ochre and cobalt—assembled in a strange and outlandish flotilla of containers: pots and pans and jars, broken saucers, seashells and coconut-shell halves. The three walls behind them were brilliant with color. On the floor, like a witch's caldron, was a cured, blown-out gourd, splashed and streaked with the pigments that had been mixed in it, with reds and yellows predominant—the same colors with which the goatherd's rags and Caroline's jodhpurs were stained.

For seconds I simply stood there, recording what I saw but totally unable to interpret. Then I suppose I must have made some sort of sound, for Caroline looked up. Her face was glowing, with that brightness it had worn on the threshold of arak. I thought she might be drunk—her breath smelled of it—but her voice was perfectly clear.

"Look," she said. "He paints. He's got nothing, nothing of

anything that he ought to have but he can paint. Can you see? *Do* you see?"

I could see, of course: what I did not know was if those gaudy effusions were mere daubs of color—child's play—or if it was painting; and somehow I could not believe, here in this semiwilderness, that it could be the latter. Then the child who had brought me—who had kept himself well in the wings all this time, mindful of the cudgel which still lay threateningly within easy reach of Caroline—began a restive hop in the background, though he still kept his distance, and his impatience communicated itself to me. After all, I had gone a good deal out of my way to help this Englishwoman, and I felt it was a bit cavalier to be asked to stand about admiring her chance discoveries.

"I think we'd better get back," I said abruptly. "It's late afternoon. I think you've rather lost count of time."

"And Val?"

"*Val?* Is that his name?"

"Valmiki."

"He'll stay here of course."

Caroline rose to her feet, brushing various colored powders from her clothes. "Of course not," she said. "It would be criminal. He must come away with us now, at once. He's wasted here."

I said, "Do you mean to Madras?"—for that was as far as my imagination would carry me.

"To Madras!" she repeated, staring at me in wonder. "God no. To Paris. Either Paris or London, I can't quite decide which."

She spoke without the slightest hesitation in speech or manner, as if she really expected him simply to get up and walk away from it all—all the life he had ever known—and into some new world she was shaping for him. There was not even a pause to consider whether he would like to or not; nor any recognition of him as a human being, with human ties.

"You forget," I said. "He may have a family. He may not want to leave them. They may not want him to leave."

"We'll ask them," she said briskly. "Let's go. You can ask them for me."

"You can ask them yourself," I said.

"Do you mean do my own dirty work?"

"I didn't say that."

"I think it's what you meant."

"I meant I was not going to help you," I said. "This boy's a human being, even if he's a goatherd and a simpleton. He's not a toy, to be picked up now and discarded when something else takes your fancy."

"Discard him?" she said. "Do you think I would?"

"I don't know," I said, furious by now, "but I'm not going to take a chance. I'd just like to remind you that what you wanted—so badly you were willing to drag both of us into this wilderness—was arak. You've got it now and that's as far as I'm willing to go."

She did not answer at once but went over to the pigskin case, dumped on its elegant side near scraggy bush and bird-droppings, flicked up the clasp, extracted the bottles with which it was bulging and emptied them one by one into the ground. When the last of the fizzing liquid was gone she turned with something like satisfaction.

"There," she said. "That's how much arak meant to me. But the boy's real. I'm not going to let him throw himself away here. You're not going to either."

I said, "I'm going now. Will you come?"

"No. I'm staying."

"Here?"

"Yes. I don't want to lose Val."

"You're not *likely* to!" I said, exasperated. "He's here all day and every day. I suggest you come back now with me to the village—"

"No. I'm going to his village. I must go there to get in touch with his family. There's bound to be someone who speaks English, isn't there?"

"If you're lucky, yes. But if you do go you go under your own steam."

"Yes."

"It'll be entirely your responsibility."

"Yes."

During all this acrimony the goatherd had remained a little apart, neither with us nor with the child guide. Now he came up to me—rags, goat smell and all—and said:

"What does the lady want? Is it to do with me?"

I turned to him, looking at him properly for the first time, realizing as I did so that whatever the villagers might think this was no simpleton standing before me, that their description was simply one of a variety reserved by any community for those of its unorthodox members who disturb its conscience. His eyes, deep-set, gray—exactly the color of Caroline's, I saw with a slight shock, though it looked different from the different skin setting—gazed steadily into mine. He held himself well—neither awkward, nor impudent, nor obsequious—the three commoner attitudes in Indian backwaters; and there was about him an air of stillness, like serenity, far removed from the dull stagnation of vacancy. Looking at him I was suddenly uneasy, wondering if perhaps Caroline was right, if all that he had labored on alone here on this stony hillside was more than mere child's play: suddenly anxious that, whether it were or no, he should not be uplifted too high, let fall too far, for he was neither old enough nor calloused enough to bear it.

"It is to do with me, isn't it?" he repeated, his disturbing eyes searching mine.

"Yes," I said. "The lady thinks all this is—well done. But it may not be so. Do you understand?"

"I understand."

"She wishes to speak with your family," I went on. "But you need not take her to them. It is only if you wish."

The unfairness of it tore at me, this asking of a child to take the future into his immature hands; but neither could I wrench it away in his name.

"Only if you wish," I emphasized.

The boy nodded—he seemed to understand.

"They are in the next village," he said clearly. "I will take her to them."

Then he did a curious thing. He went over to Caroline, who had been watching us intently all this time, took her hand and gently, briefly laid his cheek against it the way a dog will sometimes thrust its muzzle into your palm. It astonished me, I could hardly think what she could have done in so short a time to gain his affection; and then I realized that the few grains of admiration she had proffered might well be food and drink to him, after the simpleton's fare with which he had so far been fed.

Walking back with the morose child who had brought me—our palaver had cost him his evening meal, he said, but I was in no mood to recompense him; he need not have stayed—my earlier irritations revived. I promised myself that I would do nothing further to help Caroline, her preposterous affairs should remain her own. I would simply leave her and go away. But when we reached the village I remembered the fright I had had earlier, which had not been pleasant; and thinking of that, my imagination began etching out other disasters—remote, but not impossible. I could not quite forget, either, that this was not her country—in any sense. So once again I dug out the headman and consigned Caroline to his care.

The headman had his objections. He could not patrol sheep grazings to ensure the lady's safety. He had no jurisdiction over the neighboring village to which she intended to go. Why could I not take her away in the same way in which I had brought her?

"Because she won't come," I said. "She is negotiating for this goatherd."

He goggled. "In marriage?"

"Don't be so foolish!" I snapped. "He is fourteen—about half her age. And since when do ladies marry goatherds?"

"That is why I was astonished," he retorted. "What then does she negotiate?"

I gave some garbled version, and the headman said again, grimly this time, "The lady is bizarre."

In the end I wrung from him the promise that he would call on his counterpart in the next village and enjoin him to keep an eye on Caroline. And then, heartily tired of each other, we parted.

3

I RETURNED to Madras alone, believing that the rigors of rural living would soon drive Caroline back to town; or, if it did not, hoping that the waning of her latest enthusiasm assuredly would. A week went by, without my having come across her anywhere. I let another week go, brooding on her, on the boy, on what she was doing to gain her own way; and when she had not returned then, curiosity as well as anxiety drove me back to the village to see how she was faring.

She was faring, needless to say, extremely well. Wherever the British go, as the whole of the East knows, they live on the fat of the land, though the British themselves have no inkling of it. Simply by taking it for granted they have the hypnotized natives piling it onto their plates. So I was not really surprised to find Caroline parked in the headman's house—a brick-and-mortar structure, the only one of its kind in the village—while he and his family camped in a hut. The headman's wife sent in cooked meals. A maid and a washerwoman waited on her. And she had pressed into service, as interpreter, the village schoolmaster. She was more pleased about him than about any of her other cossets and comforts—of which, indeed, she scarcely seemed aware. I gathered the first few days of no English spoken had been almost too much for her.

"I was frantic," she said. "Just sitting there, you know, dumb, when there was something so important to say. I wept with rage—oh yes, literally. Val's parents were horribly upset."

"So you've actually got in touch with them."

"Yes of course," she said, looking puzzled. "That was the whole point of staying. I told you."

"I know," I said. "I wasn't sure you would—I rather hoped you wouldn't go so far."

"Why not?" she said, still puzzled, and then her face cleared. "Oh yes of course, you don't think anything of Val or his work, do you?"

"I don't know what to think."

"I do." She was supremely confident, born and brought up to be so, with as little thought of fallibility as a colonial in the first flush of empire, as a missionary in the full armor of his mission, dogged by none of the hesitances that handicap lesser breeds. "He's a born painter. I don't know where he gets it from, but he's got it. You haven't seen half his work yet."

"Enough to judge, if one had the knowledge."

"Knowledge," she said contemptuously. "One doesn't need knowledge! All one needs is half an eye—come and see."

She took me into the first of the three rooms of which the house consisted. I nearly gasped. Sprawled over all four walls was a monstrous vine, sprung from the realm of Jack's beanstalk, so proliferous was it with giant tendrils, enormous turgid fruit that hung like swollen bladders, leaves of violent green as large as platters, and the whole of it done in bold chalk.

"He did that in a week, working nights only," said Caroline with pride. "He loved doing it—he's never had so much free surface to work on before, do you know? I told him to go ahead, and that's what he produced. It's wonderful, isn't it?"

"I hope the headman thinks so."

"He's a vandal," said Caroline. "He says he's going to wash down the walls as soon as we leave. He can't be very sound, can he?"

We moved to the next room, and here on the floor was the same spread of paints and colors and containers I had seen on the hillside, but in even greater profusion. In one corner stood a pestle and mortar, used evidently for crushing pigments from the mixture of colors encrusted in the grain of the stone. In another, soused in a bowl of what I took to be some sort of oil base, were discolored, disintegrating pulps of several cactusfruit.

"It makes a splendid purple," said Caroline, prodding the ooze. "Some of these native dyes are really quite remarkable. They make a wonderful terracotta too, from crushed leaves. But of course none of it's practical, it takes far too long. When I've got Val away he won't waste his time as he has to here."

I followed her silently into the next room. This was bare except for two charpoys, one piled high with the headman's possessions and pushed unceremoniously against the wall, the other with a small pillow and Caroline's pigskin case on it.

"Look at this." She opened her case and handed me a sheet of paper—the cheap, yellowish kind on which village school primers are printed. On it was a drawing of a peasant in his middle years, sitting in his doorway looking out at his plot of land. It was a very rough sketch, with hardly any detail, yet there was something in the pose—the exaggerated outthrust of chest to ease the ache of long stooping, the hands hanging from the wrists as if nerveless at the end of long laboring, the permanent question mark in the furrows of the temporarily relaxed brow—that made the whole curiously poignant.

"That's Val's father," said Caroline. "You can tell it's good, can't you, simply by looking. Unfortunately he isn't very sound."

"Who?"

"The father."

"In what way?"

"He wants to keep Val."

"The boy's his son, after all."

"He's got seven others," said Caroline. "Three sons and four daughters that he can't even feed."

"It doesn't stop him having some feeling for this child."

"He doesn't see him from one day to the next," said Caroline relentlessly. "Val's the simpleton, useless on the land, useless at home, they keep him as far from them as possible. No. He's thinking of who'll look after his goats. Incredible, isn't it?"

It was, of course. Yet when I spoke to him—the original of that disquieting sketch—it seemed less incredible, and by the time he had finished speaking I had to grope for my own vanishing perspective.

"It is true what the lady says," he said haltingly, his peasant's hands knotting in the effort to find the unaccustomed words, his face working as he tried to grapple with a problem so grossly beyond his range of experience that it seemed like cruelty to set it before him. "If my son goes with her another must take his place, but I am not young, I need both my sons if the land is not to lie fallow. We could not afford that, being as many as we are. Yet I could not sell my goats . . . the seasons are not always kind, you understand, it would be foolish to rely only on one pot to fill one's belly."

All the time he spoke the other members of his family were nodding in agreement—the sons and daughters, home from the fields with the ending of daylight, his wife, even the two little girls, all of them endorsing everything that he said. Valmiki, alone, made no sign. He had already detached himself from his family and sat in line with us—with Caroline and me, denizens of a world which did not, quite, think a painter a simpleton fit only for goats; and with the schoolmaster, in temporary uneasy alliance with us because of his uncertain gift of two tongues.

The schoolmaster translated what had been said, laboriously, inaccurately. He was a conscientious man, intent on giving the service for which he had been paid. Even Caroline had not been able to ditch him.

"Tell him I'll compensate him for his son," said Caroline. "Say a couple of thousand rupees. Five thousand."

The schoolmaster recoiled, equating "compensate" with "pay," his mild soul balking at this buying and selling of human beings. Nevertheless, dutifully, he translated. I intervened, as gently as I could.

"Not pay for the boy. She means to compensate you for the loss of his services . . . enough for you to pay some other lad to mind your flock."

"Five thousand rupees?"

"Yes."

The man was wavering, at last giving way to forces that could, with such magical ease, dispose of Himalayan obstacles. It seemed so unfair, this tempting of a man, that I could hardly bear to look on. Then his wife broke forth, letting loose a torrent of words meant, I felt sure, only to drown her husband's agreement, for little of it made sense. By the time she had finished we were all silent, and having achieved her purpose she turned to me, quite calm now, and said she would speak with me alone, for we were of the same race and sex, and I would understand her feelings even if she could not utter them.

So we went outside, to the small paved square where the grain was threshed, and she said, "Is it true that the English-woman wants to take our son because of his skill with his hands?"

"Yes."

"*Only* because of that? Can that be true?"

"It is true."

"And she will have him taught?"

"Yes. Whatever he still needs to know."

"Give him food and shelter?"

"More than he has here."

She looked ashamed, hesitantly explained away her guilt: "For he was no help to us here, you understand . . . he could not do anything, and he would not be taught . . . just sat idle all day long while his brothers and sisters worked and all the village laughing at him . . . so in the end we bought the animals and he to shepherd them but he is no good even at that, they are forever straying. People say it is because his brain is addled. Do you think it could be so?"

"No," I said, "I am sure that is not so. He is different from other people, which is always difficult to understand."

"Yes," she said, smoothing and smoothing the same square

inch of threadbare sari, her face very tired and worn. "He has always been different from my other children, always so difficult, I do not know why . . . he has brought us nothing but shame and sorrow."

"Yet you will not let him go," I said.

"Because he is still my son!" she said. "Because I am still his mother and unless I am turned to stone I cannot put that from me."

She was crying. I turned away, thinking Caroline's instinct had been right, she had wanted simply to take the boy away, which might have been better than to demand this crucifying decision, a decision which they themselves, the hapless parents of this strangely endowed boy, might well have been glad to see taken from their hands.

The minutes ticked by, while I wondered how much longer Caroline could contain herself: but she must have learned patience even in the few weeks she had been in the village, for we were left undisturbed.

Presently as the gloom thickened the woman said, "This English lady—you know her well?"

"Not well. A little."

"And she will look after my son, care for him properly?"

"I think so. I do not know, but I think she will."

"Bring him to see us sometimes?"

"Perhaps. You must ask her that yourself."

"I have asked, she said she would if he wished it . . . it is just that it is a far country and she may not be able to bring him."

"She is a rich woman," I said gently. "She can travel when and how she likes and your son could be by your side in a day or two even though it seems a far country."

She pondered this, the slow thoughts reflected in her somber eyes, and at last she said, quietly, as if some peace had come with the decision: "Perhaps it is his destiny that she should come so far to seek him."

"Then you will let him go?"

"Yes."

"Your husband?"

"He has already decided," she said bitterly. "Did you not hear him? It was the money—it was too much for him. But it is always so, men are ever free and easy with that for which they have neither suffered nor labored."

The matter was settled then. We went inside, and Caroline must have known at once she had won for she put her arm around the boy, as it were taking possession of him in full view of his family. There were a few loose ends still to be tied, and when that was done we left—Caroline, the boy, the schoolmaster and I, with one small hurricane lantern to light our way across the inky black country and a tireless host of fireflies for company.

4

WE had meant to leave first thing in the morning; but when morning came the boy had other plans. There was the Swami, whom he must see before leaving the village; he could not possibly leave before this had been done. Who was this Swami, I asked. Oh, some holy man or other, answered Caroline impatiently and dismissively: a man she hadn't seen, who appeared to be keeping an eye on the boy.

She turned on Valmiki fiercely: why hadn't he, she demanded, thought of it before, in all the days she had been cooling her heels in this backwater? He didn't know. Or last night? He didn't *know*, he repeated, and his fierce face and tousled hair, the sudden wildness in his strange light eyes, made it easier to understand why the villagers had grown uneasy about him. Where was this holy man? In the wilderness, needless to say, on the hillside of the sheep grazings, but on the farther slopes of a neighboring peak.

"It's quite out of the question," said Caroline, in the firm tone one uses to a child to indicate the final word has been spoken. She sat down on the charpoy and began to pack her suitcase, putting in the four ravikais she had had made to supplement her only shirt, the two pairs of handmade sandals, the sketch of Valmiki's father which the boy had given her, and various of the headman's possessions—a palmyra fan, a fly-whisk, some trichinopoly cheroots—which she thought would come in useful, selecting all these from the heap on the second charpoy. Then spruce and trim once more in jodhpurs and silk shirt, she announced she was going off to see the headman, and on her return Valmiki was to be ready to leave.

When she returned, a few minutes later—the farewell had been unwontedly brief—Valmiki was still standing where she had left him, rooted there like one of those sturdy thorn trees that seem able to ride the worst storm.

"We're going now," she said coldly. "Are you ready?"

It was a silly question. Provided his spirit was willing Valmiki could have left at any time, he had nothing to pack—not so much as a toothbrush; and as for his work, most of it was on rock slabs and mud walls which a pack mule could not have transported. Nevertheless I put the question.

"No," said Valmiki, plain and distinct. It was one of the first English words he had learned—Caroline had taught him.

"Come along," said Caroline firmly, moving toward the door.

"No," said Valmiki.

"Oh, come *on!*"

"No."

I said to Caroline, "Can't we go and see this holy man and get it over?"

"No," said Caroline.

"It might be quicker."

"No."

"It would be better than hanging about here another day."

"No!"

It was Caroline who broke the brassbound silence that followed.

"Tell him," she said to me, "he is to come at once and I don't want any more argument."

"No," I said.

"*Tell* him."

"There's no point."

"Oh Christ. Why not?"

"Because I don't think it would do any good."

"Well just remind him I'm his guardian now and he is to do as I say," she said furiously. "You can do that, can't you?"

I did; and when I had finished the boy said scornfully, "She has not bought me. She has only compensated my family for the loss of a laborer."

In a way I couldn't help admiring him—this nobody in rags who was not to be moved by Caroline, whose birthright had been to get her own way, matching her inherited arrogance with an arrogance of his own which came from God knows where. But it was also irritating that a grown woman and a stubborn child—and I too, for that matter—should be locked in this absurd impasse. I said abruptly, "If you go to this man, will you be long?"

"Not long." The boy began to smile. "He does not speak much unless he is in the mood."

"How long?"

"A half hour."

"Will he be there now?"

"Yes."

"Are you sure?"

"Yes. And while I am there I can also see my gods, so it will be two things done."

"Your *gods?*" I asked.

"Yes," he confirmed. "They are all there in the cave. I want to take leave of them before I go."

He spoke seriously, with the baffling assurance of a child who describes explicitly the minutiae of invisible company. I did not know what to make of this, and while I hesitated Caroline came to life.

"Deva," she said. "God—gods. Is that what he said?"

"Yes. Something about gods in a cave."

Before I could say any more the boy broke in, repeating "deva" over and over again, distinctly, glancing at Caroline as if to see whether she remembered the lesson; obviously it was one of the first words he had taught her. And Caroline said, her eagerness almost equaling the boy's, "Yes, he's told me about them before. They're paintings. He never would take me to them. Has he changed his mind?"

"Let's take it he has," I said. "Just let's go."

The rocky, inhospitable hill we were climbing, which I had assumed to be untenanted save for the holy man, turned out to have other inhabitants. The first we came upon was an old man, a hunchback who hobbled off as fast as he could as soon as he saw us. Farther on we caught sight of smoke, and presently came to the small brushwood fire, over which a cooking pot was suspended. Two women sat near, one with shorn head who seemed peaceable enough, the other a half-naked witch who broke into shrill gibberish as we passed, clanking the empty tin cans she had slung round her waist. I questioned the boy, and he said vaguely yes, perhaps there were one or two others . . . it seemed clear that this hill, suitably distant from the village, had been made the preserve of its misfits, in much the same way as the sweeper caste, or crow-catchers or gypsies, used to form settlements well outside city limits, beyond range of city noses.

The holy man, however, was in no sense a misfit edged out by his fellowmen. More likely he had fled them, coming to rest in the crumbling upper reaches of this hill in the name of peace. He was deep in meditation when we came, a thin, muscular figure with not an ounce of spare flesh anywhere, not a stitch of clothing on his body; a man probably of middle years, though he looked younger; in a meditation so deep that his closed eyelids did not so much as pucker, his pose alter by a fraction of an inch, at our noisy approach. Nearby was a lean-to shelter like Valmiki's, but better constructed, less ramshackle, with inside it the mess of paints I had grown used to seeing wherever the boy was about; and on the spur of the hill, under a rocky cliff that jutted out from the hillside, we could just make out the mouth of a cave.

"This is it," said Valmiki, halting abruptly. "Swami's cave, though he does not go to it often save in the monsoon. The gods are within."

He walked on, and while I was trying to decide whether to go with him or not—his halt had seemed purposive—Caroline followed. I thought this would precipitate a crisis, for there was something forbidding and inaccessible in the boy's attitude to the cave—a blend between reverence and a jealous possessiveness —that Caroline had not and probably could not gather from the bald translation which was her only method of communication with him; and in any case she was too intent, concentrated on entering this cave to which she had so long been denied access, to respond to atmosphere. She strode forward; and the boy stopped dead, barring her way.

Physically he was nowhere her equal. Equally plainly, she would not stoop to lay hands on him. It was a matter of spirit, and they both simply stood there, locked in this sweated contest of wills which brought identical expressions of near-hate to their eyes. I waited, and the heat and isolation clamped in on me, producing a nightmare in which it seemed the three of us would never move again, there was no reason why we should; we would just go on standing there until we turned to stone, monoliths as inexplicably positioned on the brow of this barren hill as many another. Then the lonely figure of the ascetic below us stirred, a hundred feet below; and it was enough to break the fantasy.

After that brief movement he did not move again for a few moments, retaining his relaxed pose with his hands held loosely in front of him, his legs crossed heel upon thigh; then still unhurriedly he rose, felt for his loincloth and wound it round him, and so turned to the tableau we presented. I don't know what he made of it, for at least on the two of us he had never in his life set eyes. Yet his acceptance was complete. He merely looked at Caroline, then at me, neither querying us nor our presence there; finally at the boy; and having bared the bones of the situation he said, seeming hardly to raise his voice, though it carried clearly: "Let her pass. There is no reason why you should stop her."

The boy hesitated; then the mutiny faded from his face, leaving behind not even ill grace.

"Come quickly," he said, briefly, quietly, "or the sun will be in the wrong place," and he set a pace up the gradient which we could only with difficulty match.

I assumed his haste had something to do with *raukalam*, the "dark period" during which it is inauspicious to undertake anything of note, whose ramifications were ill-defined now, though I had known them well enough once; but it was much more practical than that. It was a question of light, of entering the cave at a time when the rays of the sun, pouring through an irregular fissure in the roof, fell transversely across the rock chamber, illuminating the whole main wall of sheet rock. On this wall, lovingly sculpted and frieze upon frieze, were Valmiki's gods and goddesses. There must have been scores of them, some with rough outlines where the rock had presumably been difficult to work, others precisely executed, with the symbols and attributes of each god and goddess clearly defined. These latter, obviously more pleasing to the craftsman's eye, had been caressed into further beauty, gilded and jeweled with gold leaf and paint. Flecks of paint lay on the dark earth floor, mingling with rock chips and the diamond dust of rock filings, the glitter of flakes of gold leaf.

Nor was this all. At the foot of the wall was an opening, an aperture little more than a foot wide and perhaps as high through which the boy crawled, beckoning us to follow. We did so, and found ourselves in a cavern similar to the first one, from which we could see the opening of yet another. Probably the hill was honeycombed with caves, though the boy indicated we were to go no farther.

The cave we were now in was even larger than the first, lit by stray beams let in through slots in the rock, with sheer flanks of rock rising to support the domed irregular roof. Here were no carvings at all; instead were representations of gods and goddesses, mostly painted onto the surface of the rock, a few done on palm leaf and stuck to the walls, and all as meticulously interpreted as the figurines in the first chamber.

I gazed and gazed and it was almost too much for me, too rich, too crammed with creation for me to absorb much or to comment. I turned away at last, wondering where this child of peasants could have gained his knowledge of the Hindu pantheon, a knowledge which so far as I could tell enabled him to accurately portray the deities, each with its divine attribute. Perhaps it was memory, a study of the *gopuram* of any temple. Or perhaps it was the Swami who had instructed him. The latter seemed more likely: it explained the use of gold leaf, so incongruous in these surroundings, and certainly beyond the resources of a goatherd.

There was a mat in one corner, presumably used by the Swami on his rare tenancies, and I sat down on it to wait for the other two, for somehow—I could hardly make out how it had happened—we seemed to have become a kind of trinity, and it was unthinkable that I should break away from them now. Yet as far as they were concerned I might not have existed. Caroline was rapt. She moved around slowly, in silence but for occasional low exclamations where some detail of exceptional craftsmanship took her eye, sometimes briefly touching the sculptured stone as if her other senses were not enough and she had to feel to experience to the full. The boy followed her closely, seeing only her, occasionally pointing out to her—and to her only—some particular facet she had missed, glowing at every murmured word of commendation. It seemed incredible that this same boy, not so long ago, had been intent only on thwarting her; one could only watch and marvel.

In the short time we had been there the earth had spun away from the light, leaving the cave in semi-gloom, draining color and shape from the rock face.

I went out, dazzled by the sudden strong sunlight, and sat down to wait; and was presently joined by Caroline and the boy, blinking too as they emerged, and still bound in that strange harmony which seemed to make them impatient of externals. At last I said, feeling like a clodhopper strayed into ethereal regions, "Shall we go? It's very hot. We have a train to catch."

We began the descent, all of us retracted into ourselves again, locked away one from the other as most people are for most of their lives, until presently we came to where the Swami was sitting, waiting for us.

Valmiki had been walking a few paces behind all this time. Now he had advanced and, bending down, touched the Swami's feet while the Swami's hands rested briefly and gently on his bowed head. It was a common enough gesture, this touching of the feet, to be seen many thousand times in any temple: but there was not in it the same impassioned abandonment to God, it was more a gesture of filial reverence; and I could not help wondering whether in some slight way—it could not but be slight in a man to whom detachment from the world was life—the Swami had taken the place of Valmiki's father. The boy seemed happy in his presence, with none of that tension which had kept him tongue-tied and gauche with his parents, whose limitations had made them come to expect little else from him because even the simple skills their living required he was not able to muster.

Now he sat companionably beside the Swami, like him cross-legged and comfortable on the bare earth, and presently he said, without preliminaries as if he were taking up an interrupted conversation, "Do you think it is right I should go?"

The Swami laughed. "Go and ask a donkey. He is the only one who can tell you that. Have I not said so before?"

Instead of dismay, the boy's face was radiant.

"I have asked the donkey. It is true that he knows, but he will not tell."

"Then you must ask the bearded monkey, the one who is grown so wise that he will not speak."

"He will not unseal his lips for me. Nor can I scale his tree."

"Then what remains?"

"My heart."

"What else?"

"My self."

"You have learned your lesson well," said the Swami, laughing again. "Yet still you come to me."

"Because people say you are a wise man and a holy man," said Valmiki, wheedling, soft soap in his voice, "and so I would have the answer from you, not from donkey or monkey, or my heart or my self."

"Whether it is right for you to go?" The Swami spoke gently, no longer teasing.

"Yes."

"Do you want to go, still?"

"Yes. More than anything else."

"If you want to, then you must. Because if you did not you would have no peace yourself and you would take it from whomever you met, for the sound of chafing is like the croaking of bullfrogs, it has little charm. And once you have gone, and looked and found in yourself the answer, then you will know whether to stay or return."

The boy pondered this, giving it time and silence, his face grave; then his features lightened and he said with a child's lively curiosity, "Do you think—will I enjoy it?"—as if this were a holiday—a festival outing—on which he was going, instead of the beginning of a new way of life.

"You will and you will not." The Swami's answer was un-compromising, but his eyes were like a woman's. "The world offers its fruit in plenty, but they come in halves, the bitter and the sweet. That is a lesson you should have learned by now."

The boy nodded; and indeed who could have known it better than he, paying for the pleasure his work and vision brought him with the physical, spiritual isolation of an outcast?

All this time the Swami had not concerned himself with Caroline, not so much ignoring her as dealing with first things first. Now it was her turn, and addressing her directly he said, in slow careful English, "Look after him. He is young and no shell has formed to protect him yet."

Caroline nodded; she looked a little startled and was probably beyond words. From the very beginning he was the only human being with whom she was ill at ease.

The interview was over, we rose to go. But now the boy hung back, last-minute hesitant, his doubtful eyes beseeching the Swami.

"Shall I?"

"Yes, go. Go quickly."

The voice was steady, but its edges were raw. I moved quickly on, and somehow found myself unable to turn and look again at the lonely figure we were leaving behind on the hillside.

5

I WAS staying with relatives in Madras. Their orthodoxy barely managed to contain me, with my graceless, none-too-clean, learned-in-England ways; it would certainly not countenance either Caroline or the boy. Caroline was lodged, inevitably and comfortably, at the Club; but the Club would not take the boy and Caroline refused to be parted from him. The Western hotels were full. So were the Eastern—we must have tried them all, one after the other from sumptuous to seedy. Caroline, blazing, went to Jumbo; but he, usually so helpful, turned reproachful eyes on her and backed away, his whole person sagging like an unfairly punctured balloon.

All that day the boy came with us in his rags, wretched, alien, made to feel at one stroke the full organized enormity of a hostile society, his small thin face growing more and more pinched and anxious at each fresh rebuff.

Towards evening Caroline said, her eyes burning bright, "*What* shall we do?"

I said: "I'll find him lodgings in the bazaar, but he'll have to stay alone. They won't take you."

Caroline's mouth set firmly. "No. I've told you I'm not going to leave him alone on his first night here."

"I should have thought it would have been preferable."

"Preferable to what?"

"To the sort of welcome he's been getting with you."

"Are you suggesting it's my fault?"

"I'm suggesting nothing. Except that he might have been acclimatized first. Or even bought some reasonable clothes instead of those rags he's trailing around like glory-be."

"Anyone can be wise, can't they, afterwards?"

We went on wrangling, drearily, as our only way of relieving the shame and misery we felt over the heartlessness of it all; and the boy waited dejectedly, like a child who knows his parents are quarreling even if he doesn't fully know what it is all about.

At last, hesitantly, to help us he said, "There is an ashram— the Swami said to go there if—"

An ashram, of course. It would shelter him as it would shelter anyone who needed it, and its religious foundation would ensure his safekeeping. In his wilderness, miles from anywhere, the Swami had yet foreseen what should have been plain to us sophisticates but hadn't; had taken care even from that distance that his mantle should cover the child, whom our own derelection had left so exposed.

I said, "Which ashram? Did he say?"

"The one near Thousand Lights."

So we took him there, having first awakened the taximan, who had gone to sleep cradling his head on the steering wheel while we debated; and there, to expiate in some way our guilt, we lay down to sleep on the hard, uncomfortable, but hospitable and tolerant floor of the ashram, in the section reserved for women.

We could only have slept fitfully, if at all, in that swarming ashram—in a way it was a revelation, the amount of activity that went on throughout the night, people coming in and going out like insomniac bees on unimaginable missions. Toward dawn I accepted defeat and sat up. Caroline was before me, wide-awake, leaning back on an elbow, long legs outstretched in that bony pose models assume to show off tapered pants, and taking up more room than any other squashed and uncomplaining ashramite.

She said, in a well-modulated voice that woke a dozen determined sleepers, "It isn't any good, is it?"

"What isn't?" I asked cloudily. "Trying to sleep, do you mean?"

"No," she said impatiently. "I wasn't thinking of that. I meant trying to get him in anywhere."

"No," I agreed.

"So I think I'll buy a house," she went on. "It can be sold when we leave, the solicitors will take care of that . . . we've got to be here some time anyway, settling Val's papers and one thing and another."

She said it as if it were the easiest thing in the world, this acquisition of property; perhaps for her it was. Certainly it was as good a solution of the problem as any. The two of them could stay there in comfort, voluntarily isolated in preference to ostracism, while the boy slowly acquired herd-color—or as much of it as his hide would ever assume—until he could pass without arousing too much hostility. Then I remembered the small house I had inherited, a box of a place near the Fort which my agents let with great ease to clerks, whose incomes were precisely calculated for box-living, but which was now briefly vacant. Caroline could move in at once, that was its chief virtue; it would save us the tedium of house-hunting by day, and goodness knows how many sleepless ashram nights.

Caroline agreed; nor did she back out when she saw the

house, as I had half been expecting her to do. By nightfall they were installed, complete with pots, pans and furniture, and three servants—a cook, a chokra and an ayah—to fend for them. Then I left to walk along the Marina to Mylapore, where I was staying, my heart at least a fraction lighter than it had been. Dreary as it was, the house meant shelter, most particularly for the boy, at its least in a concrete sense. The rest must come from pity and generosity, if such could be found, until such time, if ever, as his own stature made this exercise in charity superfluous.

The next few days I concentrated on finishing a lamentably neglected article on Madras which a magazine had commissioned me to do, and when that was over I had a peremptory telegram summoning me to my home, farther south, to attend to urgent family matters, so that it was some weeks before I saw Caroline again.

Meanwhile the grapevine had been humming, and three hundred miles away everyone down to the night watchman knew that I had been, as they put it, mixed up with a village boy and an English lady.

The night watchman said, alert in his own province, "Lock up your jewels. You can't trust these villagers."

"He's not a thief and he's only a child."

"They're the worst, the young ones. Wily as monkeys. Once they run you'll never catch them."

My uncle said, "Be careful with her. She's half American, and Americans are not stable."

"In what way?"

"They're not sure of themselves," he said, "so you can't be too sure which way they'll go. Erratic, that's the word. They're erratic."

I had to smile. "I've never met anyone more assured than Caroline. Besides she's hardly American at all. She was born in India and brought up in England except for trips back here."

"Blood will tell," he answered, and after a pause he went on: "The mother was a bit wild, I'm told . . . that was part of her attraction . . ." and he let the sentence hang delicately in the air, for me to finish with a requiem for the daughter. But I was too involved to come to easy verdicts, though I could not help thinking to myself that Caroline certainly seemed to have more than a little of her mother in her, and no doubt it was part of her attraction too. But this wildness that magnetized a woman was not the most reassuring quality in the self-appointed guardian of a child with no known or foreseeable alignment. Equally, of course, no one who had been tamed by the world would have undertaken so daunting an assignment; and for perhaps the first time since its inception, and the irritations, the stupefaction, the weariness that had followed, I began to feel something like admiration for Caroline.

A month after this there was a telegram from her.

LEAVING MADRAS BANANA BOAT SEVENTEENTH, it said. VAL'S PRESENT TO YOU WITH COOK'S PLEASE COLLECT STOP SEE YOU LONDON SOME TIME CAROLINE.

The seventeenth was one day away, so I flew. I wanted to see Valmiki again, partly out of curiosity, to see what city life had done to him, partly because in the way that some children have he had got under my skin. I wanted also to make amends to Caroline for my strictures on her, manifest when unspoken, and outspoken more often than not. And I wanted a better address from Caroline than the one she had given me—a pinpoint on which I could look with some hope of finding them, rather than the sweeping arc that see-you-in-London meant, particularly if, as I suspected, the arc she described seldom touched mine.

There was only one cargo boat leaving Madras on the seventeenth, said Cook's man: it was leaving at midnight; and yes, among the passengers was Lady Caroline Bell and one Valmiki, a boy, who was accompanying her. That gave me ample time—almost twelve hours. I thanked the man, walked down Mount Road and hailing a passing taxi drove to the Fort House. It was closed—doors locked, windows shuttered, a padlock on the narrow grille at the entrance. The servants had vanished.

I wondered briefly if it was any use going to the house agent, dismissed the thought, hung about the empty house for a demoralizing hour in case she should come back, and eventually drove down to the harbor. The boat was in, lashed to bollards on the jetty and loading, not bananas but great bales of dry-salted hides that a dockside crane was methodically depositing in her open hold. The gangplank was down and unattended, but when I began to ascend it an officer appeared from nowhere to say that passenger embarkation was not until six o'clock. To make quite sure I asked him to confirm that Caroline was not on board, which he did; and after that I had to give up. She might be anywhere: and although I knew some of her haunts, I certainly didn't know what these might be when she was linked with the boy.

After some zombie hours—for there could be no question of anything like positive living in these unwanted, extending pockets of spun-out time—I went back to the harbor. It was after seven, darkening, and lights had come on all along the quay, laying a sheen on the water and giving a pale kind of glamour to the choke and clutter of the docks. Caroline, manifestly, had already arrived. Several cubic feet of the quay were stacked with her belongings, over which, in lieu of the owner, a number of officials were dancing attendance. Caroline was on board, said one of them; and the boy? Yes, yes, he too. Just then I heard her hail me, and looking up saw her leaning over the taffrail, in one hand one of those formal, stylized bouquets of roses and jasmine with a lime in the middle which is a charming industry of Indian flower markets, and in the other a replica of the Taj Mahal, a less captivating bazaar industry. As soon as they saw her the twittering of the officials ceased, and from the height of the stern her voice carried clearly:

"Come up—Val's longing to see you. Just walk up—they're not fussy on a tub like this."

So I did, this time without query, and Caroline was on deck to meet me, in dazzling sharkskin that made the white duck of the officers' uniforms look dingy.

"I didn't think you'd come," she said. "Val said you would. Why didn't you let me know? I'd have met your plane."

"I wish I had," I said. "I've been cooling my heels here since midday. Where *were* you?"

She smiled. "On our last day here? We were beating it up."

"Yes, but where?"

"In the People's Park. It sounds incredible, doesn't it? It was in a way, but not the way you think. In fact I'm not sure I've seen anything quite like it. There was a sort of exhibition going on—cottage industries, I think—and there were all sorts of sideshows—like a fair, like an Elizabethan fair probably was, with clowns and tumblers and cockfights, and then there was a tiger-dancer and a fire-walker. . . . Val loved it. I did too, it was all so—fantastic."

"I can't think," I said, "how you ever managed to find your way there."

"I probably never would have," she agreed. "It was the chokra. He's been invaluable, taken us to all sorts of places."

We went up the companionway, onto "A" deck where the two cabins were, one at each end of a narrow corridor, and in this stifling cul-de-sac squatted the invaluable chokra, flanked by the ayah and cook, the three of them presenting that tableau of limitless patience and monumental devotion so characteristic of Indian servants who have been treated, however briefly and absentmindedly, like human beings. They rose as we entered, flattening themselves against the wall to let us pass.

Inside, alone in Caroline's cabin, sat the boy clutching a shiny new red-lacquered box, evidently a memento of the exhibition. His face was grave, immobile, until indicating the box I asked if he had enjoyed himself, and then the somber gravity vanished, his eyes lit up and danced.

"Yes! It was not like anything I have seen before. At first I thought it was a shandy—I have been to a shandy, you know—but it was bigger, oh so much bigger, and there were no cattle so I knew it could not be a shandy. And there were so many things—I have never before seen so many things but we could not see them all, I am sure there was a lot that we missed."

What a pair, I thought, listening to him: both of them exclaiming over the simplest things, both of them with a refrain they might jointly have coined, so rarely was it to be heard in the blasé world without, that it was not like anything they had seen before, and yet each so different, the one as beautifully cut and cultivated as the other was rough and raw. Valmiki, I noticed now, had shed his rags. In their place he was wearing long white trousers and a cotton shirt with the shirttails hanging out, which made him look exactly like any other Madrasi youngster; it was this unobtrusive conformity which had kept me from registering the alteration sooner. I studied him, discreetly enough, wondering whether the change went deeper, beyond his clothes, but soon his eyes sought mine and held them, and as if in answer to the query he grinned and said, "I e-speak English."

"Do you?" I said, taken by surprise, and then recovering myself, "So you do. You speak it very well."

"Yes, doesn't he?" Caroline added her praises to mine. "He can write his name, too, can't you, Val?" She turned to me, glowing, asking admiration for her creation.

"Yes indeed," I said, "I congratulate you."

There was a silence. "Well of course," she said at length, "it wasn't all me. He's quick at learning, there wasn't much for me to do. And then there was Cook to help. He did all the e-spadework—did you guess?"

I had to laugh. "I noticed the intrusive 'e,' " I said. "I guessed it wasn't from you, but I didn't specifically think of Cook."

"That came from him too," she said, grimacing down at the Taj Mahal. "Revolting, isn't it? He should have said it with flowers, like chokra."

"And ayah?"

"Ayah said it with a cross," said Caroline, indicating the small gilt cross pinned to her dress. "She's a Catholic."

Valmiki had been silent so far, but now he produced from his pocket a replica of Caroline's cross and displayed it to me.

"A present, for me," he said.

"From ayah?"

He nodded, and I felt momentarily that he was watching me closely, but I could not think why and the impression faded. I got up to go.

"Stay till we sail," said Caroline. "It's not long now—half an hour."

"Cook's man said midnight."

"It's been changed to nine."

So I sat down again, and though there was not much conversation—not because there was nothing to say, but because
what there was to say could not be encompassed in the time left
to us—there was no constraint either; perhaps that kind of con-
striction can never occur when one has moved from acrimony
to admiration, shared a hut and an ashram together.

Presently the ship began to throb and hum, the tempo steadily
heightened on board and ashore.

"Well, this is it," said Caroline. "Do you think I'm being
foolish?"

"You're doing what I wouldn't do," I said, "but it's only
because I know I wouldn't have the nerve or the strength to
carry it through."

We went up on deck, the servants in tow. The other visitors
had already left and were huddled in groups on the quay. The
crew was standing by, ready to haul in the gangway. I said
good-bye to Caroline, and then I turned to the boy. To my
surprise he took my hand and clung to it, and his mouth was
suddenly unsteady. My own throat drew tight. I knew I could
not mean much to him; yet I was the last link with all that was
familiar, and looking down into the misery in his eyes I felt I
knew what it must be like for him now, while his fingers were
pried away from this final hold.

"I'll come and see you in London before long," I said gently.
"I think you will like it, it is a kindly place, there is no reason
to be afraid."

He did not respond, simply stood there with his hands tightly
around mine, looking up at me with enormous dilated eyes.

"There is no reason to be afraid," I said again. "This is not
the end. If you are not happy, come back."

It seemed to rouse him.

43

"Can I?" His voice was so husky I had to strain to hear.

"Yes."

"Are you sure?"

"Quite sure."

Overhead, the single funnel was throwing thick black coils of smoke into the sapphire night. There came the deep boom of departure, powerful, final. I freed myself quickly, and went down the gangway and stood on the quayside with the servants, a little in front of ayah, who was crying; and the four of us waited while tugs hauled at the ship, heading her toward the harbor's mouth and beyond the open sea. As long as I could see the boy did not move, and watching that lonely figure transfixed to the deck the rammed-down memory of my own first leaving returned, and I knew the same paralysis would hold him there until the land had fallen away, and the lights on shore been eclipsed one by one; and then feeling would return, bringing with it pain.

I had booked my return flight through Cook's. In the morning a messenger arrived from them with a parcel for me. It was large and rectangular, brown-paper wrapped and marked *To await collection*. It was only then that I remembered Caroline's telegram, and realized almost at once, of course, why Valmiki had shown me the cheap little gilt cross the ayah had given him and watched me with such intensity while he spoke. It was, I thought with useless compunction, probably one of the very few presents he had ever been able to make in his life: what on earth had I been thinking of to forget it? I tore off string and wrappings. Inside was a canvas, unmounted, a painting in oils of me with lowering brows and brooding eyes and a somber mouth—of me, I could not help thinking, at my forbidding worst. I stared at myself, not flattered, perhaps too astonished by the truth to be hurt; and then I saw the small tag attached, on which Caroline had written: *This is what Val says you look like when you think about his future,* and I did not know whether to laugh or to cry, or to be grateful for this most subtle of gifts which showed me at my best—forgetful of self and absorbed in another.

6

WHAT it must have been like for Caroline introducing Valmiki to the regimented England of 1949 I cannot imagine. The inference must be that she had not spent much time or thought on imaginings at anything like a prosaic level, for within a few months she had taken the boy and herself off to Switzerland. Caroline's letter gave no reason for the move, apart from a brief mention of some awful little man who had pestered her with unnecessary questions; and it was not until I got a subsequent letter, written from her Swiss sanctuary, that I realized the awful little man was none other than the divisional education officer, and the pestering he had indulged in was on behalf of Valmiki, who was unschooled, and who as a British national could not for scandal thus be left. "But school," wrote Caroline passionately, definitively, and in disregard of historical example, "is only for people who want things put in their heads, not for someone like Val who already has all that he needs. School is no place for him."

From Switzerland they moved to France; then to Italy and on to Greece. From there she whisked him off to the Nile delta, "to see if the sun can get his circulation going again," ran Caroline's bulletin to me—a figure of speech I found tantalizing, for I could not divine what exactly had stopped and needed to be got going again: certainly not his circulation. She had given up writing letters by the end of the first year: now she sent me these small square cards, each with the picturesque stamp, and about three lines telling me of the new move. After that, in 1951, in the summer, they returned to England. By now Valmiki was sixteen, and presumably the threat of schooling was over.

Later that year I was in London myself, doing some research for a film script I was writing, and as soon as I had found myself a flat as near as I could get to the British Museum, where my mornings were spent, I went to call on Caroline. She was not at the Belgravia address she had given me; she had more or less closed the house, said the housekeeper who came to the door, and was now living in Silvertown with the boy. Could she give me the address? She could, she said, she had been told to expect me; and in a neat hand she wrote it down.

Silvertown, E., was not the sort of district one associated with Caroline. It was not rich, or fashionable, or eccentric, merely workaday and difficult to get to. What, I wondered, could have sent her into this kind of exile—another awful little man, some other dragon's head of officialdom which she could not draw her sword and sever as she might have done in another age? Not at all. Caroline had chosen the district because she felt the boy would be happier in it, because Belgravia overawed him, and the two English servants made him uneasy. After this little speech one might have expected them to be living either in modest dreariness, or possibly even imitation squalor. Wrong again. The house, one in a terraced row, only presented a façade of conformity with its drab neighbors: the transformation lay within, casketed, discreet, wrought by the hand of one of those interior decorators whose simple good taste runs up four-figure bills.

The street door, painted railway-station green outside, opened onto a black-and-white interior. Black-and-white marble gleamed in diamond shapes on the minute hall floor. The Chinese white walls had a finish like porcelain. The stairs were covered in black sleek carpet like a puma's coat. One vivid Shiraz rug was splayed on the wall; and replacing the usual clumping wooden banisters were spindle-legged balusters and a graceful handrail of shining sycamore.

I stood there silenced by the unexpected, extreme elegance, wondering about Caroline, that strange woman—the bizarre woman of the headman's description—who had the courage and the imagination to secure for the boy a milieu in which he could breathe, who could yet not perceive these surroundings might make him uneasy. Perhaps to her they were not extreme, not luxurious, merely livable. Or perhaps there was a limit to her endurance and she could not live in this scruffy street unless she was able to shut it out once she had closed her front door behind her.

Caroline had put my coat away. "Come up," she said, leading the way. "My room's on the first floor. Val's is the one above, our man's in the one below."

"Your man?"

"Sort of cook-houseboy."

"Indian?"

"Yes. Quite useless, needless to say. I don't know why I keep him."

"Perhaps he's better than nothing."

"Perhaps. Yes. But he takes up so much *room*."

"How much?"

"One. One room. But there're only three *altogether*—one on each floor. And something that looked like a kitchen cupboard which was the *kitchen*. How *could* people live like that? Can you imagine? And there were two families living here when we came."

"People get used to things. Perhaps they had no option."

She shrugged slightly; to her way of thinking, and indeed to one of her leonine endowments, neither proposition could have made much sense.

Caroline's one-room-on-each-floor, however, turned out to be a little exaggerated. There was in fact a first floor back—the kitchen cupboard which had once been some woman's kitchen, which was now a bathroom though all it could take was a hip bath, a water closet and a corner basin so small it had probably been specially made. The first floor front was a large room, by comparison. It overlooked the street, but venetian blinds took the worst edge off the view and anyway there was in the room enough to draw the eye and engage it. Caroline, clearly, did not travel for nothing; nor like a tourist, exulting home with yellowed ivories, molting pelts, shoddy silk, chryselephantine boxes, mother-o'-pearl inlay—wholesale tributes to the merchant endeavor of every export-minded casbah and bazaar from Port Said to Marrakesh. There were no ivories; only one skin, a magnificent snow leopard's; brilliant Thai silk covers on the sofa and chairs; a beautiful little terracotta nude; and an Arabic prayer mat on which Caroline was sitting cross-legged, her knees not lying flat but risen, European fashion, at ungainly angles from the floor.

"Well," she said. "Now you've seen how we live, what do you think?"

"Of living here? Pleasant enough," I said, "but I can imagine it might be a strain too, sometimes."

"The hip bath?"

"And the street."

She shrugged. "They're maddening, of course. But they're not what you'd call a big worry."

"Have you a big worry?"

"I'm not sure whether I have or not."

"Valmiki?"

"Yes."

"He's not adjusting the way you'd like him to."

"Adjusting himself to London, do you mean?" She disposed of the suggestion. "Of course he is—why shouldn't he? London isn't exactly farfetched is it? It's full of foreigners who've adjusted themselves."

Caroline's pronouncements were so casually made, so cool and overpoweringly confident, that there was always a time lag before you caught up with their inaccuracy. Before I could protest she had moved on.

"It's nothing like that. But you know how he worked in India—perhaps you don't, you never lived with him, did you?— but he used to be at it all the time and when he wasn't actually working he used to dream and scheme—I know he did because I used to get the schoolmaster to find out for me." She laughed. "Funny little man, wasn't he? So terribly earnest."

"But not a very good interpreter."

"I don't know . . . he used to find out what I wanted to know even if it maddened Val. 'Madam, he is thinking: where I am to get red dyestuffs for picture?' Or, 'Madam, he says his wish is to paint all the people in one face.' Val used to dance with rage."

Caroline was a good mimic. I could well imagine the scene—

the painstaking schoolmaster with his ponderous questions, his face haggard with anxiety as he strove for the literal accuracy on which he prided himself and which had produced some startling translations; and the badgered angry child, forced to give form to unformed, barely visible nebulae beginning to shine in his mind.

I said, "Didn't you feel sorry for him?"

"For Val? Oh yes. But it was insupportable not to know what he was thinking. He dreamed all the time. And schemed, and worked. But now—" She broke off and got to her feet. "Now nothing," she said bleakly. "Come up and see."

Valmiki was out, his room was empty. It seemed an intrusion to enter, but Caroline walked in without qualm and I followed. It was a tidy room, plainly intended as an artist's workroom, though the capable hands that had so equipped it had not in the process been reckless of comfort. There was an armchair, velvet-upholstered, deep enough to get lost in; a couch; a beautifully proportioned bachelor chest; a plain wooden kitchen chair, and a wooden bench such as is used in schools. At an angle to the window, where it caught the most light, stood a new-looking easel. Next to that, in neat racks and holders, were canvases, brushes, paper, a palette, fat tubes of paint, oils and watercolors, jars full of powders, bottles full of oil, and a pile of clean rags and cotton waste. Except for one painting of what looked vaguely like a desert, the walls were clean and bare. The palette bore traces of paint, there were desultory flecks of color on easel and floor. Despite these the room looked decorous, almost sterile; and although I had not expected quite the clutter he had thrown up around him in India, the absence of uproar was disquieting.

"You see?" said Caroline. "He has everything he needs, and nothing has come of it."

I looked around the ordered room again, and all the painstaking provision that had been made, and thought about India—
not mine but his—and its extraordinary confusion, the passionate
agglomeration of color with which he had surrounded himself,
the strange flotilla of basins and bowls assembled with hard
labor, the squelchy dyes, the fruit for which he had to search,
the gold leaf for which he had had no money, the knowledge
he had garnered from infrequent excursions on foot to the nearest town, the goats whose wanderings must have driven him
frantic; thought of it, and it needed no great imaginative effort
to guess that the lifting of these pressures might have left him
dizzy, in an atmosphere so weightless it might have been a new
element which he had yet to learn to manipulate.

"It was always a gamble." Caroline stood with her back to
me, looking up at the painted desert on the wall. "You always
thought so, didn't you. I didn't, because I didn't think talent
like his could simply dry up. I still don't, except at moments.
I feel it must still be there, though I don't know what if anything is ever going to set it moving again."

The question was in her voice, not in the words. I could tell
she was waiting for me to answer, but I did not know what to
reply because of course there could be no certain knowing. I
hesitated, and then I said: "I don't know how talent works . . .
does anyone? But some people work best when they have a
little peace, and some people only work when they're pushed,
when they're under pressure."

"Under reasonable pressure." She turned and faced me. "But
the conditions Val was working in were gross, disgusting. He
couldn't have kept going for long—he'd have been washed up
by twenty. That's why I took him away, and when I did I meant
him never to have to grovel like that again, I wanted him to
be free to work as he wanted, and never anything else. What
are you asking me to do—make some sort of ghastly mock-up

of those conditions? Or take him back—return him to the exact crevice in the rocks I found him in?"

Before I could answer, the half-shut door was pushed open, and Valmiki came into the room. "Crevice," he said. "What is crevice?"—and those were his first words, concerned with what exercised him and taking natural precedence over commoner greetings and loyal addresses.

7

TWO years had gone by, the skeleton had put on flesh, the human being stood taller, straighter, broader, ruddy with health instead of touched with the yellow of creeping enervation; and looking on him so, I could not help reflecting on the tenacity of nature, divinely blind to futility, producing generation after generation a frame of such enduring potential in the hope that someday, somewhere, it might be hung with the dignity that befitted it. Whatever else might be in balance, this much Caroline had done for him: she had put an end to his half-stomach rice-and-water diet, and with food and care given him the decency of a healthy body.

"Crevice," the boy repeated again. "What is crevice?" He had advanced into the center of the room and was looking straight at Caroline, not at all at me; and for the first time since I had known her, I saw her flush.

"It's a—a cleft, no, not quite—" She stopped, pulled herself together. "I'll look it up for you, later. But really, Val, you do choose the oddest times for your questions."

"I wish to know. Now." His voice was stubborn, but by now Caroline had regained her composure and the brief battle of wills was over, in her favor.

"Now is hardly the right time." She spoke briskly, with an undercurrent of coldness that subdued the boy. "Do you realize it's two years since you last saw Anasuya and you haven't so much as noticed her?"

"I see her. Not blind." The boy turned to me, sulky, but looking a little sheepish as well. "You well? Make safe trip to London?"

He spoke in English, a curious laconic English with an accent hovering between Tamil and Arabic—all the tortured *s*'s, the *p* sounds for *f*, of the first, the rolling *r*'s of the second—and little of the fluency I had somehow expected. Then I recalled he had not been to school, and that Caroline, with her characteristic unconcern for the practical ordinary, had probably scorned to engage a tutor; and no doubt, and understandably, her own teaching enthusiasm had waned; and his English had come in scraps from India, England, his travels, and I could not help surmising, from cook-houseboy on the ground floor.

The same source, I felt, accounted for the suit. What I could not make out was Caroline of all people condoning it, it was so awful—a splendid, unmuted blue, short in the arm so that two inches of wrist showed, so long in the leg that threadbare turn-ups flopped dismally over the uppers of his boots, and the collar of such peculiar cut that he seemed neckless, his head set squarely onto his shoulders. It made him look for all the world like one of those Indian students one sees in Gower Street or the Strand—newly arrived, badly off, and pathetically and obviously lacking one single English friend to do him the service of pointing out mistakes.

But Valmiki had presence, a finer variation of the magnetism that was Caroline's, which would never allow him to pass without notice, as a nobody. Somewhere implanted within him, however deep and dormant, lay the seed of the knowledge of his power, and it gave him the bearing which is also conferred on the truly innocent, the walking saint. It had kept his head high even when he was a discredited goatherd; and it sustained him even now, in full-fretted knowledge of the shackling of his strength—a wasteland of the spirit most dreadful for man to inhabit because he cannot compute its term, or be certain of enduring till its end.

The courtesies were over now, the banalities Caroline had insisted we engage in while covers were laid on those edged exchanges. Valmiki said, abrupt as before, "I not work. Only finish one picture." He waved his hand toward it. "That one."

"I know."

"She tell you?"

He asked the question bluntly, in English, ignoring Caroline although she stood next to him, and sharply as though it might have been a betrayal for her to have done so.

"No need to," I said diplomatically. "I can see for myself. I'm not blind either."

"You see now? Just now?"

"Yes of course, I haven't been here before."

"Then you not know from letter?"

He seemed oddly agitated, as if it were somehow of moment that I should not have known.

"No," I said, suppressing my impatience, and honestly enough.

"Then you not tell Swami."

"Swami?" I had all but forgotten him, but now he strode powerfully into the room, I recalled with clarity every detail about him down to the last gentle nuances of his voice.

"No," I said, gently too, "I have not said anything to him. How could I when I knew nothing?"

I might have added I had not even seen the man—not since the day we had left him on that faraway hillside and walked away without once looking back; and I wished I had when Valmiki said, his eyes lit with eagerness, "You have seen him? He is well?"

I shook my head, feeling abject, and thought uselessly of the disproportionate proliferations of misery small omissions can make, for the boy's face was wretched, touched with a gray that seemed shabby and wrong on anyone so young. I wished I could retract: pretend to some nonexistent communication: but when I tried to lie I found I had not the courage.

There was a short silence. Caroline, who so far had been following our conversation, but with no great attention, un-coiled herself from the depths of the velvet armchair and sat up. I had the impression that she was instantly, coolly alert, and the atmosphere of calculation made me vaguely uneasy, but the words were innocuous enough.

"Val," she said, "the Swami means a great deal to you, doesn't he?"

He nodded at once, in full acknowledgment, without that supercilious desiccation of the emotions which sophistication postulates.

"Yes. He was like father and mother and friend. Always good. Always help."

"Help? In what way?"

"Many ways."

"Buying you things? In that way?"

"That way also." He frowned, struggling to be fair to her and at the same time to him. "But he not rich like you, not buy much. Few things, few times."

"Yet you say he helped in many ways."

"Yes." He stopped, and the tussle with thought and remembrance and finding some English to fit knotted the veins of his forehead, his gesturing hands: "It was so. I not know how, only it was so. He say good, I feel good. He say work for God, I work for God. He say you paint well, I paint well."

"It's not the same, is it," said Caroline, "if I say you paint well. It doesn't work, there's no magic in it."

He was instantly contrite. He threw himself at her feet, with the unconscious dramatics of a desperate child, and began hammering his forehead against the arm of her chair as if the infliction of pain were the least he could offer in atonement—vainly, for the arm was velvet-cushioned.

"Same, yes, same. You say good, I feel good. Here. Here." He thumped his heart and head with his fists, shaken by his own sense of guilt, his vehemence.

"But it still doesn't work, does it?"

"No. Not work."

He lowered his fists, his violence unstrung by her cool, almost gentle voice, and was quiet.

The brief day was ending; one became aware of it in the long, gray silence. Caroline broke it, abruptly.

"It's dark," she said briskly, brightly, and the shattering light clicked on, the curtains twitched into place with a screech of the abused runners.

Valmiki looked up at me. "I not paint," he said flatly, without raging or recrimination. "Why so?"

The bleak white light fell full on his upturned face and he allowed it to with a kind of deliberate acceptance—as if beyond that dissecting light lay the confessional of compassion and comprehension, and perhaps a working creed.

And all I could find to say, though gently enough, was, "It will come."

"When?"

"Nobody can tell you that."

"Long time already."

"Not so long. Some people lie fallow much longer than that."

"Fallow." He frowned. "What is fallow?"

"Like a field. Leaving it until it can yield again."

But he, land peasant, having turned from it early knew nothing whatever of the land except what it looked like; and he had not the English to understand me further, and my Tamil refused to cope with the explanations involved; and the evening closed in mutual irritation.

I was no more than a few hundred yards from the house, looking in the fog-ridden street for an unlikely cab which I could not afford, when I heard footsteps clamoring along the pavement behind me and turned to confront Valmiki—hatless, coatless, his absurd unbuttoned jacket flapping as he ran.

I thought I must have forgotten something fairly essential— perhaps my purse.

He said, halting and breathing hard, "What is crevice?"

I had to take breath too. "Really, Valmiki," I began, and then I stopped, because the tone was so exactly Caroline's. Perhaps it was how most women reacted to his behavior—preposterous behavior that turned out on reflection to be wholly logical. He wanted to know: he had to ask to find out.

I said, "Look it up in a dictionary. It will give you more meanings than I can, and you can choose the best."

"Dictionary?"

"Book, of words. Caroline will give it to you. Ask her."

"No!" He shouted at me, at what I recognized was my stupidity, my fool's words. "You tell! No use book. No read ABC. You tell—now!"

People were turning, English ears assaulted by the loud jerky English, peering through the sulfuric murk to ensure being in at the savory start to a domestic quarrel.

"Come away," I said, and taking his arm walked him forcefully on until, blessedly, the lit sign of a café loomed through the fog.

It was a pull-up for bus crews; warm, smoke-filled, smelling of stale chips and cheap cooking fat. The coffee came from a bottle, diluted with water in the cup.

"Drink it," I said, "if you don't want to die of pneumonia."

He looked at me with his mule's face. "You tell now," he said, "what crevice is. I drink afterwards."

I was tiring of his what-this-is, what-that-is. I said, "It means a small crack."

"A small crack, in rocks." He said the words as if they were brands on his thin-skinned back, monstrous on human hide. His anger flared, bright, violent. "No. I not crawl out like lice—you go tell her I not lice! She not find me in crevice—she beg me, I come. She not like, I go back to Swami. To Swami, not hole in stone like belly-lizard. You go tell her that!"

His voice rose with each broken sentence, carrying him toward hysteria. I said sharply, "*You* do that. I'm going home now, as soon as I've finished my coffee."

He quieted a little. "No. I not go back to her."

"What will you do?"

"I come with you."

"You can't. There's no room—not even a spare bed you could sleep in."

"Sleep on floor. Anywhere."

"You can't sleep on the floor in this country."

"Then not sleep. No matter. Not caring."

He really did not care. He sat with his head lowered, his coffee cooling before him, in that depressed ashen misery, like the aftermath of drugs, that follows anger. Even his hands were quiet—long brown hands, on whose sparrow bones Caroline had put flesh, into which she would gladly have thrust whatever he asked were it only within reach of her formidable power, and for which she had with so little ado deliberately broken and recast the molds of her life.

I said, "You can come with me if you like. It'll be an embarrassment, but we can get over that. But you'll have to tell Caroline first. She's responsible for you, she brought you to England because she cared about you, she's entitled to know where you're going and that you're going simply because of a slip of the tongue, which is all that crevice is."

He said, bitterly, speaking in Tamil so that the rush of thought should not be dammed by a dearth of words, "She does not care for *me*. She cares only for what I can do, and if I do it well it is like one more diamond she can put on the necklace round her throat for her friends to admire; but when I do nothing I am nothing to her, no more than a small insect in a small crack in the ground. It was not a slip of the tongue, a manner of speaking: it is what she thinks of me when I am as I am now."

In a way the maturity of his words astonished me, for he seemed scarcely more than a child: and yet of course he was only saying what every child—implicitly, in his own way, however young—says: love *me*, *as* me, not because I am obedient, good, clever, pretty—love me for myself. But the bitterness was not like a child's but spiked, unfair, that of an adult.

I said, "You have forgotten what it was like in the beginning
—who it was that praised you, showering you with sweet words
you had never heard before which made you feel like a god
whose feet are washed in honey; who had faith in you though
the whole village laughed, saying like had met like; who cared
enough to insist you were never alone—not even one single
night in all that dreadful time when no one would take you
both in."

He seemed surprised. That particular night was clear enough
to me, but for him perhaps its detail was lost in the general fog
of misery. He said, "That was so?"

"That was certainly so."

"You are not lying?"

"Why should I?"

"Because you do not wish me to sleep on your floor."

"I do not wish it," I said, "but I would not lie simply to save
your skin."

He pondered this, biting his ravaged nails, his face wracked
by indecision, his gangling body taut and awkward in his chair.
Of all ages, I thought, it had fallen to Caroline to pick the
worst—the time between childhood and manhood, hotbed of
the unpredictable—the age at which, if it happens at all, mothers
are driven quietly insane. And Caroline was not even his
mother, to achieve a kind of patience. All she had was her
feeling for him, whatever it was, double-locked away beyond
access; and an impulsiveness to match his unpredictability
which could as easily produce peace as war.

Quite suddenly the boy's face relaxed. He rose to his feet
and said, in English, and as magnanimously as if Caroline were
present, "I forgive her. I go back to her now."

When he had gone the café seemed to shake itself back into
the ordinary. The girl behind the counter came around, her

heels clacking, to wipe down the tables. The clatter of fork and knives on thick white plates resumed. There was that audible sign of people riveted in unnatural attention. The disturbing alien had gone.

8

I DID not see much of Valmiki for some months after that—perhaps three or four times, no more. The distance was daunting, time was limited, and it had been a hard winter, more conducive to brief sorties into the open than an interminable safari to Silvertown. Caroline, who with a car was less bound by externals, might have brought him: but she was absorbed by and fully occupied in the curious little ménage she had set up for herself and the boy. There were, moreover, the love affairs in which she engaged—which for some reason she preferred to keep from Valmiki, though she never made any bones about them, about what she called her nymphean needs, to me.

It was spring by the calendar, but cold enough for a fire—which I had just lit, after the usual English ceremonial of newspaper and wood-chips—when the bell rang. I went down expecting to see the postman, and there on the doorstep stood Valmiki, beaming, carrying under one arm a rectangular package wrapped in brown paper, and in the other, improbably, a straggling bunch of narcissus which he thrust at me. "For you," he said, grinning away with this new cheerfulness which became him so much better, I felt, than either apathy or scowls. "Spring flowers."

"You're becoming almost English." I couldn't help smiling. "Whose idea was it—Caroline's?"

He denied this vigorously. "No, not Caroline. She not think about you. *I* see, I like, I buy for you. You like them?"

"Yes. They smell so nice," I said, leading the way into the small flat. "Like parijata—that's what the smell reminds me of."

He said, "You remember my sister?"

I said gently, "I wasn't with your family very long. I don't really think I remember any of them, except perhaps your mother. Besides there were so many sisters."

"The oldest one," he said, frowning, stubbornly sticking to English though Tamil would have been easier. "She was widow, she live with us . . . but when it was her wedding day I pick parijata flowers for her and I tie them with grass—so"—his fingers moved, lucidly, I could see the fine chain-stitches forming to hold the delicate coral stalks—"for her hair. She like much."

"Do you miss them, Valmiki? Your sisters? Your home?"

"No," he said, so definitely that returning anxieties retreated. "I not happy there, I not live with them always, only sometimes."

"And now never."

"Now never. I not mind."

"But was it always so, Valmiki? Were you always unhappy in your own home?"

He considered this, crouched like an animal in front of the fire, his arms outstretched for warmth.

"When I am small, no: I am happy then. But when I am bigger, my father wish me to work like him, like my brothers. But I am no good, I not do it well, then they are angry and my mother weeps. I hate when a woman weeps."

"She could hardly help it."

"Maybe no. But it is terrible. And in the village the people—" He paused and looked at me somberly. "You remember what you said?"

I did remember; I looked back at him speechlessly and he nodded, confirming the words I had thrown at him in another cause, now twisted round to discomfit me. "Yes, they laugh at me, saying my brain is soft . . . then one day—it is a bad year, no rain, no rice, and my father is full of arak—he shout at me: 'Go, get out! You no use to me, no use, no work, nothing.'"

"It was the arak," I said with that sudden ache Valmiki could start more easily than anyone else, perhaps because I knew I had, like some lesser reluctant god, impinged so infernally on his life.

"Maybe. Maybe so. But no work?" His mouth was tight and bitter. "When my father is finished with the fields, it is done, finished. He comes home and our mother gives him best from the cooking-pot and rubs his shoulders because he has done this work. When I have finished it is one hand of rice and rice water, because I have not worked. But my work is not stopping." He turned abruptly from the fire, and those queer light eyes of his were a little wild, as they had been the day Caroline had tried to breach his caves. "When I stop *it* does not—it goes on—here in my head. You understand?"

I said, "It is very difficult for ordinary people to understand, Valmiki."

"But when you can see?" he cried. "With your own two eyes? That is not enough? My father comes one day, see what I do. I show. He spits, it is nothing, useless, I am useless, a mouth to take from his fields, give nothing back . . . he has not drunk arak that day."

I sat quietly, aching; taken far from this firelit London flat into which these painful words were pouring, back to that rocky hillside whose stones had seen such bitter strife.

The story was ending—the dark chapter I had guessed at, or pieced together, about which the boy himself had never deliberately spoken before.

"After that," he continued, more calmly now, "they make me goatherd, send me to hill where you have seen me."

"And you lived there alone?"

"No, no," he said impatiently. "There were the goats, always the goats. I have *told* you."

"Alone, except for the goats."

"Yes. No. My mother send word sometimes she wish to see me, then I go. My father and brothers are coming too, many times, because of the goats you understand, they not wish lose goats . . . then one day I am alone, and there is Swami. He sees what I do, and he does not spit. After that," he concluded with satisfaction, "I am not alone."

"You went to live with him?"

He gazed at me, at first puzzled, then with amusement; and I realized with a shock that he was commenting on me, my middle-class attitudes which insisted one must live in defined circumscription—in house or dwelling with specific company— and that otherwise was not done. Yet, as was clear enough now, it was preposterous to apply these standards to such spiritual nomads as the Swami and this boy.

It was new, this comment upon me—the first time, since I had known him, that I had not been the critic and he the submissive recipient of criticism—and while I struggled to extricate myself from the confusions it engendered he said gently, in the explanatory tone I recognized as one I often used toward him, "Is not possible live with Swami . . . sometimes he is one place, sometimes another. Also is not necessary . . . when I wish to see him, I go."

"But if you were never sure where he was?"

"I search, I find," he said simply.

"You couldn't have been able to, always," I suggested.

"Oh yes, always," he answered, with the unimpeachable authority displayed by children lost in fantasy, by peasants who have felt the grace of God. "When I want he is always near."

"Here—in England—too?" It was, I suppose, a cruel question —the desire to draw blood that logically refutable but staunchly defended statements like these provoke. He was not shaken.

"Oh yes," he said. "He is always near, in the spirit, you understand . . . it is what he says himself, in letter."

"Letter? To you?" I was surprised. "Has he written to you?"

"Yes, yes, yes." Valmiki's head was nodding in repeated blissful confirmation. He drew from his breast pocket a square of folded writing paper which he thrust at me. "Here is letter, for me. You read, you see it is as I said."

I had not believed the man would write. The true Indian ascetic—and in my mind I had no doubt the Swami was one—is not a parish priest, a missionary, a revivalist, concerned with keeping tabs on a human being to plot his spiritual progress. His whole aim is to achieve detachment from the world: and even if the Swami could not completely master his heart, it seemed unlikely he would seek to continue an earthly attachment by letter-writing. There are, however, exceptions: and perhaps, I reasoned, the Swami was one, unable to snuff out all feeling for the boy despite the austere demands of his creed. But it was oddly disquieting—like seeing a meaningless jumble of lines, where one had expected a clear picture.

I took the letter. It was grimy with frequent handling, worn into holes along the folded edges, and it looked like one of those tattered chits, testifying to their various excellences, that un-employed servants in India carry around.

The message was brief—written in artless Tamil, a few lines to say the Swami was well as he hoped Valmiki was, that he often thought of the boy, whom he greatly missed, that his dearest wish was to hear he was working hard at his painting, and that he was always near, in spirit, to him.

Granted the exception, the sentiments were valid enough. I folded the letter and handed it back to Valmiki, trying to forget the writing in which each character had been formed with assiduous care, as if by someone whose knowledge of language was too slight to permit a casual script—certainly by no one as skilled and adept in its use as was the Swami.

"You read? Is what I have said—he is always near me?" Valmiki was chattering on, loud and tipsy in his triumph, his eyes brilliant with the wonder of being remembered. I felt sick with pity, looking, listening; and suddenly and savagely angry with Caroline, who had proved herself so thoroughly capable of kicking aside the decent observances and usages by which ordinary people felt themselves bound. Then, stepping in icy disdain on the heels of such easy anger, came the reminder that I had nearly lied too, and had refrained only because I lacked the courage; and this force-fed truth turned sour, into exasperation with the boy.

"What makes you so sure it's from the Swami?" I asked coldly.

"Sure, sure," he answered happily. "Is in Tamil, no? Swami is Tamilian."

"So are a good many other people, who can also write Tamil."

"No, no, is from Swamiji," he said, hugging himself with foolproof, imbecilic pleasure. "Why you try say no? Is nobody else to send me letter."

So be it, I thought, weary of his gullibility—not so much disarmed as rendered powerless by it.

"Now I am happy." Magnanimously he overlooked my mood. "I feel good—here—I work again, much work. I bring, show you. You like to see?"

He was cajoling. He knew I was ruffled, although to my fury he had not guessed why, and was doing his best to smooth me down. I stirred myself.

"You've been working again? Painting?"

"Painting, yes." His head kept nodding up and down like a mandarin's. "I feel good, I do work, plenty work. Not feel good, do not work. Same with you, no?"

"No," I said bleakly, and truthfully, for at the thought of writing my spirits always dropped. Only the act of sitting down to it ever got me going.

"You can work when your heart is sick?" His eyes were round with unbelief.

"I work whatever I feel like," I said shortly, and I thought how wonderful it must be to be spurred to work by excitement, by this "feeling good" which might come from the weather, or glands, or the receipt of a letter, to be indiscriminately transformed into a creative urge.

Valmiki was at last silent, his carefree chatter killed by my sour bludgeoning. He could not know, I thought uneasily, the reason for these senseless blows: and looking at him, brooding and withdrawn now as on his own showing he had been for many long months, I knew he must touch depths of depression, unknown to me, as a price of the excitement I had both envied and openly scorned.

"I'm sorry," I said, stiff with misery and compunction. "It was wretched of me. Of course people have to work in different ways . . . some plod along, some like you need to have the lightning."

He did not answer, but took my hand and laid his cheek against it in a gesture of affection that accepted my overture completely, forgave completely, with the total, heartbreaking abandon of a child. But what, I thought, had I done to deserve his affection? Nothing except bring him and Caroline together in a venture imperial in its presumption, that already showed signs of going rank. The tug of responsibility began again, old, familiar, dogged company in darker moods for two years and more; but now there was something else, an answering affection for this strange, lonely boy—the stirrings of a feeling that lies dormant in every woman, awaiting issue from her own loins to spring into fierce life. I thrust it under. I knew I had not yet done with travel, with going and seeing and experiencing for myself: and he was not mine to take with me. Nor could I stay and guarantee being near him, for his moves were equally unpredictable, in the hands of an erratic woman. To foster any such feeling now was folly, an open invitation to pain. I said, in deliberate breakaway: "You were going to show me your painting."

"Yes." He had not noticed the calculation, perhaps because it was something he was not capable of. He smiled and smiled, his small white teeth in continuous show, like a cherub, an ingenue, his fallen, idle hands voluble again. "I paint, I bring you to show. But only one—I not able carry more on bus. But I paint more, many more . . ." He crooned and mumbled in excitement, noisily tearing the wrappings off his picture, dropping the torn bits on the carpet, standing back in rapture as the last layer fell.

"You look," he said. "Is good, no?"

"It's splendid," I said. "You've captured the exact atmosphere."

The fraudulent phrases came tripping out. Only a few months in London and I knew what to say, although my head was as empty of knowledge as before. Partly that; and partly I could not do it now—could not beat him down in his triumph, this high jubilee of achievement which had soared up so pitiably out of a lie.

"Splendid, good painting yes, oh yes very good—" he gabbled away, jigging with excitement in front of his unveiled picture. "Now I paint more, many many more, yes, and then—" He stopped suddenly, chanting and jigging together as if to underline with stillness the importance of what he was going to say. "Then we hold shandy."

"A shandy?"

"A show. Show to people."

"An exhibition?"

"Exhibition, yes. People come, they see, they clap me. You think yes they clap me?"

I took breath and said, "Has Caroline arranged it? Really? Or is it something you've imagined?"

"No, no, is true," he said impatiently. "All arrange. In Anver Gallery."

"Hanover Gallery?"

"Yes. In autumn." He paused. "You think people clap me?"

"Yes, of course they will."

"Because I paint good?"

"Yes."

He began humming, a gay little tune that I remembered our servants' children singing as they played on the squares of beaten earth outside their godowns. Listening to him I felt disposed to be glad too, even virtuous, that I had given those robust reassurances which, but for my halfhearted complicity in and consequent guilt over the Swami's letter, I might easily have withheld, and which had contributed at least a few notes to his blithe song.

He was still humming as he followed me into the kitchen—for by now it was late evening, and I had no great wish to foray out for a meal; but when I had pushed him out—the kitchen being too small to take two in comfort—and prepared the food, and the pans were simmering on their rings, I came back to find him locked in silence, and as motionless as if held by unseen bonds.

All of him was still—eyes, body, even his voluble hands were fallen and quiet. Minutes before, he had been prancing from peak to peak like one of his crazy goats, now he sat like a stone lodged in an abandoned quarry. Or was it a morass? The quiet seemed airless somehow, cagelike, stifling. "What is it?" I asked uneasily, my nerves beginning to jangle in the sustained silence. He said nothing—not even the curt "nothing" that impales you on accusing horns and leaves you to bleed until perforce you ask again.

I went back into the kitchen, and after a while he followed me in. "I sorry," he said. "I not mean hurt you."

"I'm not hurt," I said. "I wondered if you were."

"No."

"You were so quiet, so suddenly."

"Is because I was thinking."

"About the exhibition?"

"No."

"About whether people clap you?"

"No."

"About your Swami?"

"About many things, many people, and him too," he

answered, and his face was neutral like his voice, sponged clean of all expression in a way I could not remember before. So he had learned, I thought, and how quickly; it came as a small shock to realize he could do it, put on—when he wanted to badly enough to make the effort—this bland sophisticated manner that gave away nothing, that disdained the naïve revealing denial and attacked instead by breeding from your own insinuation, so that you were left with a host of elver possibilities too numerous for any to be grasped.

I turned away, feeling a little helpless, and began assembling the meal on a tray to carry into the living room where the dining table stood—a round mahogany one, with a patina like satin on it, which was one of the nicer points about the flat. We sat down, the firelight brandishing spears on the beautiful wood, the sweet-smelling narcissus in a jug, the snow-white rice piled high before us, and Valmiki smiled, though only fleetingly.

"To eat is good, yes?"

All the time we ate I could feel my mind working around his silence, trying to bare its cause, wondering with sudden jets of panic like ice in the bloodstream if he had guessed about the letter, for I had moved from a surly exasperation against his blindness to fervently hoping, since matters had gone so far, that he would never find out; and I began going back word by word on what I had said, for a clue.

His face showed little; but halfway through the gropings, the careful retracing of footsteps, I became aware, with that curious knowledge beyond tampering with or doubt which can suddenly invade you, that he was doing precisely what I was —picking a meticulous way back, going over the words I had used, the intonations, and sounding them for suppression and dissonance.

Somehow, perhaps instinctively, he had felt that something

71

was wrong; and although for all his probing he could not pin-point it (for if he had he would have attacked), he was not yet the full-blown sophisticate, prepared to mistrust instincts that were part of his nature.

9

CAROLINE had never been fainthearted—not in all my experience of her which, though limited, had encompassed more than one critical phase. She was also thoroughgoing in a way that made you respect her, even if respect was sometimes fringed with misgiving as to how far, in any cause, she would go.

Shortly after Valmiki had come to see me—it must have been within the month, for it was still spring, the green in the parks still dewy and tender—Caroline telephoned to say she was going back to the house in Belgravia. The leasehold of the Silvertown house had been sold—at a nice profit, said Caroline, with the cream that came into her voice when she made money on a deal (which was by no means a novelty, for she had told me of other nice profits made on the stock market, though God and she both knew she had had enough money to start with).

I thought she was moving because the district had worn her down—too dull, far too inconvenient, not squalid enough to begin to be interesting—in fact a plain working Jane of a place and rather a bore. Which was about the worst stricture Caroline could apply to anything.

I was wrong. She was moving so that Valmiki could get to know a few people.

Months ahead, probably within minutes of knowing the date of the exhibition, she had coolly begun laying foundations, making her plans. I put the receiver down slowly, wondering how the boy would react, whether he would recoil against the notion that knowing a few people might help. Then I realized Caroline would simply have told him what she had told me: the words themselves were irreproachable, and he would accept them equally simply, with no hint of the implications which to the worldly would be obvious in the excruciating extreme, beyond need of stating. Following the telephone conversation Caroline came herself, and again her theme was the exhibition, and Valmiki's contribution, in roles other than painter, to its success.

"He'll have to dress better," she said. "That awful suit. He simply can't go on wearing it and wearing it out and having it copied and wearing it again."

I had not realized the suit was one of many; I had admired her for putting up with even that one model.

"I wouldn't mind if it reproduced itself forever," she said, "but I think it's important for him. And speaking better English. I've forbidden him to speak anything else, even to Cook. Did you find him more fluent?"

"Considerably more," I said. I had noticed his studied non-use of Tamil, and speculated about it without a hint of the reason.

"And French," she said. "He ought to have some French. I hope he'll pick some up when we go abroad."

"Are you going abroad?"

"Of course. He ought to exhibit abroad to get really known —France, America, perhaps Italy . . . besides, there's all the experience, he won't get it all just from London."

There was the faintest emphasis on the word "London," as if it were a little parochial to think everything sprang from there, which marked the difference between Caroline and the memsahibs who had queened it over India, to whom everything did. Or perhaps it was new, postwar thinking.

I said, "He'll have to work, won't he, exhibiting so widely?"

Caroline smiled. "Yes, like hell. You can't keep showing the same pictures to the same people halfway round the world."

"Not the same people, surely."

"My dear, yes! You really wouldn't believe the way the art crowd gets around."

Caroline could say atrocious things, and things that sounded atrocious. Unless you belonged to her world you could never be sure which was which. While I hesitated she had swept on, outlining glittering and to me faintly menacing plans for the future—Valmiki's future—until at last I said, "It's all a little ambitious, isn't it? I hope it won't turn out to have been too ambitious."

"Too ambitious?" Caroline laughed, a woman's tinkling laugh that prefaces insult. "Of course not. You are being a typical timid little Indian babu."

"Because I know a little better than you what it's like to work," I said, caught on the raw by the half-truth as a total lie could never have done. "It isn't mass production. You can't expect Valmiki to guarantee output. What'll you hang on all these walls you're chartering if there's another bad patch like the one he's been through? Nag him?"

"There won't be another one," she said, slowly fitting a cigarette into the long black holder she carried and used like an irritant weapon. "Teething troubles and homesickness—he's over them both now. I think I can recognize the symptoms if they occur again."

"And deal with them?"

"And deal with them." She was very calm, very confident, without a qualm as far as I could see. It was in my mind then to pillory her about the letter—more as a form of self-indulgence, to relieve my feelings, than for any earthly good it would do— but she spoke first.

"Do you know," she said, "we go out of our way to meet, and we squabble every time we do. It's a sort of love-hate relationship, don't you think? Like the kind Britain and India used to have."

I wouldn't have called it that, I thought; it would have been difficult, with majestic exceptions, to have found much love lurking in the old relationship. Perhaps, indeed, relationship was not the word to describe a forcible possessing which had established nothing so clearly as that there could be no reasonable relationship—merely a straddling of one stranger by another with little out of it for either.

I didn't answer. She didn't notice and went on: "Perhaps it comes from the same thing—we can't do without each other."

In that respect I suppose she was right. The boy had brought us together, and our common interest in him still kept us in contact, defying the pull of orbits in space that we normally occupied.

There was a long silence after this. Caroline was wandering around the room, looking at my books, the prints on the wall, the fine collection of records left behind for some inexplicable reason by the previous tenant; and giving a good impression of a boy who longs to kick the legs of the furniture as he passes. At last she said, moodily, "I don't know what will happen after we move . . . I'm expecting the worst, though I haven't prepared it."

"What is the worst?"

"It's Hargreaves," she said gloomily, and I remembered the staid housekeeper who had written down the Silvertown address for me. "I don't think she'll stay on much longer—" She stopped suddenly and began to laugh. "I mean there's Val, and me, and Cook—just a *leetle* bewildering for an English housekeeper, are we not?"

We grinned away at each other—one of those rare moments when we could laugh about the same thing.

"Still, not to despair," she said. "There's always Ellie."

"Who is Ellie?"

"A refugee, a domestic," she said and sighed. "Last bastion of the servantless era. Better than nothing, I suppose."

She moved to the door, I had almost closed it on her when she turned and came back into the room. "I nearly forgot," she said, taking down the portrait in oils Valmiki had done of me and presented me with long ago, which I had had framed and hung. "I think this ought to be on view—it's rather good. You don't mind, do you?"

I cannot remember that I said either yes or no, but there was the gap on the wall, the painting wrapped and tied, the parcel in the crook of Caroline's arm, and Caroline's beautifully tailored back retreating down the pavement. Of course it was done for the boy's good—an end as much desired by me as by her; yet I could not escape the obscure feeling, as I watched her go, that somehow I had been outwitted.

10

SO the move to Belgravia was accomplished; and as Caroline had predicted—surprisingly, for she seldom dribbled her strength away in suffering by identification, by useless fitting into other men's shoes—Hargreaves made it understood it was too much for her and left. As Caroline had said, you couldn't blame her. There was the boy himself, then Cook, whom I had never seen before, who turned out to be a seedy-looking middle-aged Indian in a suit, whom Caroline had suborned from one of London's numerous Indian restaurants—and then the laugh had been on her, for he certainly couldn't cook; and finally there was Ellie.

Ellie was a girl of twenty, but her face was very much older and her body, from its abnormal thinness, looked considerably younger. She seemed to shrink when you spoke to her, disintegrating almost in front of your eyes, then gathering herself together for the effort she would smile—a nervous, ingratiating smile like a salesman doing his sickly best to stave off imminent dismissal and disaster—or whatever terrible thing it was she had had to stave off. Her head was cropped; her limbs like matchsticks, and because they were white they shocked me in a way brown and black could no longer do, for I had seen enough of those. She had no parents, no state, no passport, no papers—none of those hollow stacking blocks on which the acceptable social being is built. Her one asset was that she was a trained and fully experienced domestic help, which may or may not have been so, but that was the rumor put about by those in whose care she had been. She had gone from concentration camp to liberation center to resettlement camp; thence, on guarantee of menial employment, to Britain and Caroline.

Caroline had not expected much of Ellie, but even her "better-than-nothing" hope proved optimistic. If Ellie washed up, the job nearly always had to be done again. She seemed incapable of sewing, her fingers curved stiffly and stubbily around the needle as if she had never handled one before in her life. Moreover she seemed to have been born clumsy, so that Ellie in the kitchen meant an appalling series of chips and breakages that one might have called sheer carelessness but for the trembling horror with which she stood rooted after each crash.

Caroline, busy with her social engagements, and the move, and all the detail involved in the forthcoming exhibition, bore it with fortitude day after day while her china and glass were decimated. Until one evening we were sitting in the drawing room looking at Valmiki's latest canvas—still on its stretcher, the paint still wet where it lay thickest, in beautiful emphatic laminae on the rough surface—and suddenly there was a startling crash, louder than usual, which betokened the end of the coffee service Ellie had just carried out; and this time Caroline got to her feet and went out of the room. She had been lounging in housecoat and slippers—soft black ones with a velvet tread, so that we could not hear her movements—but presently there came a high yelp of fear from Ellie, then there was silence. In a little while Caroline came back and without comment took up where she had left off. Except for a slight paleness she looked no different than when she had gone from the room; and she said nothing, then or later, to either Valmiki or me—perhaps from a secret shame, a powerful unreasoning wish to keep European crime in European confine—within the family, so to speak, as far as possible. But soon there was Ellie going to Harley Street, and Ellie expensively lodged in a bone-setting clinic, and we both knew—as children learn from voiced fragments, freak silences, about sex or sin—that one of her hands was useless, had been deliberately ground into uselessness under a Nazi jackboot, and that she had concealed this mutilation—clumsily, at great cost to herself—out of the knowledge, common to the stateless, of the unanimity with which the crippled and the sick are rejected.

Ellie herself confirmed this when she came out, holding a shoe over her rigid hand and going through the motions of grinding the heel into tendon and bone. Then she wept, lowering her cropped head into her arms while Valmiki knelt beside her, blanched with the horror of it, unable to believe that this could happen, anguished because he had no option—poor Valmiki, gentle member of the gentle clans of the southern plains, taught by a Brahmin teacher, a man of the one caste which above others could disclaim a particular guilt, even if stained by the general dishonor, and stand some chance of being upheld in a neutral court. After this, humbly, in the kind of atonement we all feel we must make when nakedly confronted by calvary if at no other time, there was nothing he would not do for her, fetching and carrying when there was no need, for she had learned to manage with her one hand, while the second was mending well.

Ellie responded only with her cringing, slack-mouthed servility—an expression of the fear which seemed to be the only reaction left in her toward human beings. But before hope could finally gutter out, there came signs that—under the cumulative effect of Caroline, Valmiki, the clinic, England itself—the extensive cauterization that had closed whole areas in her mind was at last breaking down. There were occasional sorties into feeling, into attenuated emotion, an occasional feeler put out, pallid as an anemone's, followed by a barely perceptible move toward tentative human connection which in another would have been the most genial open overtures of friendship.

It was in one of these moments—months later, for the bones had knit, her hand had been free for some time of splints and plaster—that she offered to do sewing and mending for the household; and soon after this, when everyone had fallen on her neck in grateful acceptance, I came upon her one day holding an armful of Caroline's and Valmiki's clothes, crooning over them like an Ophelia. Harsh with fright, I grasped her arm roughly, but even as her face changed with the fright she in turn had received I realized she had been at peace.

I said something lame, which must have sounded quite crippled by the time it crossed the barrier of language into meaning. She laughed; and with complete unself-consciousness hugged the clothing to her again as if it was some kind of teddy bear, the missing badge of security of her lost childhood.

During these months Valmiki's work stopped abruptly. It did not seem to perturb him, there was none of the moody despair that had characterized the last arid gap. Indeed, he hardly even seemed aware of it, so preoccupied was he with Ellie; and for the first time I began to realize exactly how isolated his illiteracy had made him, ignorant of history to an extent that encounter with only one of its victims should have shocked him so profoundly. And yet he had traveled widely, with Caroline, for two years and more: it seemed incredible that in all that time he should not have become at least acquainted with European suffering. Then, looking back, the conundrum resolved itself. He had known no language except

Tamil; his English had been rudimentary, and included neither reading nor writing. Conversation had therefore been limited; and the industrious outpourings from the vast media of communication could have been little more to him than babel. Moreover, there was the fact of their anomalous association, on which at the very beginning society had imposed its sanctions. Few of Caroline's class would have anything to say to him; and his kind would not approach while she was near.

The weeks raced by, eating up with frightening speed what time was left before the November exhibition. Spring had gone; summer was over its best, and had settled into a full-blown blowsiness, with rust fringes to flower petals, and people shedding coats and cardigans and smelling rank in the heat.

Valmiki, in his state of shock, seemed unaware of time; and the painting we had admired one spring evening in the drawing room now hung framed in mute reminder on the wall, seemingly the last of its line. The situation would have daunted most people; and even Caroline, for all her iron nerve, was clearly under strain, snapping not only at poor expendable Ellie, but even at her precious newfound daily, a cheerful woman from Bow who riposted with verve and dash.

To Valmiki, however, Caroline said nothing; a forbearance so strongly against her nature that she must have torn her guts to achieve it, though the bleeding was kept internal. I made some comment, and she explained it with candor.

"Well," she said, transparently frank, "I didn't want to be told I was nagging."

I remembered our earlier conversation, my pointed rhetorical questioning as to what she would do in just such a contingency, and my own tart answers; and felt thoroughly ashamed of myself. But then I thought again, and knew her reply to be at best only a minute part of the truth, for she was almost completely indifferent to what people said. When she saw acceptance was not forthcoming she laughed, not at all put out, and explained again.

"My dear, the sheerest self-interest, I assure you. I don't think anything I say will do any good, and I'm afraid it'll anchor him even more firmly in the bog he's in now. So, I am being patient."

I would have settled for that alone, it had the ring of truth; but she went on: "The other's true too."

"What other?"

"About not wanting to be told I was nagging."

"I hardly thought you'd mind," I said, "*what* I told you."

"It just shows, doesn't it," she said with an ironic edge to her voice, "how little you know me."

"I shall never really understand you," I said, and she nodded at once, looking at me with faint amusement.

"No. It's the classic ailment, isn't it?"

"What is?"

"That England and India never did understand one another."

With the words she had deliberately moved away from the particular to a generality: yet despite them, with that superb egotism with which the mind goes its own way, establishing its own connections, I could think only of her and the boy, and wonder if what she had said were not a tacit admission of waning confidence in herself, in her power to take him over, or having taken him over, to hold him. But when I reflected again, looked at her once more, I knew it could not be. She was too strong, too sure of herself, even to countenance that the original act might have been wrong.

To her it was only a question of biding her time, however incidentally inconvenient this was, until the problem resolved itself; or if it did not, of finding a formula to cure it as she had already done for his teething troubles and homesickness. It would take many more knocks, I thought, hard ones, to topple her off that pinnacle of infallibility, so proudly and powerfully based on her faith in herself.

11

IF Caroline said nothing about working to Valmiki, neither did I; there was simply nothing to be said. He had been introduced, at firsthand and without even such preparation as a reading of Grimm might have given, to rabid cruelty, and the shock had swept everything from his mind except a horrified contemplation of the diseased landscape Ellie's presence had revealed. Caroline however would have none of it.

"Of course not," she said. "India's full of cruelty. He's seen enough without going green at the gills at the first whiff of it."

"This is different," I said.

"Different?" She raised satiric eyebrows, her voice disdainful as if she had caught me in the act of hypocrisy. "Of course it is. It's Christians behaving like methodical beasts—not Hindus doing the same thing haphazard."

It did indeed, then, sound very much like hypocrisy. I dropped the matter, without however changing my opinion. But the anatomy of shock remained hidden—how it functioned, or even why—as puzzling as physical shock which is so often coupled with bodily injury to explain why someone dies. Did he, I sometimes wondered, now equate his work with frivolity?

feel he had not the right to dabble with paint while people like Ellie lived, were tortured, and died? Or was it an interregnum, while he fought against the nobility and the savagery which are two faces of an inscrutable universal pattern, and at last learned to accept both?

The only person totally unaffected by the strain and un-certainty of those months was the precious daily, Mrs. Peabody. In the beginning there had been, I believe, some kind of ar-rangement about hours and wages; but in a very few weeks Caroline had capitulated, with sighs of gratitude, to her abun-dant energy and her passion for cleaning, so that Mrs. Peabody was to be seen at all hours of the day indefatigably working about the house—in marked contrast to the rest of the household. "I don't like to see nothink dirty," she would say, kneeling and scrubbing, her hair in a sort of dismal snood, wisps that had escaped the snare lying wilted on her nape, her sleeves rolled back to show broad white washerwoman's forearms. Or, breathing and rubbing hard, the "tidy" of rags and tins in her lap, "It brings it up beautiful, it do," she would say, with beatitude, of some wax or polish, smirking at dwindled-down reflections of herself in surfaces left winking and shining with her efforts.

Sometimes I came across her late at night, rasping about in the kitchen after one of those dinner parties to get Val to know a few people that Caroline still gave, though less and less fre-quently. I think she was fascinated by the people who came— the elegant, well-groomed, effortlessly rich of Caroline's back-ground, as well as the sprinkling of arty eccentrics—their sins redeemed by money or fashionable talent—whom she also affected. Mrs. Peabody did not cook, or wait at table—com-petent hired servants did both; but washing-up afterwards had been taken from clumsy Ellie and awarded to her and she could be seen, lurking about the hall or scullery, long before the first guest arrived. "No, Mr. Peabody don't mind, dear," she said, when I commented on the remarkable complaisance shown by her husband. "He's on night shift, in the Post Office."

"Permanently?"

"Yes, permanent," she explained. "He gets a bit extra like, working nights. Besides he wouldn't know what to do if he was at home, bless his heart!"

"Couldn't he sleep?"

"No, dear, no," she said patiently. "He's got out of the habit like. It's that quiet, he just can't get off."

She addressed everyone, incorrigibly, as "dear"; a habit which Caroline did not like, and which Valmiki pompously called untruthful because we were not dear to her. Despite this, and the spirited defense she put up against Caroline's unjust if sporadic attacks, she was liked by and got on well with everyone except Ellie.

"Don't she jaw!" she said in hoarse wonder of the silent girl, and indignantly, having been startled more than was bearable, "Fair gives you the creeps, she do, walking about in them soft shoes."

Valmiki was her favorite: partly because he was so obviously alone, partly because he was young, about the age of her own sons, partly because he was Indian. She liked Indians; an improbable attitude that had flickered into being in the mid-thirties, when she had been living as a young married woman in Bow, and Gandhi had come to stay in the next street. "He was a lad, he was," she would say, with the chuckle that came into her voice whenever she spoke of him, her eyes kindling with the memory of whatever it was that had captivated her. "Always smiling, and a word for everyone, and the kids splitting their sides with his jokes and that . . ." and then, with reverence, "He was a gentleman, no clothes and all." Coming from her this was handsome praise, for gentlemen (and ladies too for that matter, despite her sparring with Caroline) occupied predestined places at the apex of the pyramid of her very lively sense of social values, and she must have warred against equally fortified persuasions that equated nudity with savages to have set him there.

That Valmiki had not painted any nudes was a point in his favor; Mrs. Peabody knew about this side of an artist's work, of which she disapproved. Also, he occupied no social niche as far as she was concerned, inhabiting a kind of limbo, or utopia —from her conversation it was never clear which—where classlessness was the order.

Accordingly she felt no inhibitions in inviting him to her home; and when he turned his blank, dark, withdrawn eyes on her and refused, her astonishment was plain and painful to see. Underlying the contradictory codes and convictions that actuated her—many of them inherited and persistent, but knocked ludicrously askew by such episodes as the war and Gandhi— beneath this general muddle ran a solid, impermeable stratum: the knowledge that she was British, and that being British was best; which in a way was Caroline's attitude—a battered and watered-down but still recognizable variant. Therefore, it was an honor for anyone who wasn't English to be asked to Sunday dinner by anyone who was; and its decline she treated as a national insult. In all fairness, possibly she also felt it as a sharp personal snub, for Englishmen in their castles do not lightly let down the drawbridge: and having done so, mainly out of kindness whatever her other unconscious motives, it must have been galling to see the gesture pass almost unheeded.

To resuscitate, presumably, her sagging sense of values, Mrs.

Peabody repeated her invitation to the cook, which he, a lay-about in the grand Indian manner, happy to live off anyone foolish enough to make the offer, instantly accepted. She was as instantly sorry, having wanted only to buttress her shaken position and not wishing, understandably, to exhibit so supreme an example of successful sloth to her family. But she still would not hear a word said against any Indian, even those whose sloth raised all her hardworking hackles, and rather than hurt his feelings she doggedly confirmed the invitation—not realizing she could hardly have done so, for his Madras-pavement origins, and living as an alien, had combined to give him a plating of armor.

Alternate Sundays were the cook's day off, but whether he was off or not seemed to make little difference to him, he re-mained solitarily in his room, or inside the kitchen, grudgingly cooking sketchy meals of rice and eggs which few but himself could stomach. Until the advent of Ellie he had been able (though furtively, and not often, for Caroline had forbidden him this association) to go out with Valmiki and introduce him to his London—the cut-price, teeming London of steam-filled, curry-haunted eating places, seamen's union clubs and raucous street markets which is the world of waiters in Indian restaurants.

Now when Valmiki went out he dragged Ellie along with him—to get a little fresh air in the parks, or to see me, or out for a meal when the cook's efforts became noxious beyond endurance. Or else he went out, politely, with the people whom Caroline was trying to get him to know—the liberal section of it which was the only section of it that asked; and you would see them falling over themselves with benevolence, invisible wings sprouting from their shoulders with the pleasurable con-sciousness that they were treating Valmiki as an equal. He sensed it—the oversweetness, the perfervid kindness, the bowing before his every wish that verged on the idiotic; but was too intrigued by behavior which he at last called, with a philosophic shrug, "simply their way" to be resentful. Being patronized was new to him, for Caroline had never indulged in it. She respected what she believed a high talent, was determined to see her judgment vindicated, and with her sights set firm on this was at once completely indifferent to his class and race, and secure enough in her own position to be able to maintain this indifference. Beyond this, she cared for him with zeal and efficiency as she might have a property—the necklace of diamonds around her throat that Valmiki had spoken of with bitterness.

And still beyond was the affection that had come—though it might easily have been the reverse—from close association with a boy whose moments of ugly intractibility were matched by impulses of extreme gentleness and generosity.

Caroline could be generous too—in many ways, and certainly over money, though by no means because she was careless with it. From the beginning I knew she had made Valmiki a handsome allowance, and there were frequent hushed revelations from Mrs. Peabody about the satisfactory size of the cook's and her own pay packets, as well as nods and hints about Ellie's affluence, deduced from the fact that she could afford to eat out—which, said Mrs. Peabody, was quite beyond *her* purse, but then everyone knew the Jews were always better off than anyone else. "They salt it away," said Mrs. Peabody, with pursed lips and simple conviction, as if the ways of the Jews were part of proven folklore.

In fact, of course, when Ellie ate out, Valmiki paid as he could well afford to do; and indeed, despite Mrs. Peabody, there was never any evidence that she had much beyond pocket money. Her clothes were of the cheapest, ill-cut tweed sacks in which she looked even more gaunt than she was; she possessed only one pair of shoes, and that with its frugal millimeter of stick-on sole showing; and although she had a passion for stockings—it was almost a perversion, the way she handled the silk, as if preserving this one last feminine attribute in the midst of horror had exacted its own price—she could not often have indulged it, judging from the regularity with which beige rayon clad her legs.

Sometimes I wondered—since entertaining, instead of being entertained, was new in his life—how Valmiki managed in restaurants, totally illiterate as he was; and concluded that either Ellie or the waiters helped. But his method was much more direct and effective, as I discovered when he asked me to accompany him to a rather nice restaurant he had found. "A rather nice restaurant"—he said it quite simply. The disparity was in phrasing and tone, with their hint of inspired unearthing of exclusive excellence to be guarded from vulgar invasion, that sounded odd in the extreme, coming from him, until I realized it was not really an attitude—that he was merely repeating, parrot-wise, what he had heard.

In fact it turned out to be an unpretentious little place in one of those small streets off Piccadilly, with a cosmopolitan bill of fare which Valmiki waved aside. Then he ordered onion soup, an omelette with saffron rice and pimentos, and cheese and fruit. He said it all with complete assurance—a blend of Caroline's decisiveness and what, I reflected, was sheer necessity: he could not tell what was available, he simply had to ask for what he wanted and dominate them into bringing it. Either that, or depend on waiter or companion—an exercise in debility he had clearly decided was not for him.

The meal came—everything down to the saffron rice and pimentos. I congratulated him on his selection, meaning more the technique that got him so neatly over a hurdle, and he nodded and accepted both compliments.

"I know what you like, I know you for a long time. And to ask is the best way, yes? For me the only way."

I said, "What's happened to Ellie tonight? Wouldn't she come?"

"I not wish her to," he answered, and then he switched to Tamil—the first time he had done so since the ban Caroline had imposed on him many months ago. "I did not want her to hear what we are saying, and I must say it because not to know is eating me up. . . . I must know if it is as the woman cleaner says, that in the camps like where Ellie was, the young women were given to the soldiers to do with as they liked. Is it true? Was this so? I would ask Ellie myself, but she still bleeds within."

The question was so strange, so unexpected, I could not take it in at once. I stared at him, trying to work out what had prompted it, what lay in his mind, and in place of that glimmer of communication more usual between us, confronted by a blank wall—a deliberate stone wall. Moreover, considering the question in definite terms—although I had read as much about the subject with as much avid vagueness as anyone—I found I did not know. Did brothels flourish inside concentration camps? Or was the race so detested that its women were spared this one indecency?

I shook my head, feeling helpless, and he said, "If you do not know, do you think it was so?"

"Probably it was so," I said, because it seemed to me unlikely that any restraints had held.

It was not an honest answer. I should have insisted that I did not know, and refused to gamble with the truth. But by now I had concluded he was so obsessed with Ellie's suffering it was imperative for him to have the whole picture instead of snatched glimpses that led him one step at a time up an endless tormented flight, in the way that women in fratricidal wars deliberately uncover the bodies of their dead, to come to terms with the worst. This belief prompted—and colored—my answer. For some reason it never occurred to me to relate the question to more personal issues.

12

AUGUST came, and Londoners went speeding from the city as fast as huge new quotas of foreigners poured in. An impossible month, Caroline declared it, and took herself off to the country—for once without Valmiki, who, though usually malleable, had stoutly insisted on his preference for London. In a way this probably fitted in with her plans, for Caroline was in the middle of one of those brittle love affairs with which she spiced her life, and I remembered vaguely having heard her complain about her current lover's loathing of London. By now the exhibition had of course been canceled—postponed, said Caroline, but as far as I could gather no further date had been fixed.

Meanwhile I was leaving for India. The script I was working on had been finally accepted, and filming was reputedly about to begin at the Santa Cruz studios near Bombay. As early as May the film moguls had cabled acceptance and requested my immediate attendance; at the same time my agent had written, urgently counseling me to stay where I was until the financial position improved, which now apparently it had. This was confirmed by the arrival of a check, and a snowfall of further cables emphasizing the key nature of my job and my presence all of which, I knew from experience, would be repudiated at the earliest opportunity. Nevertheless I booked my flight, wrote to Caroline and to various people in India, sublet the flat, the lease on which still had three years to run, and began the dreary business of packing and moving out.

The day before I left, Valmiki came, bringing Ellie with him, and with the news that he was hard at work again—indeed that he had been for some weeks. This time there was no evidence of it: no unwieldy parcel, no sketches thrust under my nose, no leaping, ebullient excitement; instead a deeper, more contained, yet no less evident pleasure.

I was in the middle of packing, but I pushed everything aside while I congratulated him, feeling absurdly pleased myself that he should be working again—no doubt from some puritan streak within me which asserted it was better for him so than loafing around London—even with as effective a brake as the gaunt Ellie.

Ellie, indeed, seemed almost as gaunt as the first time I had seen her, and very nearly as silent, but there was little of that tense contaminating nervousness that could put an entire roomful of people on edge. Now she had moved quietly into the background and was putting records on my ancient record player—Mozart and Handel, with the volume so low that the music was reduced to a whine, though even that seemed to satisfy her. She had no particular musical ability, but for music itself she had real love as well as a deep insatiable need, so that there was hardly an occasion when she came to the flat that she did not creep up with her halting, timid request to play records, and then sit rapt in her corner as she was doing now.

On an impulse, as they were leaving, I presented Ellie with the entire collection of records. I had never been able to trace the owner, and it would save me the trouble of packing and storage. To my surprise she refused, only consenting to accept them after I had pressed her and then on condition that I take them back on my return—because, she said, she had always played them here and they would never sound the same anywhere else. I agreed. The distinct flavor given by the combination of small room, obsolete player, and minuscule volume could probably never be reproduced elsewhere; and on reflection I realized how much of our conversation—Valmiki's and mine—had, since Ellie's coming, been conducted against this faintly incongruous background of murmuring Bach, Mozart and Beethoven.

Incongruity. That, I thought as the aircraft skimmed over massed banks of cloud, was the due exacted from anyone stepping outside the bounds set by birth. It worked quite impartially, whether by making a monkey out of Caroline, with her gloves and her art enthusiasms in the artless backwoods of a tropical country, or by laying the same bizarre wand on Valmiki, hatted and suited on his way to the Savoy, or listening with me to Bach. Yet the end results were not uniformly dismal. Given courage they could rise beyond grotesquerie to become unique and splendid, like the British in India, like Caroline overcoming the worst of foreign temperament and terrain: and perhaps, I thought, one day like Valmiki too.

Going by air, as always, thoughts came and went in a fractious, disjointed way that I hated. I hated flying too, which gave me a mild version of diver's bends, a painful inability to

adjust rapidly to my surroundings that became acute each time
we plunged into a new environment to be fed, fueled and
watered. Even Bombay seemed strange—the Bombay that I had
lived and worked in and knew well—and the vultures of strange-
ness flapped dismally along in my wake for unconscionable
lengths of time—not invisibly either, to judge from the stares I
drew—until I would gladly have traded all I possessed for a
merging anonymity. But gradually my English pallor, accent,
manners and disemphasis—tenuous overlays all—began to fade,
forcing those predatory vulture faces to give way too until
nothing was left but a grim, under-the-skin reminder of what
prolonged European sojourn might mean for Valmiki.

I was staying, inexorably, at that resplendent hotel in Bombay
to which all visitors gravitate, and which, from the sheer convenience and comfort it offers, is amazingly difficult to bypass.
Here, in a modest room that overlooked the bay, smelling
alternately of sea-spray and balsam, the *Rani of Jhansi* came to
life, dominating the typewritten pages as if this extraordinary,
doomed, dead queen still kept stringent watch to see that not
even the film moguls tampered with her memory.

I, indeed, had no wish to do so. Her exploits, even in dry
straightforward chronicle, had absorbed me for months as undoubtedly they would have done the most meager imagination.
But those box-office twins, love interest and local color, had
also to be placated—my capacity for doing which seemed to
have been in doubt, since a collaborator had been yoked to me
whose job it was to keep ushering the twins into full view.
Several frustrating months went by, therefore, before an acceptable compromise could be reached and written in; but by
the end of the year the first firm draft of the screenplay was
completed, my part in it was over, and blowing on my burned
fingers I went home to recuperate.

13

HAVING gone as far south as my home, I knew that sooner or later I would have to revisit Valmiki's village. There was his mother, no doubt kept informed of her son's well-being in brief brittle notes from Caroline, duly translated by the school-master, but thirsting for word-of-mouth news for which, to the unlettered, there is no real substitute. There was the Swami, though here it would be less for his sake than for mine, to try and resolve some of the doubts that beset me. And there was the pull of, as it were, the place of decision, rousing in me a furtive curiosity to see again the exact spot on which the odd, enormous experiment had begun.

South to Madras, farther south still to the village, and of course nothing had changed. The same stony hillside, the same lozenges of emerald paddy briefly lighting the scrawny land-scape, the same sense of expanded time and silence—for accelera-tion and pitch undoubtedly vary from point to point in the world—even the same smells of well-water, cow dung, coconut fiber and thatch and, approaching the headman's hut, the faint pall of fermentation.

The headman came to the door of his house at my step, his welcome becoming charged with apprehension when he saw it was I. There was nothing, however, that I wanted from him this time, seeing which he relaxed, shouting to his wife to bring tumblers of tea, over which he grew amiable. When the formalities of imbibing were over, he asked cautiously after Valmiki, his face taking on an expression of hushed, intense curiosity as if inquiring of someone who had been shot into space.

"He's doing well," I said. "His work is highly thought of."

"We always knew he was clever." The headman clasped complacent hands across his paunch. "Our whole village felt proud to have him in our midst."

"He was never in your midst," I said shortly. "He lived alone, as you know perfectly well. Moreover it was nothing to do with your village, since he was born in the next one, where I believe his people still are."

The headman was not one whit discomfited by this realism— if anything, a little pained by its gracelessness.

"They are, yes," he said. "In the next village, as you say. You wish to see them? I will arrange . . . yes at once."

With zeal and courtesy he procured a bullock cart, which got me to the outskirts of Valmiki's village in about the same time it would have taken me to walk. From there it was only a few minutes to the hut I remembered so well, and an interview which by now I had begun to dread.

It was not, of course, as bad as my imaginings.

The hut was empty save for the mother, who sat on a tattered mat with her back against the wall and her knees splayed, rather as if she were giving birth, though it was not the pangs of bearing she had braced herself against but the rigor of malaria. It was the fifth day, the worst of the attack was over, but it had left her with a characteristic languor which only willpower, ruthlessly applied, had briefly overcome.

"You bring news of my son? He is well?" The sunken, dull eyes managed a brightness, the faded blanket fell back as she

pressed forward to gaze into my face, read the news there before I could give it.

Yes, he was well, I said, and added the fiction about his
doing well too. She made no comment on this, but started rum-
maging in the voluminous folds of the blanket draped around
her, eventually producing a small bundle of postcards and letters
that she mutely handed to me. They were all from Caroline,
variously stamped and postmarked as when she had been writing
to me; and looking down at that clear bold hand on the graying
paper it seemed suddenly preposterous, unreal, that anything of
Caroline, even her writing, should enter this baked mud hut
with cow-pats plastered on its walls.

"That one." Unerringly, though she could not read, the
woman indicated the letter she wanted extracted. Unwillingly,
under her gaze, I opened and read it—the months-old brief
message in three short lines. Then I folded and put it back in
its flimsy blue envelope and waited.

"You see," she said, "the lady has written that he has not
worked, and her plans for him have come to nothing."

"Yes." It was pointless denying it. Caroline had been quite
frank about the abortive exhibition, casually and uncaringly
truthful as I might have known she would be, although now
that the truth was out my own well-meant sedation seemed
worse than her brutality.

"If she is tired of him, he must come back." She pulled the
disarranged blanket around her and huddled into it, though it
was a baking hot day. "He is my son, he will always be welcome here in his own home."

The words were uncontrived, the lined face innocent. A
shutter had come down in her mind, sealing off her guilt—the
memory of chidings and petulances that had gone into his long
day, the coldness, the isolation, the final casting out—all of it.

Her emotions had insisted that this call of flesh and blood be passionately received and answered, and her solicitous mind had cleared the way by efficiently clamping off all intimations and evidence to the contrary.

And Valmiki? If ever he stepped over that threshold again, hung about as it would undoubtedly be with the rattling symbols of welcome, would he be—not happy, for that he had never been and it was unlikely now could be—but capable still of that blatantly powerful step he had taken before, of turning his back on it? Or would he be ridden by a guilt as paltry as hers, concentrated on that malarial mask of which there were a thousand similars in India, until his own vision blackened and shriveled as though under the maliciously focused rays of a burning-glass?

And this, I thought, was what Caroline had taken him from. I had never come before as close to deifying her as then.

"You will tell him what I have said? That if he is not at peace abroad he must come back to us, to his home?"

The cracked febrile voice besought me, and although her anxiety sprang from the poisoned bed of her delusions, it was not thereby less moving.

I pressed her hand, meaning her to interpret it as acquiescence, which she probably did. There were a few small presents I had brought with me; I laid these at her feet, and then I went out, stooping to get through the doorway which was about half my height.

There was one more call that I had to make, but I hesitated, wondering if I had the time. Twilight was not far off, and it would flare and fade as quickly as a match-head, leaving a black void which no town can know, and no townsman cares to be out in. Finally I decided to be prudent and went back to my hotel, getting in just before seven—the hour traditionally hallowed by cocktails. There were now, of course, few cocktails, but nevertheless the place was beginning to fill, people drifting up to the bar aimlessly, like conditioned rats.

There was a small stack of mail waiting for me at the desk, and in it a letter from Caroline, which I collected and took up to my room. I had a shower and changed into fresh clothes, meticulously laid out by the room boy, and then I settled down to read—leaving Caroline's letter to the last, only to be disappointed for there were only two scribbled lines on the large sheet that had fed my expectations. But the news was good: Valmiki was working prodigiously, and there was to be an exhibition in April.

Some of my depression began to lift—the depression inevitably engendered by a contemplation of poverty and sickness—and I went down in better heart to order my dinner.

I was sipping a preliminary tomato juice, iced, spiced, glowing in a glass rimed with the cold, when I felt my arm taken and there was Jumbo, beaming, incredulous that he should have come across a friend here, though in fact his friends were spread over just these gilded parts of the globe, and with a friendliness and charm that must have wrung governmental hearts—British and Indian successively—even as they systematically stripped him of his iniquitous wealth and estates, I greeted him warmly; we were old friends, had known each other so long there was not even sex left, just this easy relaxing warmth that is sometimes found between well-disposed brother and sister.

"Why didn't you let me know you were coming?" He looked around for a chair, and obsequious waiters jostled each other to give him one. "We might have had a party. . . . There's precious little excuse these days."

"I nearly did," I said. "It was thinking of that party stopped me."

He wagged a finger at me, his face crinkling with genuine laughter—a buoyancy that had never deserted him during the long sad ritual of divestment that had been his lot.

"You'll regret that, you know. When nobody asks you then you'll be sorry."

"I know," I said. "Human nature is difficult, isn't it?"

"Impossible—impossible to live with. Best thing I've found is to be artificial." He conjured a bottle from his pocket and began pouring vodka into my glass. "I'm making a Bloody Mary. You prefer it, don't you? You should get yourself some, you don't need me to tell you where."

"It's not a passionate preference," I said.

"One pampers preferences, passionate or not. What else is life for?" He raised his glass. "Besides, you can't deny it imparts a sparkle? I thought not. Well, now you're back, is it for good?"

"Not this time. The next, I hope."

"I've heard that from so many people." He chuckled. "They commute between continent and continent thinking they're free, then one day they find they can't face India. London's got them. Or Geneva or New York. It always does in the end."

"But not me," I said, "because . . ."

He waited, drawing his eyebrows up derisively.

"Simply because I can always come back here," I said, "feel at home with my own family, and be received by people like you. Which unfortunately isn't true of those whose status has been altered in the West—indeed, by its courtesy."

He leaned forward. "My dear," he said, spreading his hands, adroitly avoiding the future by returning to the past, "you're thinking of that boy. But what else could I do? The servants would have walked out en bloc. You can't run a palace without servants, even if it's only one wing."

"That wasn't Caroline's experience."

"Ah yes." He smiled reminiscently. "Dear, delightful Caroline. She always could get away with anything. Comes of being that special class of Englishwoman, you know. Few of us could emulate her."

"You're still in thrall," I said, "to the British ruling classes."

He smiled gracefully and agreed; barbs on that polished surface were so much waste of time. Indeed, sometimes they acted as boomerangs, making you wince with the thought of his great good nature, and all it had been made to take.

"Now tell me all about Caroline," he went on, his face bland and receptive though he had probably already heard more than there was to tell. "All about her and her street arab, this shepherd boy."

"He has never been the one," I said, "and has ceased to be the other."

"Whatever he is then," he said equably. "There have been the most delicious, piquant rumors floating around about them."

"What kind?"

"Unkind, my dear, unkind. That she is in thrall, to use your own phrase, to this boy."

"Not to the boy—to his talent," I said. "He comes a rather poor second. Sometimes he and I both wonder if she ever thinks of him as a human being. But there's no doubt what she thinks of his work."

"That he's good?"

"Very good."

"And you?"

"I? I'm not a critic, it doesn't matter what I think."

"Critics?" His eyes were wide and avid for the gossip which

made the wheels of his life whir louder in the emptiness. "Is there to be an exhibition? Rumor was, it had collapsed almost at conception."

"Then rumor was wrong," I said with pleasure. "There is to be an exhibition in the spring."

"An exhibition, by this innocent. My dear, that promises to be most interesting." He cupped his hands about his glass, smiling down at it as if it were a woman. "You know, I'm half tempted to offer my congratulations in person to this gifted compatriot of mine—not to mention the enchanting Caroline . . . more than half tempted to exchange my cumbersome private bar"—he tapped his loaded sides—"for something more public and convivial—in fact, to take an overdue holiday."

I laughed—an echo of old laughter; and he grinned too and said, a little wryly, "You still believe it has been a perpetual holiday? But then you've never been a rajah. I assure you, only the sheerest coolie labor preserved even a tithe from the hands of rapacious Residents."

"No doubt for the coolies."

"For the rajah." He shrugged philosophically. "After all, your peasant was too dumb to get it. Better indigenous ruler, don't you agree, than imperial government via their incorruptible collectors, the Residents?" He paused. "Lady Caroline's father was Resident when I succeeded my father, did you know?—though it wasn't a long tenure."

"I gathered she had imperial connections. I didn't know it was as close as your State."

"My ex-State . . . Yes, a handsome man. Quite unrapacious. Wonderful cricketer, too. We got on excellently, most of the time." He was briefly silent, his face gentle and melancholy; then up came his glass again. "Well, here's to all peasants, especially yours."

"Caroline's."

"To Caroline's peasant."

"He's no longer a peasant."

"To ex-peasant, query present status, query future artist, whose plebeian name—"

"Patrician."

"Whose name I cannot remember. To him."

He drained his glass. I drank too. The sparkle was undoubtedly there, as undoubtedly vanished when Jumbo had gone; and I grew morose, pointlessly drinking in a hostile climate.

14

I HAD asked for an early call, so that my visit to the Swami would be over before it started getting really hot—or perhaps, indeed, before the thought of the tedium of the journey perished the intention.

At seven exactly the bearer came to wake me, bringing tea, bananas, and those Indian-manufactured biscuits which are skillful copies of the Reading ones. After a brief salutation he paid no more attention to me, but parting the mosquito net gathered up soft armfuls and massed them over the bed, straddled a small bed table over my still-recumbent body and set out the tea on it, brought in fresh towels, ran my bath, laid out sari, underskirt, blouse, brassière—all freshly laundered—and then padded unobtrusively out, all without a second glance at me, in the tradition that his caste and mine both acquiesced in—that a manservant could perform almost any service for his mistress, and providing only she never swerved from her attitude that he was an unthinking eunuch, he could be trusted to behave like one.

I drank my tea, bathed, dressed, and was down to breakfast by half-past seven. Even at that early hour there were a good many people about, most of whom seemed to be in or making for the big sun terrace that opened off the dining room. Three steps led down to it, flanked by huge brass jardinieres filled with luxuriant fern, and the terrace itself terminated in a graceful low balustrade whose coping displayed a further fine selection of fern from maidenhair to bracken, and interspersed among them a profuse variety of flowers in pots—canna and lily, orchid and cacti, the gaudy poinsettia, and the gentle hibiscus. Here were set out chairs and tables of painted rattan, each small grouping shaded by sun umbrella or potted palm, so that it was not easy to see exactly what went on at any of them.

With thoughts of an early start still dominant, I almost shrugged off my natural curiosity, telling myself that the preponderance of women meant either a business women's conference or a fashion show; then my dislodged sense of place worked back into position, making me realize that either of the explanations so casually presented would be remarkable for India. So I finished breakfasting rapidly and went down to the terrace, and there on a cane chair among the greenery, in a white loin cloth and shoulder cloth, surrounded by women, was the Swami.

At once material frontiers began to crumble. I had been thinking about him a good deal, said my confused mind, and here was the palpable result. Such evocations were rare, not unknown; and the precipitants were as varied as they were at times incongruous or, as now, utterly innocent of design. What else could be the explanation of the sudden appearance here—in this fashionable hotel, among affluent women—of a man I had last seen naked on a barren hillside lost in single mystic contemplation of God?

It was the same man beyond any doubt—the same ascetic face, with the faintly bleached look of too little flesh to hide the white bone, the same thin, weathered frame, pared and disciplined to fineness like the face; the same gentle, reasonable voice. It was the voice that steadied me, and the calm precise observation it was making on the properties of some flower. No hallucination of my brain, I thought with faint distant amusement, would exhibit this detailed botanical knowledge. It was only the violent contrast between the rigor of his past living, its present apparent plush, that had split reality.

My plan for the day made pointless now, I stood patiently with the throng, for there was not a single seat to be had. Except for a sprinkling of sheepish-looking men, the crowd was mostly of women, and mostly of middle-aged women: European, American, a few Parisians, fewer Hindus: all of course affluent, for it cost money to breathe this rarefied air, and all with a less-evident common factor of subtle deformity—the pinched, down-drawn mouths of permanent discontent, the outthrust bosom and shoulders of an unrelenting aggressiveness, the painted, shadowed, wary eyes of people exhausted by their evolutionary move from being women happy to surrender, to women doomed to conquer, like those distant sea creatures that took their first steps onto land to collapse gasping upon the beach.

The key being there the picture became clear, the presence of the Swami explicit. They craved tranquillity, he embodied it, the two had come together. The intervening process of encounter and suasion, like the postures and mock battles of mating byplay, was no more than intriguing trivia. The irreconcilable was the Swami himself, returning to a world he had renounced, and particularly to this morbid section of it; it was a conundrum only he could resolve.

I settled down to wait, edging closer as the opportunity occurred in the accepted fashion for those seeking audience. Public audience, in the natural, shameless, uninhibited manner of India; and oddly enough when I stood before him the Western yen for privacy, the castle to contain oneself, no longer mattered. Here we were, two people alone in the crowd, both caring in varying degrees for the same boy, and I said simply, "I have come about Valmiki."

He said, equally simply, "I shall be happy to hear anything about him. Despite myself I have not been able to forget him entirely."

So room was made for me by his side, and I told him what there was to tell with a large admixture of my own misgivings; and when I had done he said, peacefully, "There is no difficulty, except what you have created. The boy, should he want to, can always come back here."

"He cannot. I have told you, he is a misfit. With his family, his country, the life that he led—"

He stopped me gently but decisively: "One can never be," he said, "a misfit in the service of God."

Valmiki, in the service of God? I could not visualize him in those terms, less than ever because I knew him in the context of prosaic London, alternately moping and obsessed. The nearest that he came to God, I thought, was when he was driven by his devils. I did not say so: I had not come to spread calumny and cause pain; but in a few moments he had taken up the unspoken.

"He came to me as a child," he said. "He was my disciple,

during the formative years. Nothing will touch that. Where other men despair, he will turn to God, unlikely though it seems to you now. If he is fretted by wherever he is, he will return to me and it will not be the joyless void that you imagine, it will be a homecoming."

I could neither accept nor reject what he had said; but certainly it is not only the Jesuit who claims the man from a custody of those few deciding years in the child.

I said, "I don't know if you're right but I hope you are. I hope you're not making a mistake."

"Everyone makes mistakes." His tone had changed. Voice and words were for an audience, he was no longer speaking to me alone, as in a curious way he had so far been doing; and the audience, whose presence I had completely forgotten, reacted with a fervently concurrent chorus from which rose a solo voice, half-bantering, half-serious:

"You too, Swamiji?"

"I? Yes, certainly." His voice matched the solo performer's but it was gentle. "It is you, who invaded my solitude, who made me aware of it—made me realize I had sought the contemplative life too soon, that there were lessons yet to be learned in the world . . . what else should I be doing among you ladies here but sitting at your feet learning my lesson?"

There were denials, delightful murmurs; more questions and answers; the sort of kindly repartee that the world is first shocked and then charmed to find included in the armory of its saints.

Already the temper of the meeting had changed, moving from the tensions of an intransigent egotism to a more bearable and balanced whole, in which the problems of self and neighbor, flesh and spirit and society assumed their due and relative roles. I felt the release in myself, felt the wavelets of euphoria lapping

softly against me; and after a while I said—though even then I
sensed, remotely as in another existence, that such unworldly
things could not be of the slightest interest to him or myself—

"Valmiki is to exhibit his work in April," and I added depre-
catingly, struggling to remember why it should have seemed so
to me too: "It is an important event to him."

The Swami turned; his eyes rested on mine briefly, but
attentively.

"I will remember," he said.

I was in my room, and it was much later, before the absurdity
of it hit me hard. What could an exhibition of painting possibly
mean to him—a man whose horizons were limited to this small
corner of India, however boundless his inner vision, who lived
so meagerly and parochially—a backwoodsman, even if temporarily and startlingly denizen of an exotic hothouse?

Yet, oddly, I did not regret having told him.

15

I WENT back to London in March to begin work on the
second of the series of scripts called for in my contract. This
was much less harassing than the first: a straightforward docu-
mentary needing a good deal of research but no romantics,
and I was positively blithe as I stepped off the boat-train onto
the greasy, gale-swept, bitterly cold platform at Waterloo.

Caroline had come to meet me. With the rush of pleasure

that the unexpected gives, I saw her almost as I got out of the train, a lone figure standing aloof from the crush at the barrier.

"What a place!" She shivered as I came up to her. "I cannot understand why everybody doesn't simply get back into that train and steam away to wherever they came from . . . no, we don't want a taxi, I've brought the motorcar."

Efficiently my luggage and I were stowed in the car, vehicle of mercy in this season of gales. Caroline sat beside me, voluble, more spirited than I last remembered her. She was wrapped in a sealskin coat, her swan's neck rising above the sleek fur, her skin with the delicate pallor that English skins often assume in extreme cold.

For late March, it was extraordinarily cold. Snow still lay on the ground, churned to a gray mulch on the pavements, but on parapets and copings, on roofs and the railings to the squares, wherever it had lain as it fell it was a glittering, piercing, resplendent white. No hint of green yet; only the white and the black of the trees, charred skeletons against an ice-blue sky with a frail tracery of snow along the branches where the sun had not yet gilded the bark. It was beautiful, with that un-impeachable beauty that gives London its lovers despite every kind of fickleness and deceit.

"Well," said Caroline, "what was India like?"

"Hot. And London?"

"Cold."

She began to laugh. "That's marvelous . . . almost pure Coward. What I really want to know is, what about the parents?"

"What about them?"

She said, guardedly, "Val's becoming known now . . . sooner or later, I suppose, they'll learn about it, and then will they want him back?"

I forced myself into attention, feeling a little irked that I was to be confronted with problems again when all I wanted to do was to look at this cold, beautiful land, preserve our earlier lightness.

"Unless you tell them in one of your pretty little postcards I doubt if they will hear," I said. "But if they do, surely it'll be a simple matter to send him home for a visit? After all, that was part of the original arrangement."

"A visit," she said reflectively. "Or will it be for good?"

"Good heavens no," I said. "He's grown completely away from it all—he'll never be able to settle down with his people again, never want to either. I think if you'd seen his mother, that hut of theirs, you'd be as convinced as I am."

She nodded slightly. Her eyes were cool and shrewd, you felt she was notching up scores for and against the success of some private vendetta. Then she said, flatly, "There always is, isn't there, the medicine man . . . his Swami."

I think she saw him as in the end the real adversary—the one who could, more formidably than anyone else who had crossed her path, show up for shadows her authoritative declarations of an austere disinterestedness in and a legitimate entitlement to the boy; and resist her taking and keeping possession of what she wanted.

If so, it was a lightning assessment on her part; for that was about as much as her brief meeting with the Swami could be reckoned.

By now we were passing the British Museum, frivolously capped and laced with snow, but withal dignified and solid, with a solemnity that seemed to seep beyond the walls and the railings into the streets and even the buildings that surrounded it. Nothing had changed, as far as I could see; and in the flat a careful and thoughtful tenant had left basic provisions in the kitchen and scrupulously restored every item to its customary place, so that I felt exactly as if I had never been away.

Caroline, who could enter a crowded room and turn into marble until a few magic words of the right interest or accent restored her to life, was quite different when alone, or almost alone. Now she moved quietly about the room, companionably remembering this and that, reordering the formal arrangement of the cushions, putting cigarettes from her case into my empty box while I made coffee and lit a fire in the chill room.

When I came back with the cups she was standing in front of the record cabinet. "You used to have a good collection," she said. "What's happened to it?"

"I gave them away to Ellie," I said. "They were going begging . . . I thought she might find more use for them than I would."

"Poor Ellie," she said, and repeated the words. "Poor Ellie . . . it's funny, isn't it, the way one always puts poor before Ellie?"

"Why funny? She has so little."

"She hasn't anything as far as I can see." Caroline leaned forward and crushed out her cigarette. "It's beyond me why Val should have thought her worth putting on canvas."

"Has he?"

"Painted her?" She looked almost amused. "My dear, you *are* out of touch. You must come and see, I can promise you it'll be a surprise. *Quite* a surprise."

16

ON Monday, a week after arriving in London, duly arrayed for the cocktail party that Caroline was giving, I presented myself at the house. Driven by curiosity I got there exactly on time, which in the manner of such parties was a good half hour before anyone else.

Mrs. Peabody opened the door, perceptibly unchanged, in a woolen skirt and floral apron that I remembered, the same absurd snood around her head that only half netted her hair, her feet in working slippers.

When she saw me she stepped back dramatically.

"It's you, miss. Well, I never did!"

"Weren't you expecting me?"

"Yes I was, miss," she admitted with hoarse caution. "But seeing you there like, it fair gave me a start."

Why? Her utterances often had, for me, this enigmatic quality.

Shivering in the cold hall, I took off my various wrappings and handed them to her, for Caroline did not subscribe to any genteel usherings to upstairs bedrooms for divestment. She slung them over her arm, complimenting me on my good sense in wrapping up so well, commiserating with me on my feeling the cold so much, not so much showing me into the drawing room as propelling me there, and then standing with the door wide open to drafts while she gossiped.

All about the dreadful winter, and what her feet were doing to her, and about the cook, and, in a shocked voice, about Ellie.

"Exposing herself, she has been." Her eyes were small cold stones, her mouth a round hard button. "Not one stitch on. Not one!"

I thought of mental imbalance, a sexual aberration. Mrs. Peabody swept on. "It's not right, that's what I say, it's not right her leading him on like that and him respectable as you or me, miss, and no one's going to tell me he done it on his own because he didn't. It's her what done it and she ought to be ashamed of herself but some people—"

Here she flickered her eyebrows, closed her mouth and departed, for Caroline was coming down the stairs.

Caroline must then have been about thirty-five. In the subdued light of the drawing room, with its damask shades and luminous shadow, she looked about twenty-five. She was wearing white, a dress with a tight-cupped bodice embroidered with silver bugle beads, the skirt shaped like a bell, the material with the sway and rustle designed as expressly as drumbeat or the dance for excitation.

"Darling," she cried, and instead of the sparkling wine I expected it was vinegar. "Have I caught you gossiping with the servants again?"

"It was your servant gossiping with me," I said sourly. "I haven't your ruthless way of disposing of them."

"Gentle Hindu lamb," she said sweetly, "how *do* you survive in this jungle of English man-eaters?"

"By putting on a mask," I said.

She went over to where the drinks were grouped and got me one.

"It's champagne, darling. It's champagne all round tonight."

"Why?"

"Why not? It's a delectable drink. Tell me, what were you gossiping about?"

"Mrs. Peabody was, about Ellie not having a stitch on, indecently exposing herself. Did she?"

Caroline was shaking with laughter, the silver bugle beads shimmering on her sculpted, pointed, carefully separated breasts.

"That's dogsbody's version, is it? Poor old puritan. It's too marvelous, I must tell somebody."

"Did she?" I asked again, but Caroline slipped away without answering, gliding through the open doorway like a mute swan making a theatrical exit.

Her return was a triumphal entry.

It would equally have evoked the long low whistles of any street corner as the massive hushed murmur that rises like incense in the theatre when the curtain goes up on a sumptuous scene.

Caroline came first, all in her shining whiteness, leading by the hand Valmiki also in dazzling white, and he leading by its chain a tiny monkey wearing a scarlet hip-length jacket and a gilt leather collar. The trinity was surprising enough, but it was Valmiki who held me—a new, an astonishing Valmiki, clearly very conscious of his sudden and heady accession to self-confidence, a little too obviously careless of the striking looks guaranteed by brown skin against white clothes, light eyes against brown skin; and his uncompromising peasant attitudes exchanged, with at least questionable gain, for a glossy uniform urbanity.

I had hardly taken it in, or said more than a few words, when people began arriving, the room was suddenly full, and swirls and eddies began to form around the gorgeous and still cohering triptych. I retreated to where there was a little space, behind the grand piano which had been turned into an impromptu bar, and here among the steady drinkers parried banalities while I speculated on where exactly Valmiki fitted into the opulent picture. Had he, I wondered, already arrived and these were the prizes? Or were we all gathered here together, complete with bottles of champagne, to launch him? Caroline had not troubled to say.

By now the room resembled an alarmist view of Asia, too overcrowded to contemplate or aid. I looked around for Ellie, but there was no sign of her. Indeed, with her skill in effacement she would not have been easy to spot in the crush, though her pallid appearances could usually be counted on to create a rift in any glossy social fabric, which, smoothly repaired as it would undoubtedly be, I felt I would have noticed.

Occasionally from my corner I caught sight of Caroline, by now parted from her foil but still scintillating in her own right, moving among her guests; and there were tantalizing glimpses of the third of the trio, mostly glittering eyes and a gray small furry bottom, ludicrously bare and eye-compelling beneath the modesty jacket, hurtling between those exquisite bodies, dragging tail and chain behind it.

I knew hardly anyone; a few faces familiar from the getting-to-know-people era, a residue of the well-meaning liberal contingent whom presumably Valmiki had remembered and invited; but in the main the company was new to me—a select company, more casual and gilded and several rungs up the ladder than those that had gone before.

The glitter-dust seemed to fall agreeably on Valmiki. Assiduously attended by slim young women in black, he was floating around the room like an exotic sunflower, smiling, flushed with

the champagne continuously at his lips, at ease and ably man-
aging his attendants. His clothes seemed designed for floating—
pants that ballooned prettily about his legs, gauzy white dra-
peries only remotely related to anything worn in India, the
ensemble highly reminiscent of ballet with an Oriental theme.
It seemed unnecessary, for him; a cheap little maneuver to
garner attention more worthy of some petty starlet. As he
wafted past I said acidly, "I like your clothes. What style would
they be—South Indian devadasi?"

He examined his finery complacently, without loss of composure despite the jibe, the deliberate reference to temple
dancing girls.

"No—Muslim style," he answered equably.

"But you're not a Muslim."

"My dear, you know and I know. But how many of the
people here can tell sheep from goat?" He waved a brown
contemptuous hand at the assembly, chuckling. His votaries
closed in, laughing as if he really was the most amusing thing,
a delicious *enfant terrible*, and he was borne away.

His English was good, the accent cultivated—Caroline had
clearly made him work at it. Most of the uncouthness was gone,
and some of the honesty. Did it make him more acceptable? In
this polished Western world, obviously yes. The East was too
strident, too dissonant, too austere, too raw; it had to be muted,
toned down, tarted up—its music larded with familiar rhythms,
its literature wrenched into shapes recognized by Western
tradition, its dances made palatable by an infusion of known
idioms, its people taught to genuflect before understatement—
before a measure of acceptance came. Undilute East had always
been too much for the West; and soulful East always came
lapdog fashion to the West, mutely asking to be not too little
and not too much, but just right.

And did this acceptance mean so much, fall as sweetly upon him as the stardust? Again, I thought, yes. And yet once or twice when his eyes caught mine I was left with the feeling that he was not only ardent partaker but partly onlooker as well: that there still remained, for good augury, vestiges of a cold and watchful inner eye, as disdainful of others as of himself.

That evening was full of surprises. At nine, as I was thinking of leaving, the doors of the big double drawing room, hitherto closed against all blandishment, were thrown open. In the stripped room, against a background of severe drapes and discreet lighting like a Bond Street window, centered on one flawless dove-gray wall, was an anguished and anguishing portrait of Ellie; and flanking it six splendid paintings of an India lovingly remembered and scrupulously represented, a combination of passion and austerity that kept everyone silent, momentarily, until release came in a spate of admiration and congratulation, voiced in an audible and unfortunate but unembarrassed cascade of cliché.

"Only the minutest portion, my dears, I assure you . . . yes, several more . . . yes, rather like these, rather good I think . . ."

Caroline, powerful maestro, was directing the stream, her clear voice with its exquisite syllables riveting attention as skillfully as any fairground barker's, to which it was undoubted if improbable and silken kin. Her face, her eyes, her beautiful body in its glittering trammels, were all touched and transfigured, uplifted by triumph. The triumph of another, and that other not even her own flesh.

Or was he? The disturbing thought had not come before and would not have come now, I think, but for the radiance in Caroline, and the electric atmosphere, and the wine, subtle dismantler, pointing and revealing the sexuality latent in move and countermove, in gesture and inflection and laughter.

Were they one flesh? Were the rumors I had heard in India more solidly based than I, lulled by her series of love affairs, imagined? The thought hammered at me again as I saw her white arm encircle him, holding him as if he were hers; and then memory stirred, and I remembered this was just how she had held him long ago when he was a boy and she was establishing her claim to him as plainly as if flag in hand she were registering property rights. This stance once suggested, there were other reassuring props: the disparity in their ages, the differences of race, above all their long association and close peculiar relationship which would bring an unpleasant whiff of incest to a carnal union between them.

What I did not take into account was strength of purpose, and the terrible overpowering craving for possession.

A light touch on my arm stemmed these reflections. It was Ellie. I took her rough thin hand with the haunting sense of pity and unease that she always engendered, which Valmiki had so miraculously caught in his portrait of her.

"I've been looking for you," I said. "You manage to hide yourself most effectively."

"I am only now here. I was in my room."

"In your room when Valmiki's celebrating?"

"I did not feel well." She flushed. "I had to lie down, Lady Caroline said so to do. Now I feel better, I thought I would come."

She did not look ill; on the other hand she had never really looked well. She was wearing olive-green—another shapeless sack which emphasized her pallor: a plain crepe-silk dress embellished with a handful of sequins clumsily sewn onto the bodice—undoubtedly by Ellie herself. Poor Ellie, I thought, echoing Caroline. Poor Ellie, she tried so desperately hard and nothing ever came of it.

I said, to break the hard little shell of silence that had enclosed us, "Valmiki's become very good, hasn't he? Let's hope he'll have the success he deserves."

"He is already successful."

She said it without malice, her awkward hands hanging limply down by her sides, the sallow defeated face reflecting in microcosm the unfairness of an inexplicable universe as she gazed at the brilliant arena in which Valmiki was sunning himself.

Yet when, eventually, he saw her, he made his way at once to her side, and his words were genuinely solicitous despite his preoccupations.

"Ellie, you really feel better?"

"Yes. I am all right now. It was only a slight sickness, it has passed."

"I am so glad. Many people have asked to meet you, and I have said yes my dears, so you shall as soon as she is here and now—" He turned with a flourish, full of his newfound social graces, to introduce her to his admirers.

"May I present Ellie? She is the original of the picture which you see."

There was a slight stirring of attention in Valmiki's immediate vicinity, a murmur of polite interest, some evidence of curiosity even among these blasé people. Next to Valmiki a blonde in black, beautifully gowned, extended a languid hand. "How do you do?"

Ellie stood frozen, smiling hideously. Valmiki prodded her skillfully, as no doubt Caroline had prodded him countless times, and her hand shot out.

POSSESSION

"I am quite well, thank you," she said stiffly.

"How do you do?"

"Well—thank you."

More people came up, drifted away, their interest cooling before this shattering gaucherie. Ellie's lips were dry, her worn-out face sharpened to a shrewish ugliness under strain, her poor little body rigid as if these light social overtures were meditated assaults. Valmiki did his best, but his smile grew less and less charming, his benevolence more forced, his incredulous impatience of her poor showing more plain, and at last as he chafed to be off, one of those splendid blond creatures came to reclaim him and he bolted.

I suppose at some stage when Caroline was breaking him in he must have felt the banderillas of social inadequacy so obviously quivering between Ellie's shoulder blades; but either he had effectively suppressed it, or he did not care to revive the memory.

When he had gone, Ellie slowly began to relax. I don't think she minded what sort of figure she cut, providing only she was not overlooked by Valmiki.

She said, taking up the threads of our conversation, "I hope he will be more successful than already he is."

"Do you really?" I asked curiously.

The cropped head went up and down emphatically. "Yes. It is to him very important. Also he has so hard worked," she said with feeling, "without eating, without sleeping."

What Caroline had said came to mind, the sharp inflection of her voice, and I said suddenly, "I hear he's painted you a lot."

"Yes. I did not want him to, but he made me."

"There's no need to feel guilty about it," I said, surprised by her tone. "You aren't, are you?"

120

She lowered her head, saying nothing. In a moment or two I felt her timid touch again.

"I will show you," she said in a low voice, inclining her head toward the door. "Upstairs. Come."

17

I FOLLOWED her up to her room on the first floor, the sounds of the party trailing after us as we mounted the stairs, falling into a background hum as we closed the door behind us.

I had never been in Ellie's room before. It was medium-sized, furnished with a divan, a table and a chair, a fireside chair and a fire, and a large white-painted cupboard. Stretched across the room on thin wire was what looked like an old counterpane, the silk discolored and torn, which divided the room roughly into half. Ellie unhooked the curtain, folding it back upon itself; behind it was a sort of storeroom that Valmiki had made for himself out of the living space he had commandeered from Ellie.

There must have been thirty or forty pictures stored here—some hung, some stacked against the wall, unfinished sketches, portraits, full-length nudes, and all of them of Ellie. So this was what Mrs. Peabody had been throwing dark hints about for, I thought with amusement, picking my way over the clutter; to her this was exposure, and exposure was indecency. Then I stopped, my attention drawn to a large painting of Ellie that stood in a corner, which I had already half-noticed first time around. It was a nude, in oils, and it showed Ellie sitting in a chair, her face twisted away to show only a brief blurred profile, but the body naked and open and fully revealed, calm, with an almost blatant pride in itself. There was a hint—a slight disproportion of belly to torso, a spreading and darkening of the areolae of the small flat breasts, which made me turn sharply.

"Ellie," I said, "are you . . ."

"Yes," she said simply, folding her hands over her abdomen as if she expected a blow.

"Valmiki's?"

"Yes."

"You're quite certain?"

"Yes."

"Does he know?"

"Yes."

I sat down on the bed. The whole evening I had been aware of Caroline, her dazzling display in the odor of musk, and all the time it had been Ellie, the unenchanting orphan . . . and yet there had been ample scope for the obvious deduction. For months they had been thrown together, with opportunities for intimacy normally open only to the owners of elusive secluded flats. Valmiki had been devoted to her, explicitly so, and why neither Caroline nor I had divined its right cause I could not now imagine. There was their under-the-skin bondage, the joined experience of a calculating, maiming, actively hostile and cruel world; and the joint feeling of being without roots, top-heavy saplings struggling to keep a crazy balance in an earth that quivered and shifted, recording every move from isolate nobility to pervading madness.

So it was poor Ellie. Poor Ellie had been the desired, not

Caroline—triumphant Caroline whose brilliance had obscured these other issues.

I said, "What will you do now?"

"I do not know." Her voice was dull, uninterested.

"Is Valmiki going to marry you?"

"I do not know."

"Does he love you? Are you in love with him?"

She said a surprising thing. "I lie with a man—so. I do not talk about love, because I do not know if that is what I feel. It is not easy to feel, because I am burnt out, inside I am burnt out. But Valmiki loves me. He does not know it, but he does. At times like tonight he forgets, he cannot understand himself how it is possible to love someone so dull as I am, you can see in his face he is asking this question. Then when the others are gone and it is daytime again he comes back to me, we are of one kind."

"But aren't you interested in his coming to you at night as well?"

"It is for Valmiki to decide."

"And the baby that's coming," I said, out of patience with her lackluster submissiveness, "have you any feeling for it or must Valmiki decide that for you too?"

She looked at me queerly, without a trace of anger. "We have only been together once," she said with extreme simplicity. "If I had no feeling for a child, would I have conceived?"

One could only overlook the fallacies in statements of such faith.

"Only once," I said with pity. "The first time, Ellie?"

"First time with Valmiki," she said carefully, "but in the camp it was every night. They came for us every night. In the beginning I would ask them to kill me, but they only laughed . . . it made it worse."

"With all that," I said, "in all that time, did you never conceive or bear a child?"

"Oh no," she said in a matter-of-fact way. "It was not possible, I was too dry. Also after a few months we were not women any more . . . the flow stopped, we looked like men—no flesh, no hair—" She touched her cropped head. "For some of us it never grew properly again."

In the silence that followed I found myself shivering. Listening to her dispassionate voice the horror of it came close, all the obscenity, the wanton evil, the endless waiting for "them" to come, to be taken.

A sudden wailing cry from just outside, the clink of a chain being dragged slowly along the corridor, made me jump with fear. I glanced at Ellie and she was cowering against the wall, her skimpy arms uplifted in some sort of feeble defense. I managed to get to the door and open it. It was the ludicrous scarlet-jacketed monkey, half strangled by the silver chain which had caught in the doorjamb.

"It's all right," I called, "it's only the pet monkey."

For a moment there was no response, then Ellie came out. "It is like happiness," she said. She was shaking.

"What is?"

"The relief," she said, and knelt to hold the squirming, cross little animal while I released the chain, cradling it against her when I had eventually got it free. It lay passively in her arms, looking up at her with limpid brown eyes that were slowly regaining their sanity, until we heard the drawing room doors open, and Valmiki's voice saying good-bye to the last of the guests; and then, all action, it sprang from her clasp and bounded down the stairs, chattering wildly with the most transparent pleasure.

"Well," I said, "at least it knows to whom it belongs."

"Oh yes." Ellie licked the long scratches the monkey had left on her wrist. "It has always been Valmiki's pet. . . . He is tired of it now, but it will not go to anyone else."

It was in fact clinging tightly to his neck. Valmiki had put an arm around it in careless affection, and he was cooing to it as he negotiated the stairs—fake little love-cries that Caroline employed on her friends' toy dogs. Halfway up he spotted us and stopped to wave—a disastrous move, for the unmanageable portion of his bouffant clothes, which he had carefully assembled over his free arm, slid to his feet in muslin balloons. The monkey, delighted, clambered down at once and fell upon them, chewing and tearing and grunting in ecstasy. Valmiki, trapped and angry, attempted to fend it off with his foot, and in the process dislodged his shoe, a graceful Moorish slipper with elongated and upcurled toe. It was in a way the saving of the situation, for the monkey, diverted, abandoned the tattered material to pounce upon the shoe which it crammed under its arm, and vanished.

I think it was in both our minds then to creep away, not to face Valmiki's further embarrassment, but in fact he had rapidly recovered himself and, sitting down on the stairs, calmly removed his one remaining shoe, gathered up his clothes and came up to where we were standing.

"Good party, didn't you think?" he said, with an aplomb worthy of Caroline at her best, kissed me on the cheek (which he had never done before) and patting Ellie's behind gently with the Moorish slipper passed gracefully on to his room farther along the corridor.

Caroline, with an offhand consideration characteristic of her, had offered to put me up overnight in the dressing room that intercommunicated with her bedroom. There was a wide comfortable divan there on which a bed had been made up, and lying on it between Caroline's jade-green scented sheets, with Caroline's belongings spread around the room, I found it was not she but Ellie who dominated me. Pale ineffectual Ellie, asleep—or more probably awake—in her room across the landing, surrounded by Valmiki's work, and carrying his seed in her womb.

If when he asked I had told him she was a virgin, would he have touched her? Unquestionably, no. Basically he was Hindu, however nondescript he had become; and the atavistic reaction against unsanctioned defloration common even in relaxed societies would function as a positive interdict in his own. Why then had I not? Simply because, I thought, I had not visualized sexual connection between them, Ellie seeming to me to be sexless, and Valmiki the child I had known despite a surface recognition of his maturity. If I had, would I have lied in the hope of preventing what actually had happened? I would, I thought with useless regret, and went cold. It was what Caroline would have done, it was her way of controlling other people's lives—not involuntarily by speech, thought, the very fact of living, but with deliberation and lucidity, and it seemed to me in the mindless panic of night that not only Valmiki but I, also, had come within orbit of her powerful influence.

18

ELLIE'S hopes for Valmiki's success—and indeed the hopes
of all of us who were close to him—were amply realized in the
weeks that followed.

In an atmosphere of mounting electric tension Valmiki
opened his one-man show; and it closed in the knowledge of
success with extravagant, intoxicated relief. The critics, with
their humane tradition of generosity toward newcomers, did
not skimp their praise, and their acumen was nicely supported
by the number of sale tabs that appeared on the pictures—
though there might have been more but for the fact that
Valmiki, in a nervous frenzy, at the last moment withheld most
of the Ellie pictures, passionately declaring that he could not
abide being parted from what was a slice of himself.

"But think of the money, Valmiki. What will you live on?"

"I live on nectar." He kissed the bunched tips of his fingers,
in the Oriental extravagance that had come to be expected of
him, at the crowds, the attention, the acclaim. "What do I want
with money?"

Caroline upheld him. "There is not the slightest reason why
Val should be asked to think about money. I'm there to think
for him."

So did Ellie. "He did not eat or sleep, except a little, while
he was working. Flesh and blood are in it."

Of the occasional dissident critical voice Valmiki took no

notice. Either he was sophisticated enough to cloak his vulnerable soft core, or the avalanche of eulogy cushioned him sufficiently to disregard the pinpricks.

"What does this one say?"

He made Mrs. Peabody cut out his notices, finding this more exciting than waiting for press clippings from the agency Caroline had commissioned; but he never wanted her to read them to him, always coming to Caroline or me, or occasionally Ellie.

"It says: 'All birth is exciting; and we are witnessing here the birth of a rare and exciting talent.' "

"Good. And this one?"

" 'Feeling must be disciplined before it can burgeon into art. There are signs of an undisciplined incoherence in this artist's work.' "

" 'An artist *manqué.*' " Valmiki tore the cutting into small pieces. It was a new phrase, which he had picked up bodily and used correctly, though he had not the remotest idea of what *manqué* meant.

The clippings of which he approved he pasted painstakingly in a child's scrapbook, his delight growing as the pages filled until one day a man who wrote showed him a proper press-clippings book in black morocco with his name—the author's— on it in rich gold letters, and at once Valmiki's face fell, his eyes grew covetous.

"You could design an equally nice jacket for your book, Val. And have your name on it in gold."

Diamonds, said Caroline's voice, would not be too good for you.

So he followed her advice and painted a splendid jacket for the Woolworth scrapbook, driving the author, who had had to make do with the same book jacket in six different colors for six separate books, wild with envy. Caroline wrote his name on it in Gothic, and Valmiki illuminated the lettering with as much care as he had devoted to his cave murals.

With helpful hands, loving labor, and nothing succeeding like success, the book quickly filled. Even when it was full Valmiki, who could not read a word of English, could instantly tell, word for word, what each notice said. It got so it was almost his party piece.

"Val, what does this say?"

It sounded almost a parody of what was more frequently and pathetically on Valmiki's lips.

Valmiki obliged. Several of his responses—the Eastern emphasis and extravaganza, the predilection for champagne, the woebegone mascot-monkey—were to oblige his public.

"It says: 'There is an elegiac quality in his work, astonishing in one so young.'"

"And this?"

"This one is a libel, written by an artist *manqué*."

He never would go over the rough patches—the very few surviving instant destruction—that had managed to eel themselves into the scrapbook, although for the good ones he was prepared to spend hours learning the meaning of the long words and practicing their pronunciation.

"You will have to have several books, soon," said Caroline with rich pride, wreathed and laden with triumph. "One for every capital that shows your work."

"Will you be going away," said Ellie, her downcast eyes at last open with question, "leaving England? When? Soon? For long?"

"Dear Ellie, so impetuous!" Caroline's cold gaze swept over the insipid little Jew who held Valmiki with her weakness and

her swelling belly at least as securely as she herself did with
her power and her influence, the triumphant consummation of
a long-joined sweated ambitious endeavor.

"Dear Ellie, so impatient. Of course Val must exhibit as
widely as he can—it would be a crime if anything, or anyone,
came in the way of his doing so. But when—where—how! My
dear, I do assure you these things simply aren't arranged in
a day."

Ellie the unworldly shrank and dwindled, reduced to size.
The mounting pressures of anxiety, the weltering fears of a
gravid woman, had briefly conquered her status, given her the
nerves and the guts to speak, now she was back in the restricted
sphere inhabited by a nobody.

Valmiki rescued her whenever he remembered and whenever he could—dutifully, but with not too marked a blight on
his zest.

"Ellie!" He pranced over to her, the aigrette trembling in
the turban which was part of his ensemble for that evening.
"Lola is dying to meet you. Come on."

Girls always died to meet Ellie. They always were revivified
when they did.

You could see Lola relaxing in all the length of her beautiful
body when she saw Ellie. Lola was a top model, often seen at
art shows, oftener still at parties before and after them. Ellie
was a model too, but clearly roughcast still. Lola's alerted
professionalism subsided. She tried to be and was briefly and
impersonally kind to Ellie, who was as usual locked in a guttural
and strangulated shyness, and like so many others Lola moved
on.

Between conscience and care, Valmiki made Ellie accompany
him on his triumphal tours. He insisted that she should. It was
her right, she had been his inspiration, his model, his success

was at least partly hers. When she pleaded her condition he went back to his peasant origins, where women bore children between the completion of one day's chores and beginning the next day's crop. When Ellie complied and was stranded, he noticed and complained.

"Why can't you talk to people? They wouldn't leave you alone if you did. What do I bring you with me for?"

"I don't know what to say to them. They have experience of so many things that I do not have."

He was suddenly gentle, suddenly and nakedly the man who painted beneath the popinjay.

"Ellie, the people here who frighten you, who know so much —do they know what you know? Or have they seen the things that are hidden in human minds as you have? I tell you if I painted them as I have painted you it could all be said in one canvas and even so I would have to thin my paints— But your face! Twenty, thirty pictures and I still have not caught you."

Grievances, however, outlasted these illuminated truths.

"Why could you not be nice to Lola?" He was irritated and angry.

"I tried to be, Valmiki." Ellie, humble and cowed, invited kicks.

"You could not have tried very hard. Lola is a charming girl. She could be very useful to me, doesn't that mean anything to you?"

He strode away, his aigrette shaking with wrath, leaving Ellie stammering with guilt. Not long ago he would have balked even at deliberately getting to know a few useful people. Now he had rethought his values, or had them rethought for him.

Caroline, percipient and sensitive where her own interests

were concerned, though effortlessly perfunctory over the trials of others, watched them with a cat's concentration. It must have been a bitter pill to take, the unlikely transformation of domestic into rival, but Caroline had done it with distinction, emerging with her weapons honed to a finer, subtler edge.

"So uncouth." This was on opening day, while Ellie stood about like a potato sack—a comment on her in between the sparkling gush with which Caroline laved the elegant. "Uncouth little pig. She'll never be anything else."

"She hasn't had the benefit of your intensive training."

"My dear, one cannot make French pastry from German dough."

"The Indian kind seems to have been malleable enough."

"Suya my sweet. You're developing into quite the sharpest little needler of even my catholic circle of acquaintances. Why? Could it be because you didn't recognize the nugget lying on your land until I picked it up and polished it?"

"Little," as Caroline used it, always meant disparagement, though not inevitably dislike. The little man from the education authority, who had nagged her about Valmiki's education. Uncouth little Ellie, so pathetically set up as competitor. And Valmiki and I, who took turns regularly at being little.

Indeed the nugget was shining brightly; and beyond question Caroline was eager to be seen with it.

"Val's come on wonderfully, hasn't he?"

"Yes. He's a credit to your system."

"I think so." She was purring. "Though a system can't make you good-looking."

"Do you find you can only make friends with good-looking people?"

"I find it helps." She smiled, blowing smoke rings around

me. "Don't you? Or don't you know? You must apply your subtle Brahminical mind to it sometime."

Being handsome helped Valmiki with Caroline. Being Indian helped him generally and massively, for India had come into fashion. Fashionable to know of India, fashionable to know Indians, fashionable to admire its art, fashionable to welcome its women and even, at a pinch, its men.

Valmiki benefited. He did not suspect that his success might be due to the turning of the great political wheel that had put India on the map; or that he had come in at the beginning of a cult. He thought, blithely and charmingly, that it was due to his talent and industry and good public relationship, and so perhaps in the main it was.

Caroline benefited. She linked her arm in the clever young painter's—affectionately, proprietorially—and spoke of his beginnings in clipped narrative that had the impact of good drama.

"I discovered him in a cave. Oh yes, a real one. In India. Hideously bare and uncomfortable, except for those superb walls. And Val of course."

Oh, do tell us more of this fabulous land, this fabulous creature. Nobody actually said that, but that was the atmosphere.

Caroline luxuriated in it. She herself had never lacked attention, but here was the piquant combination of looks and talent— their looks, his talent, her talent in recognizing it; and then there were all those tart years to be requited, when he hung around gangling and dispirited, dour, intense, and dressed to annoy in his cheap blue suits.

19

TRUE to his threat, Jumbo turned up in time for the celebrations, genuinely delighted with Valmiki's success, extremely proud of his countryman, more than equable about being seen with him now that he had arrived.

"My dear boy, this calls for a libation!" He slapped Valmiki on the back, unsettling the pet monkey roosting on his shoulder. "Where shall we go? Now there's a charming little place I used to know—wonder if it's still there? Just off—"

"There's rather a nice place I know," said Valmiki, "just off—"

In the end it was the Savoy, where the waiters naturally took the gorgeous commoner for the prince and the prince as another Indian-in-a-suit, for despite his pedigree Jumbo had no presence.

"I'm no good at dressing up." Jumbo's antennae, sensitized under successive Residents, instantly picked up the fine gradations in deference, but without resentment. "Been doing it for years, but it never comes naturally . . . durbars, Viceroy's Ball, Birthday Honors . . . all that sort of thing in the old days. Now when I open crèches and factories—oh yes, the old pensioner's still in demand, you know—I struggle into the ancient finery. Mustn't disappoint the populace—cardinal rule, that—not to say scandalize them. But discretion, always discretion! Not too many of the old heirlooms showing, you know."

"Have you any left, Jumbo?" Caroline asked with curiosity and the affectionate concern which a wide variety of people felt for him.

"A few, my dear, a few." He held up a hand, on the little finger of which, in discreet permissible elegance, glimmered a sapphire ring. The rest of the permissibles were disposed about his person—gold cigarette case, the chronometer on his wrist, the Parker pen, and the slim gold propelling pencil. The jewels he kept in the bank.

"In London?" Reticences were rare in Caroline, in her imperious nature which demanded, full-stop, honestly unaware of the feelings of those on whom the indent was made.

"In London?" Jumbo had become the common man, the ancient man shielding his grain from the ancient foe, the tithe-gatherer. "I hardly know, the loot's been so dispersed. All I keep tabs on is the regalia, on which my life depends—the things I put on to do my democratic chores."

"Like apron in butcher's blue in a sensible sizing."

"My dear, we have not come to that yet." Jumbo's laugh echoed Caroline's mockery and rang through the room, causing one or two well-groomed heads to semi-turn in smiling sympathy. He pressed his hands together devoutly. "Pray God we never do. No, I mean sword with fancy hilt, and chain of princely office, and plume with jeweled clasp such as our young friend is wearing, to which he is wholly unentitled."

Valmiki, nicely balanced on the graceful points of social success and a confident *savoir-faire*, began to wobble. It was one of his turban evenings, and decorating the front of it was the damning aigrette, luminously anchored with an opal brooch of Caroline's.

"Princely privilege." Jumbo shook a finger at the pallid Valmiki. "But who should care? Not I, my dear fellow. Merely passing on the information, case you're ever on dear old home ground again."

In his own way, *au fond*, Jumbo was a kindly man with limited but humane impulses.

"Tell you something else about turbans—never start from scratch. You do, don't you? I can see you do. It's sheer spillage of nervous energy. What you do is have a cast made."

"Who by?" Caroline, at least, had a firmer grasp of London realities.

"Who by? My dear Caroline, how should I know? One of the servants. Anyone who can work papier mâché. Have a cast made, just the top of your head and give it a point you can grasp—I'm speaking literally, my dear fellow—then the winding's simplicity itself, and when it's done you flick the base away—no, no, my dear chap, you never leave it even if it doesn't show, only bearers do—and there you are, turban sits on head as firm as a nest."

He demonstrated, using a scooped-out half of breadroll and tape the waiter had been summoned to bring. Valmiki watched with interest, heady fumes from balloon brandies rising into his intent face. It had been brandies all round twice, following a superlative meal for the meat eaters and boiled vegetables for the rest.

"I do not eat meat"—this was Valmiki at his new lofty level, looking down on Jumbo who did—"because I prefer not to consume corpses."

Poor Jumbo, immersed in a splendid *boeuf Strogonoff*, raised a dripping protesting fork, but Caroline, similarly engaged, paused only to approve her protégé, acknowledging and endorsing tactics that led to the establishment of superiority of whatever outlandish genre.

For once Ellie had, by her own pleading, been left behind;

and Jumbo, less conversant with London rumor than Indian, made no comment on her absence. The monkey was absent too, having been, after an incident, suavely escorted home in a cab by a commissionaire, taking with it the nervous tension induced by its habits and idiosyncrasies which usually made miasmic combination with the peculiar brand wrought by Ellie.

"Don't know how you stand it," Jumbo spoke irritably, aware of what monkey-on-shoulder (briefly) had made him look like, though it went well with Valmiki's exoticism, and picking and pulling at threads teased free from his coat sleeve.

"It's a dear little creature," Valmiki answered mechanically, copying what women usually said while they tickled its pate with one finger.

If not the sole, it was one of the few irritants of the evening, now about to pass the first test of what constitutes a good one in that everyone was slightly drunk.

"Tell you what." Jumbo oozed benevolence. "We'll go on."

"Where?"

"It doesn't matter where. On. Anywhere."

"There's a little place I know . . ." said Valmiki.

"A little place I used to know," said Jumbo, eyes darkly reminiscent, "now what was it called—Bag o' something or other . . . no, perhaps not there . . . but there was that other place with the marvelous floor show, fillies with legs like milk-white arabs' . . ."

In the end we went to a place that Caroline knew, run by a friend from her Cheltenham days, where the fog was as thick as a Thames-side pea-souper and light filtered in hooded and strange from lurid vents in painted faces on the wall.

Jumbo sank back in his chair with relaxed sighs of recognition as if home from far-flung wandering, drawing deep drafts of the air into his lungs. Waiters, moving like gunmetal cutouts in blue light, brought bottles in buckets. There was a band, dancing in close-packed sexual rhythm, and a floor show with the legs and breasts so close you could see the veins and the powder.

"Do you know what this reminds me of?" Jumbo juggled with bottles and glasses, supremely happy, tearful with nostalgia. "Old days in Delhi. No, I'm wrong—not Delhi, too much imperial oojah. Simla, that was it. Christ, those were good days! Though they wouldn't mean anything to you, old boy, you'd have been much too young."

"Too poor." Valmiki grew tearful, hunched over his glass.

Caroline, wedged against him on the gilded, undersized banquette, caressing and possessing him in silence, turned cruel eyes on Jumbo.

"Tell you what," said the miserable Jumbo, "next time you're in India, old chap, you come up and see me, I'll do you the honors, I'll see that others do 'em for you."

"No closed doors, no nonsense," said Caroline, drinking steadily through the evening, as cool and remorseless now as when it had begun. "No being driven to sleep on ashram floors."

"Never knew it had come to that, too ghastly," Jumbo mumbled, as unnerved as if he were being interviewed by the Resident.

"Never let it come to that again."

"Never, on the word of a pensioner prince." He drank again, recovering his spirits. "Truth is, old boy, we don't know how to treat chaps like you—clever chaps, artistic chaps—but it's never too late"—he broke into song—"for a dog to mate, or a bibby to suck, or a buck to bite, or a bitch to ———, and it's never too late to learn." He stopped and looked appalled, muttered that ladies were present and apologized abjectly.

Caroline hadn't heard, or if she had wouldn't have turned a hair at this jejune dirt. She had her jade holder out, complete with showy black cigarette, her eyes were agate, but the urge to bully passed, she turned to her victim.

"Come and dance, Jumbo. I'm getting cramp."

He led her to the floor, lumbering from the liquor he carried, and they danced briefly until the cramp had gone and she led him back, for Caroline had no tolerance for poor dancing. Still charitable, she turned to see whom she could see, whom she had so far ignored, spotted friends at the next table and took Jumbo to them.

"Georgina, Sarah: Prince Jumbo. He's dying to dance."

Valmiki, who couldn't dance, watched morosely, until suddenly Caroline took his arm and rose, and hardly moving they swayed together on the packed floor.

The need to be close must have become very pressing.

Jumbo was doing well, his dapper figure unsteady but active among the dancers. Each time he passed me he waved, and each time the music stopped he said, "You don't mind being left, do you, Sue—you're a writer. You *don't* mind do you, you're looking so cross?"

"I don't mind the backhander. I loathe being called Sue."

"Never again. Never on the word of a pensioner prince. Anasuya she is, and Anasuya she shall be."

Toward dawn great steaming platters of bacon and eggs were borne in, to be applauded like caviar at a less tipsy time.

"Time to go," said Caroline, above food, tucking Valmiki's arm firmly into her own while she disentangled Jumbo from Georgina.

We walked up the cellar steps into air like snow sherbet, and an entrancingly beautiful night with the stars frozen in the cold bitter blue. The air must have been Caroline's undoing, for when I turned at the sound of her irregular titupping she was walking behind Valmiki holding one end of his uncoiling turban, and when presently they were stopped her voice grew shrill with unwise exasperation.

We walked on, Jumbo babbling to Sue. A tousled Ellie let us in, and must have heard, with greater clarity and anguish than I did, the deep snores from Jumbo downstairs mingling with, later, the intoxicated cries and sighs of Caroline and Valmiki's lovemaking.

20

DEAR Jumbo. He came like a buffer between Caroline and me, between Valmiki and Ellie, at a time when our emotions were being sharpened and abraded to wounding point, to whatever ugly climax came of the friction.

Jumbo had lost so much, he complained not at all. To those unaware of his heritage, he was the possessor of an enviable purse. He himself never alluded—except slyly and wryly among people who knew—to a time when it had literally been bottomless. His money, now, was adequate for the standards to which, without recrimination, he had adjusted himself; it was treated with respect, it saved him from the pricks which make pincushions of the poor; and he used it to dine well, to drink and to dance—sybaritic arts in India, so that Jumbo in desperate pursuit of these pleasures was merely an example not to be followed, whereas here in London he became metamorphosed into a representative of civilized man—a rare bird among Indians, refreshing to find.

Jumbo thrived on this role, which was after all closer to his reality than opening those countless crèches. He made friends, he took them out, he took us out—singly, in pairs, most frequently in a foursome. Automatically, without a word being said, Ellie was dropped, although by then Jumbo must have known something of Caroline's curious ménage; and it was easier all round not to have to labor to fit her in, or encounter those burnt-out eyes which made your conscience enlarge and fill your breast like a diseased heart.

Ellie herself had pleaded to be left, but now that she found herself increasingly taken at her word she reacted with a kind of muffled normality, saying nothing but growing if possible even more haggard and haunting. At whatever time one returned, the light in her room would be on, and though she never made a sound or came down, one knew she was awake and had it confirmed by the soft click as at last the light was switched off.

One day, brusque from a hangover, Valmiki asked if she was nervous of being alone in the house at night. Ellie flushed darkly, a kind of purple under her sallow skin. She began to deny it, realized halfway the awkwardness of an alternative explanation, and shot down the bolt-hole he had provided like a terrified rabbit.

"Yes. Sometimes in the night I am afraid. It is stupid of me."

Valmiki melted. He was basically gentle, vulnerable to any appeal from the persecuted and lonely.

"There is no need to be afraid," he said kindly, "there are always people about, even at night." An assurance that was hardly necessary, from the 2 A.M. crump of motorcar doors and the carrying decibels of clear high voices as Belgravia went to bed. Moreover Valmiki cared for Ellie; it was the implementation of caring that he found difficult, for with morning, afternoon and evening engagements, as he said he had no time to think.

"Dear boy, why *should* one think?" asked Jumbo, tutored carefully and well at expensive schools.

"Simply because one should," replied Valmiki, also well schooled in his own way.

"I never do," said Jumbo. "I did once, and once was enough. No point in stoking up your own little hells."

"Stoking?" Caroline's coaching had given Valmiki a streamlined flueney in English, but occasionally a less common word betrayed him.

"Creating, I suppose you chaps would call it. Thought. Creation."

"Create heavens," said Valmiki reasonably. "Why always hell?"

"My dear chap, our imaginations aren't all like yours," said Jumbo affably. "Mine, it's always been hell-bent—dishes up the bad things, you know. No future in that."

Valmiki agreed sympathetically, and the two went off companionably to lunch, prior to visiting a picture gallery. The passion for art-viewing was growing in Valmiki. In the early days—before success came, before the expert and intensive grooming for it initiated by Caroline—he had been chary of going to exhibitions, some instinct warning him that too great a dwelling on other painters' merits would daunt him before he began, as too great a study of their techniques would stultify his own work.

Now, with his own achievement to fall back on, it became a matter of less moment; and Jumbo, whose tastes ran to trefoil and white jade, nevertheless trailed after him happily enough from gallery to gallery, exclaiming in wonder and distaste over most of what he saw.

I asked him why he did it.

"Must move with the times, m'dear. Even if one doesn't understand 'em."

He was exceedingly adaptable, and amiable and likable; and he in his turn readily liked anyone who was amusing, or acceptable or presentable. Ellie was none of these things, and so taking his cue from us he behaved as if she did not exist, in which practice—from participation in those innumerable regal and viceregal tours past whitewashed poverty and hidden squalor— practice had made him perfect.

So, under this framework of strength and beauty that we had all had a hand in rigging up, the nonexistent problem slowly festered and swelled into evil; and meanwhile the social whirligig went on—dinners, shows and suppers, dazzling Caroline, darling Val, dear Jumbo, our delightful foursomes, splendid evenings of going *on*, hangovers of enviable and unrivaled proportions, and success: above all success.

21

THEN on my way home late one night I noticed that the light in Ellie's room was not on, and groping back realized that in fact it had not been on for weeks.

When I called the next day Mrs. Peabody said, "She's gone,

she has. Been gone a fortnight and not so much as a good-bye. Can't never trust foreigners, can you!"

"Oh, I don't know."

"Don't mean you, miss. It's the likes of her . . . scandalous, I call it."

Caroline said, "It's absolutely true and quite inexcusable. Went off without a word to dogsbody, so upsetting for the poor old dear. . . . She felt she had to sort things out for herself. She couldn't do it here—*too* distracting."

And Valmiki flanked by Caroline said, "She needed to be alone to think things out. *She* wanted it."

"What sort of things?"

"Darling, do grow up," said Caroline. "Ellie's going to have a baby. That needs thinking about, doesn't it?"

"Why not here? Why go away?"

"To be alone. Val's just told you, she wanted to be alone."

"She was alone here often enough."

"Suya, whom are you trying to blame? Nothing stopped you from enjoying her society if you wanted to, did it?"

"I'm not trying to blame anyone. I was simply trying to work out why she had to go."

"To woo and win detachment," said Caroline, yawning. "Not too bright today, are we?"

"But—"

"Don't *fuss*," she said, "it's the besetting Indian sin. Ellie's gone away, Ellie'll be back when she's had time to think. What *is* there to fuss about?"

Quick and nervous corroboration came from Valmiki. "Yes. She'll be back when she's had time to think. It's something she must do on her own."

"Why? She didn't start the baby on her own."

But Caroline had that ineffable withdrawn look as if bald truths that did not come from her were bad manners best slurred over, and Valmiki's mouth had turned sour in poor copy of the inimitable original.

In intervals between eating, sleeping, work and play—small interstices of time—I thought about Ellie. There was no bond between us, no special tie, yet that most irrational of links, the chance circumstance that had made us acquainted, constantly propped up her shrinking image in front of me. What kind of thoughts were locked in that shorn skull? What decisions would they cry for that could possibly be implemented without money, or identity, or influence? And beneath all this benign clarity ran the silt, the feeling of injury that Ellie had ever manifested herself, the terrible corollary to which was that the sooner the manifestation was over the better.

At this point I got an invitation from old friends of mine and escaped thankfully to, of all places, Northumbria in a spring that had turned out to be colder than winter.

When I returned—all thought in the meanwhile mercifully blunted by hard labor in the cold climate of a thatched cottage —there was a letter waiting for me with an Indian postmark and a week-old date stamp. It was from the Swami—writing by ordinary mail where anyone else would have cabled—to say he was on his way to London and would I tell Valmiki?

I took the letter to Caroline, who was sitting warm and luxuriant in a bathrobe in front of a leaping fire. Her skin was pink and clean from the bath, her face looked soft and relaxed in contrast to its more usual cool brittle alertness, making me wonder how much of a strain housing Ellie had been, and how much taken in her competent stride. If there, she had never shown sign of strain, and hardly did so now except by contrast. But whatever the case, she had never lost her balance. Ellie could have been dismissed out of hand at any time: but Valmiki would have followed. Caroline had elected to wait, and Ellie had been edged out, incredibly, fully acquiescent and consenting.

"Well." Caroline handed the letter back to me. "It's in Tamil. I suppose it's from the Swami. What does he want?"

"He's coming to London," I said.

She nodded indifferently, as if he meant nothing to her, as if she had never considered him an adversary, and with as much splendid impassivity as a European actress playing a Chinese peasant-woman who has just lost husband, home, children and dearly-beloved plum blossom tree in some all-too-frequent Eastern holocaust.

Nevertheless, before night fell again the Indian cook was gone—sacked, made to pack, and sent on his way dazed but jubilant with more money in his pocket than he earned in a year.

"Good riddance," said Caroline, washing her hands of him, flushing from memory the unsavory hours he had spent laboriously concocting at her bidding those wretched little counterfeit letters which would not have deceived a child but which Valmiki, illiterate gull, had swallowed whole.

"Has he actually gone?"

"Yes. Without so much as a good-bye. Poor old Peabody!" She smiled. "You know, I simply can't think why I didn't get rid of him sooner."

"Can't you?"

Caroline could with the greatest ease induce in one a feeling of awe, so monumentally false were her assumptions of innocence.

"No. His cooking was awful. I suspect his Tamil was worse. I don't know why I didn't get you to write those letters. I'm sure you would have done it better."

"You didn't because you knew I wouldn't," I said.

"Dear Suya," she said. "Running true to type. Never whole hog—singe its bristles but never do it in."

These barbs were common: an itch to pick fault and probe vulnerabilities that lay like a legacy in the blood from the long opposition of her line to mine.

"You've taken care of the cook," I said at last. "What about the Swami? He's not in your pay, and not likely to be."

"I know, my sweet. The thought had occurred he might be less accessible than you are. Still, the worst he can do is reveal he never wrote 'em; he can't produce the scribe that did."

"We hope."

"And pray." She pressed her hands together devoutly, voice and gesture mimicking Jumbo. "Direct confrontations are the very devil."

In fact the cook never crossed our tracks again. He had vanished into the vast impersonal limbo that was London, taking with him his loneliness and some inkling of puzzling minor knavery, his only requiem the relieved signs of those he had left behind. Especially Mrs. Peabody, who had borne the brunt of his masquerades and impositions.

"You couldn't help feeling sorry for him," she said, out of her large heart, wiping Brasso from her hands onto her apron. "Though he wasn't what you might call a worker. Every other Sunday—close on three year, I reckon—he'd roll in dinnertime rarin' for his grub. 'Make yourself useful,' the old man'd say— made him mad it did, watching him hanging round idle humming to himself like a blooming top—nothing you'd recon-nize, just that queer heathen singsong, if you'll pardon me saying so, miss—but it wasn't no good. You could tell he wouldn't know where to start, never having the habit of work as you might say. Now what would you say he did in his own country, miss?"

"Cooking. He was supposed to be a cook."

She raised eyes and eyebrows to heaven in mute amazement and set to work with a redoubled vigor that pointed the difference between them, her beefeater's shoulders and washerwoman's forearms achieving more in an hour than the enervated sun-dried frame of the cook could have done in days.

So the cook went and the Swami came—within a few days of his letter but, in the Indian fashion, weeks after Valmiki's exhibition of paintings had opened and closed. To Valmiki, despite his vanity, this made not one whit of difference. Where Jumbo was concerned it had mattered to Valmiki, been of proud and joyous moment, that he be seen in his hour of glory. With the Swami it became inconsequential, seen not in the light of the ordinary world but through the eyes of that extraordinary man.

The important thing, now and always, was that he was coming—this man who had been the first to lean down and wipe from his face the mark of the outcast placed there by thinking fellow-beings. From his remote scrubstone country beginnings, Valmiki had carried the seeds of a loyalty that was lifelong and steely, shaming even the mildest exponents of expediency. So now he bubbled and sang like a kettle, and cracked his knuckles like castanets—to Caroline's wrath, for she had spent some time in eradicating the habit.

"All this way to see me," he exulted, rocking on his heels like any old peasant, with an eagerness that quarreled with his sophistication and went ill with his new getup.

"Among other things," said Caroline coolly.

"I wish I had a house." Valmiki pursued his thoughts, for once deaf to Caroline. "I would have him to stay, I would like to do that."

"Darling," said Caroline, melting, melting him with the warmth of her generosity. "This is your house. Ask him if you want to. We'll get another cook—an Indian cook. Anything."

But when he was not there she said with a bleakness that in anyone else would have been panic, "There isn't an earthly, is there?"

"I don't know," I said. "I have no idea where he will be staying."

"I suppose whoever's responsible for his coming here would know."

A cloudy conscience casts ambiguous shadows over the most casual statement. "I suppose they would," I said.

" 'They'?" Again the slight inflection, real or imagined.

"They. International Guild for the Advancement of Theosophy," I said staunchly, "who are organizing the tour."

"He's coming for *them?*"—eyebrows arched and scornful.

"Yes."

"Oh well." She appeared to lose interest. "In that case somewhere big and drafty—Toynbee Hall, or Euston Station. Or Claridge's.

22

IN fact the Swami went his own way, serenely and courteously bypassing the efforts of the organization sponsoring his tour to put him in hall or hotel, and installing himself in a spacious old house in Kensington lent by a rich disciple.

These disciples were numerous. They fetched and carried, ran errands, placed themselves and their assets at his disposal. And the irony lay in the sheer superfluity, for the Swami would scarcely have noticed had any or all of it been withdrawn. Money flowed lavishly into his hands. He used what he needed, gave away the rest, never hoarded, never banked, and assuming it meant as little to others as to him never troubled to ensure, as newcoming disciples learned to their cost, that the surplus from gifts went to the giver. Or perhaps it was a deliberate lesson in the painless handling of money, an antiseptic dispersal of the ugly intensity with which it was surrounded.

In their usage of money the Swami and Caroline came curiously close: she from always having had so much, he from never having had any; the gulf lay between their attitudes, hers shrewd and knowledgeable even at its most casual, whereas he had, as it were, moved to a realm where the currency was different.

Valmiki, in this as in other things between two worlds, oscillated violently between one and the other. In fits and starts he hoarded money and spent it, alternating between reverence and contempt—although whether for it, or for himself, it would have been difficult to say. One day—in his materialist period—he came to the Swami to boast of the respectable sum for which Caroline—an excellent agent—had sold one of his pictures. It had been a cash transaction: Caroline often arranged it so for the delectation of Val, who cared nothing for checks, as she would have arranged for payment in gold coins were they but legal tender. Now with an eagerness that had been his before his blasé period and now wrangled with it, he drew out a roll of banknotes and thrust them under the Swami's nose. The Swami thrust it away.

"What is it?"

"Money." Valmiki spoke exuberantly, without the hushed note Mrs. Peabody introduced into such occasions. "Three hundred pounds, for one small picture!"

There was a silence, clearly marked in that packed room full of the sounds and movements of people—a silence not attentive but embarrassed. Valmiki looked around, puzzled. In the society he kept—the gilt-edged society whose doors his art and Caroline's class had contrived to open for him—to mention money was to secure frank and unabashed attention. Or else, some rungs down the ladder, the interest if covert was no less enraptured, manifest in an anguished and raging preoccupation whether it was or was not vulgar to talk about money. Here, under the influence of uncommon interpretations and persuasions, it was out of context, clearly without relevance to people of sense.

Valmiki, after all, did not paint as he did out of nothing. He had sense, sensitivity, instinct, all of which helped him however minutely to achieve an integrity of his own adrift in a society that redistributed its grains of value and merit, like the subtle reordering of genetic patterns at each new conception, at every step backward or forward out of class. In the silence he knew he had offended, and guessed why, but he had his answer— unready and unpracticed—but honest enough.

"Money," he said hesitantly. "It is not everything, but it is a mark, a token, people would not give it to you if you were worthless. One accepts it for—for what it signifies, as well as the other things."

"So the significance," said the Swami, "was in the painting?"

"Yes," said Valmiki simply.

"And the painting, judging from the money, was excellent?"

"Yes," said Valmiki, not without humility. "It was good work—judging from the money as well as other things."

The Swami smiled and let it go. Valmiki was all smiles too, not so much from having talked himself out of being censured as from having made peace with his mentor. They were still close, despite the years between, the transmogrification of Valmiki, the dedication of one to the spirit and the other to whatever it was; in the general welter it had become difficult to tell.

Indeed, with the arrival of the Swami, Valmiki was hardly ever to be seen with Caroline, although of course they continued to inhabit the same house.

Caroline, deprived of her gorgeous painter, went from nose-in-air unawareness to cold wrath. "It's a seduction," she said, "spiritual if you like. There's no place for it in England. He ought never to have been allowed in."

"He came by invitation," I said, "presumably from precisely those who felt there was some scope for spiritual development in England."

She looked up and smiled. "That jab went right where it was intended to," she said, "in the soft underside of the belly."

"But encountered armor," I said wearily. "I noticed no blood."

She laughed. One well-kept hand went on buffing and polishing the pink oval nails of the other.

"Do you know," she asked, "how long the medicine man will be here?"

"A month, maybe two. There's an itinerary, but he keeps it flexible."

"A month," she repeated. "A great many things could happen in that time."

"Surely nothing catastrophic," I said. "What is a month to the years you've had?"

"Nothing, of course," she said slowly, and her eyes were deep in calculation.

Nevertheless she did not go near the Swami. He subdued her, she was afraid of him, or if not of him of the power he still wielded over the clay she had molded and caressed to an image she could love. In a way he was something of an obsession, become so partly because she could not bring herself to emasculate it by personal encounter, partly because she was jealously aware of the years that had gone before, before she had had Valmiki. Instead she sought to compensate the reality by endless questioning, storing away my answers like arms in some secret arsenal to be brought into later use. . . . What did Valmiki say to him and he to Valmiki? What did he think of Valmiki, and Valmiki of the Swami? Had there been any change, either subtle or flagrant?

As far as I could see, very little. Valmiki's attachment to the Swami seemed undiminished, if less emotional than when he had been a child. It was to some extent certainly reciprocated; and perhaps it was this human tie, tenuous though it was, that had led the Swami to forsake his isolate life in the realization that he was as yet unready to meet its austere demands. Yet the link had been slight, or severely controlled. In all the years of their separation he had never once communicated with Valmiki, nor had there been any indirect inquiry; and his visit to London, though distantly connected with Valmiki, was only a matter of a few brief weeks.

So the days went by, with Caroline questing and prodding, marking the dawn of each empty one with renewed irritation, and its passing with steadily mounting relief. Meanwhile the lit fuse was quietly working toward the bomb she and I had so carefully made out of lies, deceit, and silence.

23

ON the last day of his stay in London, Valmiki said to the Swami: "I hope you will continue to write, your letters mean so much to me," and the Swami replied: "I have never written to you, not even once, although I have often been tempted to do so."

This was some time after five in the morning, when the Swami had finished his devotions at which Valmiki had joined him, in the short calm following prayer and preceding the plunge into the world's noisy affairs.

By six Valmiki, raging, the thin skin of civilization sloughed roughly off, was in my flat to which for years he had had the key in case of emergency, although this was not quite the eventuality for which I had provided.

"Is it true? Is it? Have you known all along?" He was kneeling on the bed, wrenching at the bedclothes, dragging me out to answer him. He had rushed out without even a coat, and was chattering from cold in the icy room.

I thrust him away savagely and, numb with cold and shock, managed to get to the fire and light it. When this was done he crouched beside it, still shivering and chattering but with a glimmer of returning sanity. I left him there while I made some coffee, strong and black as the ritual of emergency required, and when this was inside him he went over what had happened with rising anger, until the final furious point-blank question.

"Did you know the Swami did not write a single one of the letters I have been getting? Did *you* write them?"

"I didn't write them," I said at last, though this was small comfort, "but I knew about them."

He looked ill with anger and misery; speechless, finished with words.

"The intention was good," I said wretchedly, "meant to help you. I—"

He simply got up and walked out. I dressed hurriedly and followed, but wasn't quick enough to see which direction he had taken. Either Caroline or back to the Swami, I thought, and the first guess turned out to be correct.

I rang the bell and Caroline came to the door in her negligee, an unlit cigarette in her hand.

"Valmiki, is he—?"

"Yes," she said coolly. "In there, babbling. Come in if you want to. I'm going back to bed."

She stopped to light her cigarette before going upstairs, her mules clacking softly over the carpet. I heard the slight click as she opened her bedroom door, and Valmiki must have heard it too for he came out, looked at me without really seeing me, and followed her up. I hesitated, uncertain whether my presence would be an intrusion or not, but their voices carried clearly—the door had been left open—and after a little, I went up too.

Caroline was sitting up in bed, a fur wrap about her shoulders. You would not have thought, from her calm marble unmoved face, her underwritten manner, that she had just been accused of forgery, deliberate lying, and deception, for all of which, in her heart of hearts, she must have known herself guilty. It did not make her falter.

"Darling," she said, and it was like a cold douche, sharp and crystalline with ice splinters, "you're behaving like a gutter-snipe and it's too boring. Of course we manufactured those silly little letters, and of course you believed in them because you were a silly little fool, but it was to stop you being one that they were written in the first place and you can't pretend the trick didn't work *or* that you'd rather it hadn't and you were still the dreary little zombie that you used to be."

It was a slap in the face of hysteria. It was also a sharp tug on the halter, reminding Valmiki of the charter under which he now served, where undertones were obligatory, and narrow views on expediency frowned on, and a tolerance of venial sin expected.

Valmiki, whose self-control had reached breaking-point, began to quiet down. Now and then he trembled, in short weak spasms like the involuntary impulses left over from passion, but his anger was gone, changed into a lowering sullenness.

We sat there silent, the three of us, smoke from Caroline's cigarette curling softly around us and hanging in smudged blue trails across the room. Until at last Caroline said, with the gentleness she could now afford, "You were wasting yourself, Val. Throwing away what you believed in. I couldn't just stand by and watch."

"So you acted," said Valmiki, forlorn and bitter, rejecting reconciliation. "For my own good."

"Yes," said Caroline, "for your own good—if you must make it sound terrible."

"And what else?" said Valmiki, with the elaborate sarcasm she had taught him to use as a weapon in preference to that blunt instrument, anger. "What else have you done for my good? Or rather, at what would you stop?"

"At nothing," said Caroline simply. "At nothing at all, my dear, I assure you."

Silence fell, and out of the void suspicions began to form, bringing Ellie into the room as tangibly as in a dream while it is still being dreamt.

"Ellie," said Valmiki at last. "Where is she? What have you done with her?"

"I?" Caroline shrugged. "What should I have done with her? She wanted to go. She went."

"Weeks ago . . . how many? It doesn't matter. As long as she comes back . . . she is coming back?"

"Really, Val, how should I know? It's a decision for her to make."

"Must see her," he mumbled, "can I? Tell me where."

"I do not know where Ellie is," said Caroline distinctly.

"You must. You must know where she is."

"No."

"You arranged everything for her. She told me—that you had."

"No. I said I would if she wanted me to, but she never did."

She was lying: there had been a flicker of time while she adjusted to his knowledge and searched for the lie to checkmate it. If Valmiki had insisted on an answer then he would have got it. He no longer seemed to have the strength. He sat as if gutted, unable to care, in the kind of apathy that seeps into people whose faith, or trust, has been picked to pieces.

Then at last he made the effort to go, and went without a word to Caroline, or to me, or to the curious Mrs. Peabody who had zealously arrived as usual on the stroke of nine.

I do not think we recognized it then: but it had come, in a way, to a testing of strengths. Between Caroline, who made casualness a religion, applying its supple standards and ingratiating gloss to all aspects of living; and the Swami, whose principles of morality were both inflexible and majestic, requiring a scrutiny not only of ends but of means, and rejecting as indefensible a plea of lack of knowledge.

Valmiki, therefore—numbly and instinctively seeking out the security the Swami offered—was roundly told by him to seek the truth. This pronouncement, baffling and annoying to anyone at arm's length with themselves, Valmiki understood only too well. If he wanted to be at peace, he must ask for the truth from Ellie herself. Half-measures, an easy defeat such as Caroline had with his connivance inflicted, were a kind of betrayal, worse than the one he had felt so keenly.

All this—the flight to the Swami, the outpourings, a recital of Ellie's history (for Valmiki pursued by guilt had never been able to do more than touch on her briefly, before running)—took place between nine that morning and eleven, when the Swami was due to board the train on the first stage of his tour of Europe. The Swami must therefore have been presented with a confused and disabling picture of Valmiki's predicament. His mind was, however, a disciplined one, used to reaching through the thick mulch of decaying truths and half-lies to the clogged roots of the matter; and moreover he was under no obligations to execute those fine, precision movements that delicately balance pros against cons. Accordingly he simply referred to fundamentals and gave Valmiki the answer he did not want.

Seek for the truth. Seek for the truth from Ellie, for no one else has it.

Valmiki came to my flat that evening mumbling and muttering her name. It was dark by then; he had apparently spent the hours since the Swami's departure in roaming the streets. He looked exhausted, eyes fallen back in their sockets, and blue shadows about his lips. I tried to get him to sleep, but he wouldn't, insisting instead on going over everything the Swami had said.

"I must ask Ellie," he chanted again and again. "I must find out from her."

"I don't suppose anything very terrible has happened," I said reasonably. "You mustn't let your imagination run away with you. In any case you'll have to find out where she is first—ask Caroline again."

Instantly his mouth set hard. "I am not going back," he said. "I will not go back to her."

"But my dear, where will you stay? Here? It's minute even for one, apart from anything else."

His head lolled down on his chest, he did not answer. I had tried in vain to get him to sleep before: now, nearing midnight, just as I was trying to edge him out he had fallen deeply asleep.

The morning after loomed no better. Valmiki woke with the old refrain of must-see-Ellie, but made no effort to get out of the flat. When I left he was still lying supine on the settee, in the clothes in which he had slept—the crumpled blue suit that he put over his elegant body like a hair shirt, whenever he felt the need to mortify himself or Caroline.

I rang Caroline—from a call box, to save any ructions from Valmiki—to reassure her about him before setting off on my own work. When I got back Valmiki was still there, the coffee I had made him untouched by his side, and by now looking not only exhausted but ill. I put it down to hunger, turning instinctively to organic causes as among the simplest with which to deal. He had probably, I thought, not eaten since the day before: from experience I knew the routines of feeding and sleeping escaped him, once in the grip of a mood or an idea. But neither hot milk nor the brandy I forced on him appeared to do any good, and he declined anything more solid on the grounds that he would choke. I suggested a doctor, but he refused, and indeed except for his appearance there were no real symptoms.

That night I gave up my bed to him, sleeping instead on the narrow divan in the living room. He accepted, not remarking on or even, I think, noting the sacrifice—which remained one notwithstanding.

The morning repeated the previous day's exasperating pattern, with Valmiki looking ill and wanting to see Ellie but refusing to see Caroline, until at last I pointed out sharply that London was not like his Indian backwood, where a few hours' search was bound to reveal anyone, even someone in hiding—that the key to Ellie's whereabouts was certainly with Caroline.

"I will not," he said again, and put his head in his hands, "will not ask her. She has played with me—used me—treated me like a fool. Those letters . . . I believed them, the shame of it. Go back, no, I never want to see her again."

"I knew about them too," I said, hoping to jerk him free of his apathy. "It didn't stop you from coming here, why should it keep you from going to Caroline?"

He roused a little at that, partly no doubt from the affront, but in a little while dejection and apathy had again set in.

"I will see her soon," he said listlessly. "Yes, very soon, yes, tomorrow if you like."

On the morrow, however, his body came to the rescue of his mind, providing the excuse he craved for inaction. Fever, sweats, and a heavy chill combined to prevent his going anywhere, and I resigned myself to having him on my hands for at least a fortnight.

Caroline, duly advised, sent Valmiki's things round in a taxi, herself keeping a wary distance. A doctor was summoned and came, and scrawled an imposing prescription which when dispensed looked uncommonly like aspirin. Most blessed of all Mrs. Peabody arrived, bringing tins of soup and stew like some improbable lady-of-manor, fussing over Valmiki, who had turned his face to the wall, and generally looking after him in as obtrusive a way as possible. Nevertheless I was grateful: her daily visits got over the worst chores, and I was not as tied as I had at first feared I would be.

24

IF Mrs. Peabody's angelic ministrations stemmed partly from her large heart, there were undoubtedly less beatific side-shoots. For Caroline, shrewdly keeping well in the background, her visits were one way of keeping tabs both on Valmiki's progress and on his whereabouts—since, after all, he could have melted into London almost as easily as Ellie. The apparatus of discovery, of course, lay well within Caroline's scope: but she had never been a believer in unnecessary work. Nor did she lack patience, when it came to achieving an end of her own: or for that matter courage, or skill, or finesse.

She waited a whole three weeks, and at the end of that time on a beautiful day full of tender green lights and pale sunshine she presented herself at the door.

There was something about Caroline, when she tried, very fresh, spiritually appealing: as if she had bathed at dawn in some magic formula that took away the squalor of ordinary scheming humanity; and the illusion was fostered by the limpid pallor of her skin, the pale sheen on her hair, rather as the ascetic is glimpsed through an overbrilliant eye, the luminous flesh of a radiant denial and privation.

"Darling," she said, ignoring the three weeks that had passed, "I had to come and find out if there was anything I could do," and raising her voice she called: "Val, there's something I must tell you, do say you'll see me because Suya's just about to say you won't."

There was no response—he had not seen her, was still armored against her. At that moment there was an indignant, muffled but still shrill chattering. Caroline's fur coat began to undulate, and presently Valmiki's pet monkey emerged looking harassed and ruffled, and wearing some other animal's fur cannibalistically over its own.

"Val," said Caroline, in her clear carrying voice. "It's Minou. She's been fretting for you. I had to bring her."

This was very probably true: the poor little monkey, bought for show purposes of which it was unaware, had put out these small inconvenient tendrils of feeling and bound itself to Valmiki. But it was also a powerful second line of attack, to which Caroline must have attached a good deal of importance to tolerate those exploring destructive hands so near her exquisite silken person.

By now Valmiki had appeared, wearing one of those splendid dressing gowns which Caroline had created for him, in which he looked like a fallen shah; and we all went into the flat.

Invariably the mood at any meeting was set by Valmiki; he was so emotional—numb with depression, or incoherent with anger, or treading the delectable highlands of a lush imagination —that virtually nothing else was possible. Now as the seconds ticked by we waited for the fabric, the tenor of the day, to declare themselves; until at last Valmiki said, formally, "It was kind of you to come, Caroline"; and at once it was clear that the battens of civilization were down.

"Darling, I had to," said Caroline, maneuvering exquisitely in an element that had been over the ages fashioned and fined down for just such people as her. "Even though you were incommunicado. I knew you'd forgive me. Just think—the most wonderful thing—Léon wants you to exhibit in Boston. He's terribly impressed with your work. It'll mean opening in New York, too. Not until the fall of course, but we could go now, it would allow you to see something of the country—and, my dear, you'd love it, the color and light's so alive and brilliant, quite different from English pastel and marvelous for your painting."

Léon was one of Caroline's influential art-men, as she called them. A man of distinction and judgment, sought after and inaccessible. Caroline must have worked hard, I thought, to have engaged him in her cause.

And Valmiki's cause. For all his tempestuous life, to him painting was a part of living—the deep and absorbing part that soothed him, gave him the kind of satisfaction that others so wildly sought, each lashed to his own whirligig, and saw turn to froth in grasping hands, between urgent soliciting thighs. It had been something of value in the beginning, it was no less so now, despite the limed net that had fallen over his head, entangling him with Caroline and Ellie and slim young women in black, in class and caste and the making of money, the infinite intricate preoccupying combines and permutations of society.

Already you could see his interest mounting, the apathy pushed away from his face like an unwanted ether mask. The sense of betrayal that had caused it, the outrage, the bitterness, the piercing loss of a precious security—all seemed to be going, slowly consumed in the steady flame Caroline had once again coaxed out of embers. Also, he was better: healthy body re-acting against further domination by a sick mind—or, as the doctor put it, the illness having run its course.

"America," he repeated after her, cautiously, only nibbling the edges of delight. "I'd like to go there. I've often been told I ought."

"Really, Val? Who by?"

"Oh, people," he said vaguely. "One meets so many . . . I believe their sun can even be like ours."

"Yours, darling? Do you mean the Indian sun?"

"Yes," he said, gently contemplative. "Indian sun. Dazzling. Blinding. You never get it like that here, do you? Sometimes you'd burn your hand just touching the rock, it got so hot. Made you think of the terrible power there was up there . . . you always ended up thinking of God."

"Yes," said Caroline. Her voice was brisk as it always was when God was taken out of context—which was church, to which she scarcely ever went—and brought into everyday liv-ing. "We must certainly go, it'll do you a world of good, in all sorts of ways. Oh, I nearly forgot. Jumbo sent you this—" She pulled out a ring, gold, set with a magnificent mogok ruby flanked by smaller—though only by comparison—pink diamonds. "He asked me to tell you that if you're ever in India and you want any help, you've only got to show it. It's got his coat-of-arms, there."

She turned it over, and on the back was the usual muddled Indian coat-of-arms, with indiscriminate derivations from both East and West, of a Bengal tiger and a rampant lion holding aloft in their paws intertwined temple-type garlands.

Valmiki took the ring, handling it with reverence, his bright face reflecting the romance of it—the fairy story of a pledge, redeemable at moment of peril.

"I don't know," he said, clutching it even tighter, "if I should. I mean, Jumbo always says—" He repeated what Jumbo had said about the plight of princes. In a way his naïveté was inevitable, for Valmiki's Indian experience included peasants and priests—the ascetics, not those powerful Brahmin oligarchs who had exercised the powers of State, leaving its trappings and symbols to the throne; it had never been permitted to take in even the outermost courtyards of a prince.

"Oh Val, you mustn't believe everything he says!" said Caroline with faint impatience. "He's got packets of money, done up in bundles in deposits all over the world. I'd hang on to that if I were you."

"So kind of him," Valmiki mumbled, gingerly trying the ring on. "I must really—"

"He's gone," said Caroline. "Or going. Back to India: said his time was up. Poor old Jumbo, he can't do exactly as he likes these days."

The Swami gone, Jumbo going. And Ellie? She slid into the room, mute pathetic ghost, forcing Valmiki to push aside the alluring wares Caroline had spread before him and consider whatever limbo she was now in. He had in fact done little else for three weeks. It seemed harsh that he must mount his obsession again, at the very moment that Caroline had offered him a chance to be rid of it. Yet he had his early discipline, however overgrown by new indulgences, and he said abruptly, "I must find out about Ellie first. Before America or Léon, before anything else."

"My dear," said Caroline soberly, "that's the other thing I had to tell you about. Ellie's not coming back. She's decided to go back to her own people. She telephoned while you were

away ill. I tried to get her to speak to you but she wouldn't—
she wouldn't even tell me where she was, I suppose in case we
tried to change her mind. She wanted the decision to be entirely
hers."

"She has no people," said Valmiki.

"She's Jewish," said Caroline. "She's not like you or me,
Val. The Jews have inbred for so long they're one huge family.
They don't *think* of themselves except as related. Ellie will
never be left alone, or wanting anything."

"There's the child," said Valmiki. "I can't just let her go.
I must talk to her, even if she won't change her mind. If only
I knew—there must be some way of finding her?—of tracing
where—"

"My dear, it's too late," Caroline interrupted gently. "She's
gone. She went the day she rang me. She left it to the last
minute so that you wouldn't try to talk her out of anything."

So Ellie had returned to the fold, to her people—in Ger-
many? or would it be Israel? or America? To which state did
the stateless go? I was about to ask when I saw the look on
Valmiki's face, the thankful look of people who find that matters have been taken out of their hands, giving them rest from
action and decision—the ailing animal dead, the abortion per-
formed, the unwanted old certified and lodged. It was momen-
tary—gone already between one glance and the next, vaporized
by a furious guilt and shame; but it had been there. I was silent.

I thought Valmiki would ask. But he was silent, too.

"Come along, Val. We've a hundred things to do." Caroline
began to chivy him, affectionately but firmly; and in the rush
of packing and planning, the trapping of Minou and the bustle
of removal, what had been burning questions and irreparable
injury were hastily shelved, it being demonstrably impossible to
allot further time for their consideration.

Book II

25

SO we went our several ways: Jumbo to India, the Swami to Europe, Caroline and Valmiki to America, Minou shivering into quarantine, Ellie into the unknown, I to the hospitable cottage in Northumbria whose doors had once again been invitingly opened. It was as if a sealed capsule had exploded, distributing its forcibly assembled components over the globe.

Caroline's house was closed, the silver wrapped and stored, the furs put away in napthalene and tissue, and dust covers laid on the furniture by Mrs. Peabody, to whom these procedures were new and whom therefore Caroline—with bad grace and audible sighs for the well-trained long-gone housekeeper—was obliged to instruct. Mrs. Peabody's services were nevertheless to be retained for want of anything better, Caroline having perforce developed a capacity for putting up with the trivia of change and circumstance, if nothing more weighty; and the small retainer she paid sent Mrs. Peabody into excessive raptures.

"You'd know she was a real lady even if you didn't," she said in an awed voice, forgiving and forgetting the times when Caroline had barked at her and she had snapped back. "It's not as if she had to, is it? But there, you can always tell them that is from them that ain't."

Her more usual contention, that she was as good as the next person, seemed slightly at odds with this but left her untroubled; no doubt she had long since accepted the two faces of divine right and equality-Joe in her makeup.

"What will you do?" I asked. "Take another job?"

"Oh yes, miss," she said practically. "Can't retire on a quid, can you? But it won't be the same without him."

"Valmiki?"

"Yes, miss. Poor lamb, he's always been a bit lost like, I suppose he never had much to do with looking after himself, in his own country."

"Well," I said dryly, "he wasn't exactly a prince there." But she was off on another tack.

"If they'd asked," she said a little wistfully, "I'd have gone with them and all."

"But you've got your own family."

"I could have got my sister to see they was all right," she said. "Besides they was born here, dear, they can look after themselves. Not like that one"—here her eyes grew baleful—"prey to all them foreigners."

"I expect Lady Caroline can keep them at bay," I suggested, but Mrs. Peabody sniffed her disparagement.

"Like that Ellie what nearly got him," she said grimly, "and never a word from her. It's his luck he wasn't caught—nothing to do with *her*."

She girded up her coat about her—a coney fur, a parting present from Valmiki which he had paid for, but which she had selected amid much girlish excitement—and departed, still full of her doubts and misgivings about Caroline's capacities.

In the tranquil setting of the country cottage Mrs. Peabody's doubts took frail root—less from Caroline's angle than Valmiki's. Would he fall prey to those foreigners, the Americans, in the graphic phrase she had used, and if so would it be sexually? But this would be Caroline's preoccupation and I could not visualize failure in one season, whatever might happen long term.

Or spiritually, which would have been the Swami's preoccupation, so that he came to exalt what he created above himself: but his early training would not allow it, his religion which held that a part of God dwelt in every man and would one day reunite with the divine whole, so that to exalt man-made over man became a blasphemy.

Or morally, making him sell himself for public applause and that other coveted grail, success?

Already, I thought, here in London I had seen him play the pander, providing the attitudes and postures he was asked for whether or not they were natural to him, and reveling in his penetration of the well-kept secret of how facile, after the first time, it all was. That creeping stain had not, so far, touched his work, whose austerity and integrity his worst critics had upheld; and also, I thought, in the middle of his act I had seen him watching himself with that cold mocking unimpressed inner eye, as commonly possessed as it is uncommonly used. Or had I, I wondered bleakly, only imagined what I wanted to see?

Meanwhile the news from America was nothing if not cheerful. Caroline and Valmiki seemed to be touring the States as the whim took them—going to places, said Caroline, the sound of whose names they liked—though not, of course, quite like tourists, since almost every other city proffered someone to whom Caroline was related, or whom she knew, or had an introduction to, so that her letters only intermittently carried hotel headings, far more frequently giving the address of a town or country house which—one gathered, though not from any specific description—invariably overlooked a lake or a river or a park, when it did not actually enclose them.

The last time they had gone on tour—long before Valmiki had grown wings, when he was still a passive if unapologetic peasant and Caroline's had been the initiative—her missives to me had been brief, trailing away in the end to no more than a line or two on an infrequent postcard. Now, under Valmiki's impetus, there were slightly longer accounts of their mutual doings in letters that came at frequent intervals—*Val wants to keep in touch*, wrote Caroline frankly if peevishly, *in case you hear anything of Ellie . . . also because he says he feels it is his duty—I suppose because you've looked after him like a mother*. This made me smile. There were no more than a few months between us, yet this was a relationship Caroline constantly foisted upon me while stepping delicately to avoid it herself. *My protégé—my ward*—even *my pupil:* these labels, with their imprecise ratios of age, she was willing to accept; but never one which floodlit with the possibility of narrow calculation the fourteen years' difference between Valmiki and herself.

Valmiki, of course, could neither read nor write. He simply sent me postcards—sometimes blank, which must have mystified many a postman, sometimes with small drawings of whatever took his fancy. Once, from Baltimore, came a drawing of a sunken tub, quite empty, edged with Christmas card glitter, which must have intrigued even more postmen. It lodged in my mind, too: I wrote and asked, and it turned out that Valmiki had been introduced to that epitome of vulgarity, gold-plated taps. At one time Jumbo too, I recalled, had boasted gold taps which, with the dawning of sense and prudence, he had attempted to get rid of. Unfortunately it had been wartime, and chromium replacements were not to be had. For all I knew he was still saddled with them. Unquestionably they had impressed Valmiki: but whether by their magnificence, or sheer idiotic waste, in the absence of comment it was impossible to say.

It was this complete lack of comment which made it impossible to know what was happening to him, apart from the bland narrative of travel, people, places. He had of course already traveled widely; but America was literally and compellingly a new world, bold, virile, rich red blood in its throbbing veins and healthily free of that whiff of decadence that overhangs the overcivilized. Yet it was restless, brutal with the impatient brutality that comes from no-time-to-think, distracted and distracting, obsessed and preferring to be obsessed more by machines than by that most intricate and mysterious of machines, the mind. Which had been, of course, Valmiki's foundations.

Spring turned to summer, the cottage was wanted for holidays, and I went back to London. There was still no news of Ellie—not even a postcard, said Mrs. Peabody with some emphasis when I asked. As I had arranged for my mail to be sent directly to me, there was no real excuse to think there might be something for me at the flat either: yet somehow the hope had lingered that she would write, and a vague apprehensive depression settled over me when I found there was nothing.

The same hope—or could it be a resurgence of guilt—must have animated Valmiki, for as soon as he knew of my return to London three letters came in quick succession—dictated by him, all inquiring if I had heard anything from Ellie. Then there was silence, at least as far as that went. Presumably he felt he had done his duty.

Now when he spoke, and Caroline wrote, it was of externals: of the beauty of the country, and the friendly curiosity of the people; of the pretty young Negro maid the agency had sent Caroline (but she had not lasted long, for reasons on which there was silence); and of Minou, who had at last come out of quarantine, and who drew as much attention as a prima donna, wrote Caroline on a note of triumph and pleasure, as if besides conforming to plan this was something the monkey appreciated too.

By midsummer they were settled in Boston, where the exhibition was to be held and where, no doubt, Caroline was already casting her shimmering nets, as intent and adroit as any pearl fisher. Valmiki seemed to be working, as well as being popular, and there was, I gathered, already a gem of a collection—*and such subjects, quite unexpected*, wrote Caroline, although I could not imagine anything more unexpected, to me personally, than those nudes of Ellie had been.

Midsummer, too, in England: hot days and pavements, short cool nights, bringing reminders that this was what India offered almost all year round, the sheer opulence of never feeling cold, the freedom from fuel and fires and swaddling clothes, being able to eat out on terraces and swim in warm seas. Did Valmiki, I wondered, sometimes feel as I did this sudden tug of the land from which one was sprung, as if there was an uncut cord between the soil and the man into whose making it had gone? But, I thought wryly, such intimations were probably reserved for those fortunates of the four freedoms. What Valmiki would remember was that he had never eaten in any real sense of the word; never swum in warm seas; never, until Caroline, even glimpsed it.

August into September, the exhibition a few weeks away, and I began to feel what Valmiki was probably experiencing too—the internal tightness, the sudden painful constrictions, the jets of ice-cold adrenalin shot without warning into the hollow body. These were familiar symptoms, preceding the publication of my own books, and the vicarious suffering, since there was no book, forced me to recognize how deep a place—despite my strenuous rejections—Valmiki had gouged in me.

Then the first notices came. Valmiki had sent them, and had obviously exercised some selectivity. The second batch, from Caroline, was less unanimously acclamant: and yet, when it comes, there is no mistaking success. Critic after critic praised his fine use of color, his integrity (and here one nagging doubt was stilled), the peace and the unity of his pictures. One or two thought him an honorable failure—reaching beyond his grasp, attempting too much in trying to integrate his American experience: but these same critics would have discerned a too-narrow approach, a lack of initiative, had he confined himself to Indian experience, English landscape, and the models he occasionally used. Others, again a minority, proceeding from the dictum that art must be disciplined, found objectionable the uncontrolled passion of some of his work. But after all, I thought, the painting must somewhere reflect the painter: and for all the keen, rigid disciplines of his mind, Valmiki was also capable of the most irrational, impassioned action.

After this came the flummery: paragraphs in social columns, in women's magazines and in the slicks: photographs of Valmiki, simpering here, soulful there, wearing Oriental confections and invariably clasping a glass. There was no evidence, here, of any watchful inner eye. On the contrary, obviously frankly delighted by it all, Valmiki had actually snipped them out himself, in advance of agency clippings, to send to me in pride. Poor Valmiki, I thought, gazing at that multiplicity of faces, on each an expression suggested no doubt by the photographer, topped by well-groomed heads bearing each the sheen and gleam induced by a well-placed lamp—poor Valmiki, heir to so many lopsided values that he could glory in this kind of shoddy.

And then a sentence took my eye, an adamantine column standing alone and unexpected among the general rubble. *This young painter*, it ran, *paints as if unknown to himself he had glimpsed, beyond the horizon, the transcendent powers of Universe, and the refracted light brings a hint of the power and the menace into his own painting.*

I read it again, feeling I would like to know who had written those lines, disturbing in their insight and impact: but in Valmiki's impatience to send me his photograph the rest of the caption and review were lost. Yet the heart of it was there, and if even one human being could discern so much, I reflected, it showed Valmiki to be not entirely rapt in fatuity, or his inner eye wholly, as I had feared, extinguished.

26

THE months slipped away, 1953 was drawing to a close, when the seventeenth century erupted into the twentieth with a letter from my lawyers in India headed *Abolition of Inams*. What this amounted to was that the government was proposing to commute, by payment of a lump sum, the annual land revenues which an astute ancestor of mine had arranged to be paid in perpetuity to his descendants; and the lawyers—naturally enough, from their point of view—wanted me on hand when the sum was agreed. For my part there were several loose ends: a contract with the BBC scripting overseas broadcasts, a short story promised to a new magazine, a dozen books awaiting review: but the pull I had felt earlier in the year tugged hard, and in the end—having coped with these commitments in one frantic rush—I sailed for India.

The case was being heard in Madras, but rather than park myself on long-suffering relatives I put up at the Hindu Hotel, whose beds were of teakwood slats each one of which lodged in the back like a monk's penance, ameliorated not at all by an inch-thick biscuit; but the food was superlative.

"It's because you have become soften from the overuse of slumbereesi mattresses," said the hotel manager, a fair, fat, orthodox Brahmin as surprising in his way as those books one comes across in bazaar bookstalls, filled with charivari in extraordinary juxtaposition.

"I know," I said. "No matter. Your bed will soon undo the harm."

"The spine," he said, expounding a theory which would have induced despair in half the mattress manufacturers in England, "consists of thirty-three bones. To lie on a soft base does not give them proper support. That is why slipped disk is Western complaint—it is a common English complaint, is it not?"

I said I supposed so, which gained me his approval. He shouted loudly and a minion appeared, carrying a salver on which were arranged washed betel leaves and areca nuts. This was his hospitality—not hotel service to be added to my bill. I took one of the wet green leaves and chewed, enjoying the sharp clean taste—it is the aftertaste which is less pleasant—while he settled himself on a mat at a seemly distance from me (though it was midday and anyway we were out on the sunny open veranda which ran like a corridor the length of the rooms).

He chewed too, helping himself to pan from a separate salver. When the juice ran red he said, "You are well known in London, are you not?"

"I would like to think so," I said, "but in all honesty—no."

"But I have seen your face in papers! Was it not you?" His voice squeaked with disappointment. Once again the minion was summoned and, after prolonged shouting, appeared, disappeared, reappeared with an accounts ledger in which were pasted press clippings under the curlicued heading *Our successful kinsfolk abroad*. (God, so that bug had got in here too!)

I stared at the face he was pointing out. Certainly it was me —not me in my own right, but because I happened to be sitting next to Valmiki. It must have been taken during his first success—I could not remember the occasion; the picture taken long ago in London, reproduced in an Indian magazine, now by an odd quirk set before me again.

I disillusioned my host, who said, quickly rallying, "There are several pictures of him—*he* is well known, is he not? A mere boy!—a South Indian too, a Madrasi—it makes me very proud."

(So it was pride, another kind of bug, not quite so bad.)

I begged the book from him and bore it away to my room. There were the old clippings, and a batch of new ones still to be pasted in. I had been anxious to see what sort of reception Valmiki got from India but had thought it unlikely that I would, so long after the exhibition in America had opened and closed; yet here, months after the event, were the notices —tremulous, none too assured, wary, sometimes plagiaristic to the extent that the phrases were familiar to me from previous encounters—but still reviews, awareness, recognition. Poor old India, staggering along behind everyone else, was at last getting there, even if those centuries of ferocious paternalism had affected her growth so that she walked like an uncertain toddler instead of the adult she now was.

I had been back less than a week when Jumbo telephoned. Having a very natural interest in the fate of hereditary incomes, he closely followed all related Court actions; and he had seen my name in the list of plaintiffs.

"Of course we must," I said. "Where?"

At the Club. Jumbo lived well, in subdued splendor, in one wing of a palace that had once been all his own. The part-princely household was excellently run by his wife, a kindly and competent if shadowy figure, and by a platoon of well-trained servants; and indeed it was here that much of his official and semiofficial entertaining was done. Yet for friends, for relaxation, Jumbo always suggested the Club. Perhaps it was only here that he could freely practice among people of similar persuasions his cosmopolitan, ineradicable manners and customs from wearing the Savile Row suits in which he felt comfortable to dining alone with someone like me, a friend who neither happily nor unhappily but simply happened to be a woman.

Jumbo, however, had never flaunted his Western predilections—not even in the British era when they might have lubricated his dealings with the people in power. They were too genuinely a part of him, and he too basically gentle, for him to offend Hindu susceptibilities by making a parade of them. Instead of picking me up, therefore, as he had so happily done so many times in London, he sent his car—one of his lesser ones, an anonymous Austin calculated to do me the least harm in the eyes of Hindu Hotel inmates.

"But my dear, whatever made you park there?" These were almost his first words as he took my arm, walking me over the smooth lawns toward the clubrooms. "It's miles from any-where and anything but comfortable."

"The food," I said. "Incomparable. The fulfillment of every deprived dream I have dreamed while eating in London."

"There are compensations, all the same, are there not?" he said, and sighed. "Ah, London! Sometimes I do not know how I stop myself jumping on the first plane back. . . . It can only be my stern sense of duty, do you not agree?"

"I most certainly do," I said, and he laughed, squeezing my arm affectionately.

"Now the crucial question is: here? or inside? You will know the advantages and drawbacks of each."

"Oh, here," I said, and we sat at one of the tables on the wide terrace. There were orange silk shades on the lights, the smell of lime and rosemary in the air from the imaginative border around the swimming pool; and from the pool itself came the occasional dip and splash of late swimmers. It was all very pleasant.

Jumbo said, "People come a long way for this."

"It's not difficult to guess why."

"All sorts of people," said Jumbo. "My dear, you know quite well what I mean, though you always pretend you don't. . . . I sometimes wonder what things are coming to."

"They're changing," I said. "You've been able to change too, Jumbo—marvelously. Don't tell me you're going to give up after so long?"

"But *such* people," he said, and there were faint echoes of Caroline in the words. "People who've never been used to servants turn up here and treat 'em like dogs, bark at them, make them all bolshies . . . people who've never had money suddenly flush, behaving like mountebanks without even an inkling that they are."

I felt the sudden trickle of cold, the sweat that begins when someone you care for comes face to face with society—himself unarmed, his opponent stiff with hidden and invisible weapons.

"In fact people," I managed to say, "like Valmiki."

"Oh no," he said warmly. "Val's different. He's sensitive, a gifted artist. Why, if he came here tomorrow we'd lay on a reception in his honor."

"I daresay," I said. "The West having taken him up, the East finds it safe to join in the rush. The point is, is he going to be asked to private homes—to clubs to which people like you belong?"

Jumbo sidestepped neatly.

"My dear," he said, "I have given Caroline my assurance—Val can call upon me for any help he wants at any time. In fact he has my—a pledge, a token—"

"The ring?"

"A romantic notion of Caroline's," he said hurriedly, "one has to accede to women's whims. Shall we dine?"

When we were in, settled, snowy napkins unfurled on our laps by attentive waiters, Jumbo said, "Now tell me all about the exquisite Caroline and her young pasha. I'm starved for news, but yes, gasping! But first things first, so what shall it be, on the level or under the counter?"

"I'll join you at your level," I said. "If we're dining together it's dreary being at odds."

"Suya," he said with gentle melancholy, "you know my

level. It's too late for me to change." But his melancholy vanished as he filled our glasses beneath the carved-wood gaze of the waiters.

"Now," he said, brisk and cheerful once more, "tell me about Caroline."

"There's nothing to tell. She flourishes. Which cannot be news to anyone who knows how much work she puts into it."

"And Val?"

"In a state of pleasurable awe, after a first sight of gold taps."

He threw back his head and roared, sheer booming mirth that moved even the wood carvings to discreet smiles.

"Suya," he said, "I believe you still hold that against me."

"Not any longer," I said. "It seemed a waste at the time. Now it is only a variation of idiocy. The intriguing thing is when someone like Valmiki is dazzled by it. If he is—I'm not sure."

"*I* am." Jumbo chuckled. "Of course he is dazzled by gold, diamonds, good wine, pretty women. Quite right, too. Eminently sensible young man. Struck me from the first that he was. Only I hope he doesn't lose his head—New York and London wouldn't notice it, but people here would."

"I didn't know he was coming to India," I said, surprised.

"Nor did I," said Jumbo. "Except that eventually he must."

I accepted that. However strongly Western-influenced, it was from India that his strength came. He would have to return to it again and again when that strength was drawn, or his reserves ran low, to recharge himself.

"If—when he comes," I said, "will he get—will you give him your support?"

Again Jumbo moved adroitly.

"My dear, what is my support worth? Times are changing." He gestured toward the door, where a group of assorted Europeans were entering. "You see that lot? Riffraff. Poles, Czechs, Rumanians—technologists, we've got to have them. They know no better than to come here wearing play-shirts—but we've got to let them in. And outside? Outside princes are two per paisa, fighting Congress-wallahs for the public posts. That's where it is—the power and the influence that you want: among the representatives of the people. Go to the people, my dear, go to the people!"

But the people were still in a state of flux, undiscerning, as likely to applaud what was merely gaudy as what was good, uncertain about which features of the social system to cherish and which to cast on the nearest tip. Between people and sidestepping cognoscenti opened the pit for exceptions like Valmiki.

Strangely enough, while between us Caroline and I took into account almost every extraneous factor that might impinge on Valmiki, neither of us reckoned with his emotions. But of course this did not strike me then, as I listened to Jumbo, gazed at the sunflowers, palm trees, coral sands, kettle-drums and tropical fish that adorned the sea-cotton shirts of the tribe he called riffraff, and came to a slow and somehow confusing realization that all these brilliant evocations of pattern were Indian originals, reproduced and hardly recognizable in Western kodachrome.

27

JUMBO was not the only one to believe that times were changing. My old friend, the village headman, was vividly alive to the changes in his territory.

"Three wells in six months," he said complacently. "One dug with English money, one with American, the third the Ruskies dug themselves—that is the cheapest way, you know . . . also it made them many friends, for our people like to watch, they even prefer it to working themselves, particularly at midday when the sun is hot." He paused and swilled his tea, looking reflective. "It is wonderful, is it not, to think of such generosity? Of course it has arisen only since we were given votes, before that they did not care if we had no water. Or perhaps," he added generously, "they did not know of our need of it."

He was a shrewd man, tactful when need be, prospering with the flow of foreign aid to the village and the expansion of his flourishing illicit stills—probably an excellent headman.

I asked for news of Valmiki's family, particularly his mother for whom he had always shown the most concern. The headman did not know. The village lay within walking distance of his own, yet he had not been there for over a year. His wife proved more venturesome. She had been twice to the village in the last month to visit friends and relatives. No, she had not seen the mother but had heard she was ill.

Yes, probably the shaking sickness, but she could not be sure. She set down another two tumblers of freshly made tea, a platter of crêpes as big as dinner plates and as fine as the finest lace, spread with a fiery green-chili chutney. Would I like, she asked, for her to inquire for me, which would save me a long walk? I wavered, tempted to escape that visit with all its pointless questions, one world trying dimly to scan another nearly out of its range; but to do so would make nonsense of my having come this far, besides lumbering my conscience.

The headman would have got me a cart, but the memories of last time revived and I declined. He watched me go with a faint relief as he had done on previous occasions. The apprehensions aroused when he had first been made responsible for the English lady's safety—at a time when the rate of exchange ratified by legend was ten native lives for every British one—these apprehensions still quivered appreciably, even from contact with her at one remove. Nevertheless, courtesy impelled him to a final politeness.

"Remember me to your friend when you return," he called. "The English milady, the bizarre one. Tell her we remember her well and hope she will again honor us with her presence."

He shuddered slightly and retreated into the shaded porch of his hut.

The headman's wife had been partially right: Valmiki's mother was suffering both from malaria and from consumption, her chronically half-fed body fallen easy victim to the disease. She knew this quite well, gave herself a year to live although the doctor had said three; but then, she explained, he had meant to be kind . . . he was a kind man, who came once or twice a month to see her without making any charge. The burden of obligation on her was so great that I pointed out he was paid by the government, but this only brought gratitude for these signs of betterment in the times, without any notion that she might be entitled to it. Nor did she think to complain of dying at forty: indeed, she considered herself lucky, many of her friends having been taken at thirty. Hers was a generation thoroughly conditioned and ground into acceptance.

I told her something about Valmiki, in between bouts of coughing that arched her body as if in orgasm. She listened avidly enough but with a certain withdrawal, the remoteness of people who see on one side the falling away of a world, feel the great mystery edging up to them on the other.

Withal, though perhaps more mechanically and with less conviction than before, she made the apposite obeisances. She would like to see her son before she died. This was his home and he would always be welcome in it: and what if she were not there? his brothers' wives would see to it. They would even arrange his marriage when the time came, when Valmiki felt the need of a wife.

The words had a fantastically unreal quality: what possible kind of welcome could these forgotten brothers' wives provide for this stranger, after so many years, and sustain it? What imaginable kind of woman would make him a suitable wife? The sentences hung in the air between us like some crazed edifice whose foundations both of us saw were missing, though neither of us could acknowledge it to the other.

The long speech had tired her. She lay back on the mat, head lolling on the small hard pillow. There was sweat on her forehead, a faint line of scum on her lips. I looked round, but there was nothing with which to wipe it away. The hut was bare: pots and pans on the hearth, the bedding of each occupant—mat and pillow in a neat roll, one roll on top of

another in a corner; in another an earthenware god, a kero-
sene-oil lamp.

There was no one within call. The sickness being chronic,
and labor short, the entire family was out working in the
fields. They would rally around later, there was never any
danger that she would die alone. But the interim, I thought,
must be grim. I wondered if I should leave some money with
which she could buy herself a few comforts. (*What* comforts? wireless, television, Ovaltine, flowers?—these were the
established rights of the bedridden British, I must be mad
to think of them here.) But before I could decide, she herself
resolved the dilemma. Enlarging a tear in the tattered pillow,
she dug her fingers in, probed, pulled a small drawstring
pouch and handed it to me. Inside were ten gold sovereigns.

"They are Valmiki's," she said, "bought from the money
he has sent me. Put them where no one will find them, in
the cave of his gods. I would do it myself but it is on a hill
and I have waited too long, it is beyond my strength."

"Your husband?"

She made a gesture—the universal gesture of a woman who
is yoked to a weakling.

"It would go on arak."

"Your sons?"

"They have already had their share of Valmiki's wealth.
What remains is for him alone, it must be left for him as I
have said."

I tried to reason with her, pointing out it would be easier
for everyone if I simply sold the gold and remitted the money
to Valmiki; that there were foreigners around who would
not respect the sanctity of his gods. She was adamant. Shaking
with weakness, but adamant.

I took the pieces of gold back to my hotel, meaning to

safe-deposit them until I could find a convenient time for the trip she had foisted onto me. Of course the time never came. Nor were they deposited, for I discovered that the hoarding of gold was forbidden and I did not want incontrovertible evidence brought against me that I was doing precisely this. No matter that the gold was scarcely of hoardable proportions: principle would be invoked to crush this minuscule transgression, while bland large-scale operators looped loops around the law.

Some five months later, in May, I went to see her again. She was appreciably worse, eyes retracted deeply into the skull, body frail and skeletal and keeping a brittle shape and form like dead leaves before they crumble. Her gaunt face brought back Ellie to me, Ellie in all her tight and terrible locked-in tragedy; but there was no stain of horror here, rather a serenity, a surrender to forces that were not so much vindictive as inevitable.

She wanted to know if I had been to Valmiki's cave of gods with the gold. I said I had, filled with the superstitious certainty that anyone so near death must surely sense I was lying. She did not.

I swore to myself that I would accomplish the mission the next day; but again the months went by.

In the meanwhile I had written, after much hesitation, to Valmiki to tell him of his mother's condition. The reply came by return post: short, unmeditated, starkly illuminating how wide the growing apart had been that he could speak with such brutal realism, bereft of the gentler obliquities of his race. It was even difficult to tell, now, whether he had dictated the letter which rejected his mother, or whether he had left its composition to Caroline, so close to her had he come during her tutelage.

So mother and son did not meet; and such a meeting, after their long separation and the initial disharmonies of the household, would in any case, as Valmiki had said, have been wholly meaningless.

When I went to see her again at the end of the year she had been dead some months, and the hut was occupied by the woman—wife or concubine—who had taken her place. Valmiki's home, however impossible it had become for him to return to it, was now finally and demonstrably closed.

28

NOW I could no longer postpone, with any decency, the trip to Valmiki's cave.

After so long I had only a vague recollection of where it was, but when I had left the village behind, old memories surfaced and I found myself on a path I recognized. Indeed, although ill-defined, it was by no means concealed, and I began to wonder if Valmiki's mother had not been over-sanguine in imagining no one would pillage a deserted cave. If it still was, I thought, ascending the last sharp gradient, a deserted cave, undiscovered either by the foreign tribes that had descended on the village—those technicians, English, American and Ruskies of the headman's description, hardly to be deterred from entry by anyone's gods—or by amateur India-lovers whom one could now find, each bound to a village-life thesis, distributed in diligent single units throughout rural India.

Yet as far as I could see it was inviolate. Someone, probably the Swami, had blocked the mouth of the cave with a large boulder, building it up to the roof with smaller stones and a rough plastering of mud. There was no sign that any of this had been moved, and moss and spear grass in the interstices had clearly been growing undisturbed for some time. Nor were there any graffiti adorning the outer walls, either of Rabelaisian quality or the apologetic scratchings that nostalgic visitors leave.

I tried to peer in through the cracks between the stones, but the angle at which the cave lay to the entrance and the gloom inside made it impossible to see much. I dropped the gold pieces through, with a sense of relief that I had at last done what the woman had wanted. She had been right too, I thought, in believing the cave was left alone.

I turned away, still a little puzzled by this, and began the steep descent. Then I realized I was being followed. The steps were not loud or hurried; they might easily have belonged to someone who happened to be walking my way, except that when I stopped they stopped. Despite myself I began walking faster, and to my horror whoever it was behind me did the same. The footsteps were heavy, somehow, and exaggeratedly loud on the loose shingle. There was a queer drag in one of them, something lopsided: a long labored step as if a great weight were being lifted, followed by a quick shuffle to make up for lost time. I had to stop, to turn and look before my nerve gave way. It was a diseased man, his leg bloated and puckered with elephantiasis, his face twitching and grimacing from exertion and perhaps the pain of his grotesque leg, who did not stop when I did but came after me with renewed vigor.

I began to run. The path curved slightly here, around a clump of shrubs and thorn and westward in the direction of the village. I must have got too close in my haste. Thorn bushes seized me, imprisoned my clothes. I tore at them, feeling my fingers pricked and stinging; was almost free when I heard a low cackle rising up as it seemed from the ground in front of me. It was the old harridan I had seen on that visit long ago, toothless, slack-mouthed, crouched among one of the bushes and engaged in crushing its berries and smearing the poisoned milk over her face. The skin was already blistered, no doubt from previous applications; now she was working the milk between the rash-free areas as carefully as any beautician. Her madness seemed harmless enough, until I had wrenched myself free: and then she abandoned what she was doing, picked up a great jagged fragment of rock, and planting herself in my path began to shout offensive gibberish.

I knew I could not get past: and behind me the pursuit was closing. Then some sealed-in panel of memory slid open, I remembered that the Swami's shelter was nearby, in the wilderness of this hill slope, and the dim hope flickered that it might afford me sanctuary. I left the path and, rounding the hill, found I had been right. There, not fifty yards away, was the old lean-to, still upright after so many years. The fragile structure hardly offered any kind of refuge, yet I felt a curious sense of safety as I flung myself inside.

Several minutes went by. Presently the cripple appeared, hobbling painfully over the stony ground, followed closely by the old woman. Neither now showed any sign of haste. When in slow progress, they had reached the entrance to the shelter, they sat down, and as nonchalantly as if we had just met for the day inquired after my health.

I was breathless, speechless. I could only stare at them, these two strangely paired, self-appointed keepers of the hill, and feel again that sense of trance, of living in another medium, that this hillside had once before produced in me. I shook my head to clear it, this sensation that was almost physical; and presently the pieces of the ordinary world fell back into place, I heard the gentle voice, and realized I was being questioned by the cripple.

"Yes," I answered him. "I knew the Swami long ago, when he lived here."

"You were his disciple?"

"No. The boy was, the goatherd. He brought me here."

"Before my time," said the man. "I never saw a goatherd. Nor any goats. Only the likes of her," he nodded at his companion, "and the Swami, though *he* didn't stay long, more's the pity. When he was here there was peace, order . . . he used to keep *them* in order." He looked malevolently at the old woman, who glared savagely back before beginning her shrill unbalanced laughter.

"It's not the same without him." He shifted his position awkwardly, using both hands to lift the deadweight of the diseased limb. The skin on it was gray, a thick parchment through whose cracks lymph oozed in tiny trickles. I knew there was no risk from a direct contact, the infection was carried by subtler complicated means, yet I felt myself shrink back from that hideously enlarged leg, from any contact with the pale yellow fluid worming out of the skin; and the slight movement did not go unnoticed. "Now *he* did not mind," the faintly reproachful voice said, "what we were like—what any of us were like . . . he even tended us, as good as any doctor. When he went, we would have gone too—"

"Where?"

"Anywhere." He grinned wryly. "Doesn't matter where, for people like us. But the Swami wanted us to stay until he came back . . . he promised that he would come back. Meanwhile we look after these things which are his"—he gestured vaguely, perhaps at the lean-to shelter—or was it the cave, this entire haunted hillside?—"and keep people away, you know, interfering people who poke into this and that— no, not you, since you are known to the Swami—but others. . . ."

"Have there been many others?"

"There used to be. But word soon gets round, now there are very few who come."

I could well believe that, I thought, as I made my way back to the village. The Swami, using very simple weapons and ones already to hand, had created a formidable bastion to guard his little enclave. To guard and preserve it for himself? I wondered. Or was it an attempt, longsighted if singularly unrealistic, to maintain a retreat for Valmiki? Valmiki who no doubt at that very minute, some thousands of miles away, was savoring the sophisticated pleasures of New York night life.

29

I DID not go back to the village again that trip. There had been rumors of the Swami's return, and I toyed with the idea of going to see him; but finally I decided that with the connecting link absent there could really be no traffic between us. In any case the rumor was not verified.

Meanwhile I had finished a new novel, and I returned to England in the autumn of 1955 for its publication. Caroline and Valmiki were already back, having returned in late March after what I gathered had been a successful tour, followed by a blissful holiday in the Bahamas.

"But you *must* come and hear *all* about it," came Caroline's warm voice over the telephone. "No, not tomorrow, Val's got to see a man . . . the day after we're going to . . ." the pages of the diary whirred, eventually a free date was found, way ahead in the future as is obligatory on the successful, and the engagement fixed.

Nearly two years had gone by since our last meeting; far from it seeming like yesterday I felt a whole century had elapsed, so great was the dislocation in time created by the simple physical fact of having lived in a different continent, of having been immersed in a different way of life. I even felt we would come together like strangers, armed with discreet little icepicks with which to chip away the cold glazed blocks, but in the event, of course, Caroline was more than equal to the situation. Her warmth, bubbling, insincere, en-wrapped you: it forced you to respond, even if you suspected it was part of a training that enabled her to be amiable, an exact amiability, precisely whenever she wanted to.

"Darling, how simply marvelous to see you! You're look-ing so well too, so fresh, how do you do it?"

She turned to Valmiki, I expected her to say as she always had, "You tell her, Val: you tell her how nice she's looking," but she did not. Initiative had been handed over to him—for now? for good? Perhaps at last he was the finished article, free of further refining.

"Hello, Suya." Valmiki was smiling, relaxed, taking his cue from her and resuming easily from where we had left off. "It is good to see you again. Very much like old times."

He took my coat, piloted me in, sat me down, lit my ciga-rette—all with subtle suggestions of hothouse care, making one glow from the pampering in a way that Caroline could, or the hall porter of an older club, or a good public relations man. Caroline meanwhile was languorously arranged on the sofa, waiting to be waited on; and watching her I realized how pallid the intervening years must have been while Val-miki was learning these arts, what patience she must have exercised while inculcating them.

"—and then there was Boston," Caroline was saying, "much more soigné of course, but the reaction was good, distinctly good. And do you remember that awful little town after-wards Val?—now what was it called, some impossible Iroquois name—where we had them eating out of your hand?"

"Darling, *your* hand," said Valmiki, with the kind of af-fectionate badinage that flows in the early married years be-tween compatible husband and wife. Indeed they bore on them the invisible yet unmistakable sign of union, whether solemnized as a marriage or not—a union consummated to its fullness and settling down, no longer electric with sex but set in the calmer pattern of harmonious cohabitation. Together, now, in nostalgic narrative, each capping the other's reminiscences, they retraced those two splendid years—years, I thought, in which the pattern had been established, in which Caroline had been free to establish it, rid of rival and protagonist, with power in her hands. And now here was Caroline, delivered from the tensions of the waiting, burning years —a new and tender Caroline, rich from mating, filled with her secret knowledge, bearing on her the soft bloom of a woman taken voluptuously to bed, loins appeased with the urgent flow, body and blood nourished with the seething impregnation. Except that Caroline was not only possessed, but had also taken in possession.

Beside her, Valmiki—Valmiki with the last scales of peasantry fallen from him, shaking down with the beautiful, brilliant Caroline, who by the criteria of his own country was old enough to be his mother, and plainly satisfied with the bargain.

"—then we simply had to get away," said Caroline.

"or bust," said Valmiki. "Too many awful people, *all* sorts. You really wouldn't believe, Suya."

"Wherever," I asked, "could you possibly have met all these dreadful people, Val?"

"Well, you know, art's got popular," he answered with a faint disdain. "Art for the masses and all that . . . and those women's club affairs. Ghastly."

"I thought a log cabin somewhere," said Caroline, "shooting bear. Terribly exciting, you've no idea how exciting hunting is until you've tried. But I couldn't persuade Val."

"Killing has no appeal for me," said Valmiki smoothly,

showing no trace of the repugnance that would have been the old, crude reaction to what was in deep conflict not only with his inheritance of compassion, but with the very nature of his religion. "Never has had. Odd, isn't it?"

"And so the Bahamas," said Caroline luxuriously, "and no regrets. It was perfect, divine. The most marvelous hotels, and fruit and sun and *enormous* goldy-pink beaches, gloriously empty, I never could understand how anything so lovely could be so empty."

"It's because they were golden," said Valmiki, with a sudden descent to earth. "I'm cleaned out—couldn't have raised the fare to get back home."

"Never mind," said Caroline lazily. "What *does* it matter, darling? I've told you, I've got enough for both of us, and anyway it's only until you sell another picture."

"There's only one left to sell." Valmiki smiled. "But it isn't mine to sell."

"Oh yes. The one of me." Caroline swept aside her languor and sat up, pure nervous excitement tinging her pale skin with color, the sudden movement dislodging a casual swirl or two of her pale blond hair. "Suya my sweet, I really must show you . . . do you know it's the only one he's *ever* done of me in *all* these years?"

The omission had certainly puzzled me. One would have thought Caroline a rewarding subject, with her beauty, the immense strength that ran under it. Yet Valmiki had never had her sit for him, had never even, as far as I knew, sketched her. Was it, I wondered, that he had sheered away from an acknowledgment, in the light, of her power, subconsciously recognizing it yet lacking the courage to face revelations that the truth and high integrity of his own painting would bring? For power, of the kind that Caroline held and used with so little hesitation, to a man with Valmiki's foundations was evil. Whatever its manifestations—however excusable its manipulations, or well-favored the end—it would never be other than evil.

We went upstairs, Caroline leading. The carpet had been green, I remembered. Now it was crimson, all the way up the stairs and on the landing, along the curved corridors from one arc of which Caroline's suite opened, from the opposite Valmiki's room, the room that had been Ellie's, and finally the box assigned to the melancholy Indian cook. Across this stretch Valmiki had gone in the night to Ellie—was it from an anguished love of her as she had believed? I had thought so then, but now could never decide. Later it was Caroline, when the liaison between them was a lapse, the lubricant effect of overmuch wine in the blood, the sudden engulfing eroticism of a random touch, not the routine it had now become. Across this stretch first Ellie, then the cook, had walked many times and finally a last time and had never returned. The carpeting had been green then. Now it was crimson; and the beautiful red-gold mahogany of the doors and paneling had been restored to glow in foil to the rich deep coloring.

The door was open: Caroline's door.

"I had the whole house done while we were away," she said. "Do you like it?"

"Charming," I said. I could not remember what it had been before. Now it was white and jade-green, like the sheets I remembered and between which I had slept, with glints of gold. The bed was a double one, two pillows to each side, twin tables for the porphyry lamps. Caroline had not anticipated my glance, nor did she notice it. She simply showed me their room, their bed: a commonplace arrangement, beyond comment from long establishment.

Over the bed was the picture. It was of a nude Caroline lying in a pleasurable swoon on a sandy beach in the sun. She looked exactly like what I had years ago imagined she would without clothes: pared flanks, long fine legs and slender thighs, the swan's elegance of her long white throat carried down the length of her body, only the aphrodisiac triangle of coarse gold fuzz interrupting, and emphasizing, the smooth satin of her skin. Undoubtedly most of that beauty was still there, for beautiful women do not turn into hags overnight; but not in this miraculous, unfading youthfulness.

Her face, like her body, was upturned to the sun. It too was beautiful, and innocent, and as false and as empty as the blue illusion of sky that Valmiki had put like a meat-cover over it.

"I think it's one of the best things Val's done," said Caroline incisively. "He's managed to capture the exact quality of the light . . . and the flesh almost pulses with life. Quite extraordinary. Do you agree, Suya? Oh I forgot, you've always said you know nothing about pictures."

Which was true enough, art was largely unknown and difficult terrain for me. Yet because of Valmiki I had been to galleries and exhibitions and private viewings, and simply from looking at so many pictures I suppose a certain amount of information had rubbed off on me. Such as it was told me that the style of this painting was chocolate box, or, cheaper still, worst mid-century paperback.

Bewilderment followed this clear forthright judgment. Was I wrong, or if not what had happened to Caroline's critical faculties? I looked again, and pity for her rose in me—for Caroline, white narcissus, no more able than the rest to accept she was susceptible to change, believing that this touched-up color plate was what she looked like, equally convinced it was good art. And Valmiki? Broken mirror on the wall, he had shown her what she wanted to see. Did he think with her it was one of his best? He had not refused her praise, neither did he accept it. Uncommitted he sat with his back to the double pillows, irreproachable nonpartisan, his face scraped clean of thought and emotion in the way that Caroline had taught him.

30

WITH Caroline and Valmiki openly living together, and clearly tranquilizing each other, the contingent of solo performers that had danced around them gradually, with great good manners, melted away. Now the people with them came in safe pairs, married couples, or couples like themselves unable to marry, or unable to see the point of marrying. Occasionally there was a barrister or two, or a model, or an unattached artist (quite rare) to provide a leavening to the parties which they never seemed tired of giving; but on the whole, numbers kept even and those who came singly were mostly confirmed singulars.

I do not believe Caroline deliberately contrived this pattern. The kaleidoscope had been shaken, and it was the way the pieces had fallen. Yet she certainly acquiesced in it, no doubt glad of the respite from vigilance, or competition, or whatever else the presence of all those free-floating young women in black had entailed for her.

For her to do what she did, the respite, indeed, must have gone on too long—long enough to lull her into a kind of security, and to forget that what she possessed might well not be a freehold, but only a lease.

Or else confidence in her own power had grown, fed well on what had so far been accomplished, and it was not in the realm of her possibilities that anything could be taken away which she wanted to keep.

What she did, quite simply—if one were to judge from the action, not the consequences—was to bring Annabel to the house—Annabel who lived a stone's throw away, and who would have gone on perfectly happily ignoring Caroline as she was in turn ignored, if Caroline had not suddenly one day decided that Valmiki was not seeing enough people of his own age. She must have been bored to say a thing like that, or perhaps she was slightly drunk. Usually an almost ritual taboo prevented any mention of their age, Caroline even foregoing, and making Valmiki forego, the innocent pleasure of birthday celebrations, although both were eager seekers after any chance for junketing.

"But darling, how can he!" This was Caroline at Valmiki's first London success, stifling a yawn over someone's stupidity, someone's stupid proposal that Val should have a party, a birthday party with champagne and a cake with candles on it. "He doesn't know when he was born. He doesn't really know how old he is. *Such* a pity, but there it is."

"How exciting! Then he can *pick* his birthday," came the bright voice (it belonged to a girl called Suzanne, I remembered, who had stuck in my mind for her pertinacity, rare in anyone confronting this glittering mood of Caroline's).

"Pick it? Pick a birthday? Do you mean out of a hat?" said

Caroline's voice, and the girl Suzanne had retreated before that cold flick-knife.

Yet here was Caroline ignoring her taboo, bringing up the subject of Valmiki's age, bringing a girl of his age to him. She must have been very sure of herself, and of Valmiki.

Annabel was distantly related to Caroline, in the way that older and rich families in most parts of the world are inter-related. They shared a great many ancestors, a good many great-aunts and uncles and remote cousins. She had not met Valmiki before because she had been at school in Switzerland. She would probably not have done so now but for the fact that she was a rebel, a girl who had turned down her family's traditional plans for organized displays in the marriage market, and in doing so had taken herself beyond protection of the resplendent umbrella, with its screenings, its selection, its exquisite care, spread over debs in season, and into the ambit of people like Valmiki and Caroline.

Annabel painted. Having a little money of her own, she shared with two other girls an elegant flat in the next square to Caroline, and was among the group of people of Valmiki's age whom Caroline had asked to the party which was being given, incredibly enough, in my assistance, to boost my new book.

"Because," said Caroline, "your publishers never do, poor pet, do they?"

"They would if I asked," I said sourly.

"But you don't and they don't," she said, "and darling, you must think about your sales."

"I manage all right," I mumbled, between hurt pride and gratitude for the sheer generosity of the gesture, but not wanting a launching party. Yet here it was—Caroline needless to say having had her way—with people of Valmiki's age for him, and people from the book strata for me—publishers and their wives, writers judiciously married to critics, columnists who came in the category of useful.

And so in keeping with the strange pattern which over the years had twisted our lives together, it was at a party given by Caroline for me that Valmiki met Annabel.

Annabel was eighteen. She was small, slim, ordinary-looking: bright brown eyes, brownish-gold hair cut in ragged urchin style, the short spiky ends appearing all over her head. She had on black silk stockings, a tight skirt, a floppy purple silk matelot blouse reminiscent of Ellie's shapeless sacks—not a patch, anyone with eyes would have said, on Caroline's elegance, on Caroline. But the freshness of eighteen years was there, which nothing but being eighteen can give; and this girl's mouth was soft whether she spoke or laughed or argued or disagreed—soft all the time, not merely when she remembered the lines a hard mouth would carve on her face in time, or when people and plans fell into line exactly as she meant them to.

All evening, despite the rigors of mingling, Valmiki managed to stay close to her. Minou, the monkey, was on his shoulder—little living mascot that he carried which beat to a frazzle the teddy bears, poodles and pandas with which others made do: and when there was nothing else he used her to draw Annabel back to his side whenever she, alive to party obligations, tried conscientiously to move on.

"Annabel! Minou's losing her jacket. Hold her still, will you?"

Annabel liked Minou. Women always did: buying the monkey had been a good investment. She took hold of the gray furry arm in one hand, balancing her glass in the other while Valmiki, one of his hands similarly immobilized, struggled to hitch on the tiny scarlet jacket.

"Val, careful!"

But by now half his dry Martini was on the monkey. Minou took it well: she was a widely traveled animal, used to parties, used to party behavior, vastly different from the crazed acrobat she had been at her first appearance.

Annabel was splashed too: the loose front of her purple silk matelot mottled with Martini. Valmiki mopped her, ignoring bystanders who had also been splashed. The mopping was, of course, ineffectual, and I saw him take her upstairs (into their bedroom? his room? Ellie's?—each must have had its drawbacks) and when presently they came down she was wearing one of his shirts.

Toward half-time food appeared, all those morsels which ruin one's appetite for dinner without making up for the lost meal. There was caviar and smoked salmon—Caroline never skimped, her generosity was never confined to herself; and curly pink prawns, and some kind of cheese dip smelling of garlic which people were scooping up with potato crisps. Valmiki was forcing this on Annabel.

"Perfumes of Araby," he sang absurdly, poising a crisp over Annabel. "Open, Annabel!" She resisted, laughing, pink mouth closing over small white teeth, and suddenly she was provocative, their exchanges were alive with sexual undertones, what had been banter was love-play, an enactment of the cycle of pursuit, retreat, capture, surrender, given in shadow-play and mime.

By nine the book contingent were mostly going or gone, although the younger guests, bright and indefatigable, still hung on. There was still plenty to drink but nothing to eat, nothing much to do until, very soon, someone had the inevitable idea and in seconds the furniture had been cleared, the carpet rolled up, and dance music began to play.

Valmiki, who had been stalking Annabel all evening, instantly had his arms about her, and in company with a dozen other couples they began jogging round the room. Caroline must have regretted, then, the time she had spent persuading Valmiki to learn dancing: he had resisted all her blandishments right up to their last American trip, and it must have been galling to see the result of her efforts benefiting a rival sprung up, like a mushroom, in one night. She showed nothing. She sat quietly, refusing all offers to dance; relaxed and serene, the satisfied if slightly weary hostess contemplating the end of a successful party.

Two discs spun to a close. In the hiatus before a third record could fall, the needle find its groove, Caroline rose, and a few second later the lights went out. The music died on a shrill descending note, the dancing stopped. There was a little high-pitched giggling, some moments of indecision, but as the blackness continued matches flared, voices called to Valmiki to mend the fuse.

Valmiki, glimmering palely in the flare from his lighter, was groping his way to the fusebox when Caroline came back into the room. She was carrying a candle, and a pile of fur coats was over her arm.

"Darlings, too careless of me," she said. "Not an inch of fuse wire anywhere . . . *such* a pity, I do apologize."

"There's a bit in the cellar," said Valmiki. (Was he imper-

ceptive, really taken in by her impeccable white-lying? Or
was he asserting himself, making some kind of stand?) "It
won't take me a minute—"

"No," said Caroline flatly, and sweetened her voice and
said, "My dears, the party is over."

31

IN the next few weeks I seemed to see Valmiki and Annabel
wherever I went. There was a small spaghetti restaurant near
my flat where I often ate, whose modest pricing belied the
red candles they lit at night, the colored coffee sugar on the
table, the unlimited coffee you were left to consume in peace
—and I saw them here twice, the girl unconcerned, Valmiki
distinctly embarrassed by my presence. I saw them again at
the theatre, which I loved and went to as often as I could to
make up for those long bleak periods in India when there
was no drama at all, or only the feeblest; and as luck would
have it on three occasions they had chosen the same evening.
I saw them in the street, too, crossing the square to Annabel's
flat, dark sleek head and spiky brown one close together, so
absorbed they did not even notice me on the near pavement.

Christmas came, and I went to stay at an inn in the country
to escape the hysterical trade extravaganza being mounted in
London beneath banners and representations of the most pious
kind. On New Year's Eve, Caroline gave a party—excellently

organized, lots of fun and people, but no Annabel. Nor, as far as I can remember, was she there on subsequent occasions.

Nor, in fact, did I see Valmiki and Annabel together again. They had gone to earth, keeping either to Annabel's flat or well out of the way—and after all London is a vast place, one has only to step off the chalked lines of one's circle to achieve a kind of Siberian seclusion.

But how long was it to continue, and was the rift with Caroline a temporary one while an infatuation wore off, or the thin end of the wedge by which Valmiki meant to lever himself free to reorder his own life? I dared not ask, as I might so easily have done only a few years ago. A fledgling then, sensing his raw vulnerability in a strange country, Valmiki would have been willing to answer; now he was fully fledged, able to question the right of the questioner to question him; and if I did, sophisticate that he was he would no doubt inwardly wince at such simple barbarity before smoothly changing the subject.

So I could not ask: I could only hope that he would not use a human being as a wedge, or as any kind of instrument to shape his life, although the pagan doctrines inculcated and absorbed during his civilizing years did not leave much confidence on that score.

The weeks went by, full of an intense anxious speculation for me—and for Caroline? I shivered when I thought of her, of what she must be going through, of what she might be planning: for I could no longer accept that she knew nothing.

I had seen her once or twice since the New Year; then January passed, the whole of February, without our meeting again. In March she sent me a note—unusual for Caroline, who much preferred a brisk brusque telephone encounter—inviting me to Sunday lunch; but in a blind panic, reluctant to set eyes on whatever Valmiki had done to her, upon whatever damage his defection had wrought in her alabastrine beauty, her ruthless magnificent spirit—afraid to look, I invented a country weekend.

And fortunately for my ease of mind I did get an invitation for that weekend.

I cannot at all remember now—the shock seems to have acted like an erratic nervous drug, picking memories at random for submersion or inflation—why I came back early on Sunday evening, instead of on Tuesday morning. But I did, I crossed the street to the building without even noticing that the light in my flat was on, went rapidly past the icy hall, up the stairs with my key held ready, and opened the front room door.

Spread-eagled on a rug in front of the electric fire lay Annabel. Valmiki covered her. They were closely locked from mouth to loins until the firm white legs flared away from under him. Both were naked, and their bodies moved as if they were a unity, with a beautifully articulated urgent rhythm.

I retreated back into the passage, whose chill cold struck doubly in contrast to the warm room I had left. I was shivering, partly from cold, partly no doubt from what I had seen: yet why? I had seen enough fornicating in the overcrowded desperate hovels of India, and had not developed any emphatic attitudes either way. I wished I had had the presence of mind to walk past them to my bedroom, and remembered I had been deterred by the clothing impatiently shed and left lying in two heaps near the door. An equally insane piece of delicacy, I thought, must have restrained Valmiki from entering the bedroom and making love in comfort on my bed . . .

although their accumulated urgency had probably been too great to allow them to think about externals like comfort and security, for they had not even bolted the door.

Standing there irresolute, I could hear from within the frou-frump of clothes being hastily sorted and donned, and in a few minutes (the whole thing had only been a matter of minutes) Valmiki came to the door to let me in.

He did not say anything. Neither did I. Annabel was sitting on the sofa, running a comb through her short thick hair, her soft cheeks that curved like a child's flushed pink, her eyes heavy with the unbearable languor that follows orgasm; and it was she who broke the silence.

"May I?"

"Of course," I said, and she rose, still with that gorged tiredness, and went to the next room and presently there came the sound of a bath being run.

Constraint lifted, when she had left.

"I'm sorry," said Valmiki.

"My fault," I said automatically. "I shouldn't have come back sooner than I said."

"We should never have come here," he said, "unforgivable of me . . . it's the old problem, finding somewhere to do it in: one doesn't realize until one's up against it. The key, I'm afraid, was irresistible. You'd better have it back."

He pushed the key across the table to me—the key given to him long ago for use in emergency which had, I reflected, fulfilled its purpose very precisely. I handed it back to him.

"It doesn't matter to me, does it," I said, "where you fornicate? Though it might have been less embarrassing for Annabel if the light had not been on when I walked in."

He said gently, with care because he was speaking to someone with whom there was no sexual relation, "It's not just feeling for me, it's seeing . . . I couldn't bear not to see that look on a woman's face . . . like an animal fighting you, begging to be wounded and sucking you dry, and then everything's gone, purged clean, it's like the peace of religious absolution. Annabel isn't anything to look at, is she, but when I took her just now she was beautiful—without shame and innocent, the two go together don't they?—God, so beautiful, the kind of beauty you never see on a human face at any other time. Does this sound like nonsense to you, Suya?"

"My dear, why should it?" I said. "Do you think I've never looked at the faces of temple friezes?"

"The bodies are usually more compelling," he said, and managed to laugh.

From the next room came the strangulated sounds of the bath emptying itself. The door intercommunicating with the bedroom opened, we could hear Annabel moving softly about.

I said, "Are you in love with her, Valmiki? with Annabel?" —for there was the possibility that it might be simple: a body-and-bed affair. The question came naturally now, in the easy intimacy that in one evening had been re-established between us: and he answered simply, without a descent into that graceful lightness which would have pulped the questioner, reduced the question to an ill-bred inquisition. Which answer established Annabel as a human being, instead of as I had feared an instrument.

"There's Caroline," I said.

"There's Caroline," he repeated bleakly.

"What will you do?"

"It's going to be awful," he said. "The end of an affair . . . more than that."

"Much more than that."

"The sooner the better," he said. "Oh, God—Caroline," and in a kind of anguish for her, "what will she *do?*"

That was what held me too, although the implications of his thought were not aligned to mine.

Presently Annabel came in, washed and without any makeup, her face pink, the short spikes of her hair damp and curly with steam. She looked even younger than she was, whereas Ellie had always looked twice as old, yet time and again the two faces merged and exchanged, executing a tiring and pointless little jig in front of my eyes for the whole of the evening. I suppose it was because they were about the same age, at the end of their years of adolescence; or because they shared some quality in common—perhaps a deep need for shelter—which had drawn Valmiki to each of them in turn, and which now supplied their elusive similarity. But Ellie had been worn out with knowledge. Annabel, with her clear eyes and the insulating freedoms of her race and breed, had not, except physically, even touched its fringes.

It was—despite events—not a difficult evening to sustain. Valmiki was too close to the bleeding surfaces of living—had touched as it were the bone—to attempt poses which alone would have imposed a strain. And Annabel had a natural grace, besides the polish of her class. She also had something of Caroline's forthrightness in dealing with events, a belief in as well as an addiction to uncomplicated patterns of living which, presumably, had so far constituted her experience. The problem as she saw it was simplicity itself. Valmiki had been living with a woman very much older than himself, who must always have known that the liaison would sooner or later end. He had now met a woman of his own age. It was absolutely natural he should prefer her to the older one, a fact which the latter would find unpleasant but which she would accept. This naïveté roused Valmiki, absorbed though he was.

"Darling, I don't think you understand. It's not just giving up a sleeping partner: Caroline's been with me all along the line. She took me up. I wouldn't be here, I would never have met you—I wouldn't have meant anything to you if I had—but for her."

"I know," said Annabel. "She was fortunate, being there when no one else was. But anyone would have done what she did. You can't keep on drawing dividends on that kind of capital."

Valmiki drew his brows together in irritation. I said, "Caroline thinks Valmiki belongs to her, and in a way she's right. She won't let go. People don't easily give up what they think are their possessions. The English never have."

But Annabel only bobbed her round inexperienced head, confidently. Valmiki loved her, and she believed that was the trump card.

32

BREAKING up a marriage, even a loveless one—the moment of utterance, knowing words to be the cleaver—must always be haunted, filled with suffering, the purgatory on earth to find which no mythical skyward levitation is necessary. Valmiki must have found it ferociously intimidating, for despite his recognition of urgency he did nothing. He avoided me, he avoided the telephone. Twice Annabel rang, in the hope of reaching him at my flat. When at last I got through to him he was frozen with misery, unable to bring himself to hurt Caroline, and in the mood where a man begins seriously to think of a painless solution like having two wives.

Eventually of course—and no fitter for the long wait—he told her; and Caroline according to him had nothing to say.

"She must have," I said, astonished.

"She didn't."

"Nothing at all?"

"She said wait."

"How long?"

"Until we're both absolutely sure."

"She and you?"

"I and Annabel."

Meanwhile, in that eerie household, as far as I could gather Caroline and Valmiki continued to sleep in the same bed at night. By day it was Valmiki and Annabel.

Caroline was old enough to accept the perverse involutions of this arrangement, and had indeed advanced its sophisticated subtleties, rejecting as rustic a precipitate removal and flight. Annabel however could not. She had left her own charmed conservative circle to take up artistic life with its luring illusory freedoms, but she could not bring herself to tolerate its license.

In the end she had her way. Valmiki packed his bags and Minou's. Annabel left her flat. The three of them began the search for a living room, encountering as they went the quivering fury of landladies whose laws against oddity, animals and aliens they jointly and severally offended. Until at last they came to rest, as much from exhaustion as anything else, in a room over an Italian delicatessen in Soho.

Caroline knew about the move, she knew Valmiki was leaving her, but she did not even try to stop the course of events beyond asking him, once more, to wait and be sure of his own emotions. He had already done that, he said: at which she attempted no further stop.

So the whole thing had fizzled out, I thought. Caroline had achieved—the last lesson learned by the powerful—a measure of acceptance, to accept that not everything can be bent or bamboozled into compliance, and to live with this uncompromising fact. Or else she had looked at her hand and recognized that it was played out.

To get to Valmiki's Italian room you had to go through the shop to a small doorway, hidden by a curtain, at the back, up a narrow staircase with three twists in it, and along a cramped, shaftlike corridor hung with nostalgic cutouts from travel brochures of Rome.

This method of access was during working hours—which in defiance of all shopworking acts seemed to stretch from early morning until late evening. After these hours you would see Giuseppe, the owner, arming himself with a meathook to bring down the heavy orange shutters. This done he would clank about inside, carrying the cash register to a wall safe which he religiously ignored while his shop was in session. Then he would emerge, bent double, through the dwarf-exit cut in the big shutters, pull small self-locking shutters down on this in turn, and finally creep around to the narrow side door to let himself in. Thereafter entry was fortuitous, for the mellifluous bell had been put in in the days when he and his wife had possessed normal hearing, long ago: and Valmiki's room, overlooking the street, was so full of the clamor floating up from it that neither he nor Annabel often heard it ring.

The disadvantages of this room were legion. It was small.

There was only one window, an ill-fitting one hung on frayed sash cords that raised it in a series of irritating jerks. Delicatessen smells came up constantly and clung—a blending of pasta, tomato, salami and garlic like a young-contemporary recipe out of a smart cookbook.

But Giuseppe's wife was a woman of great warm kindness, as understanding of passion as she was of good cooking; and Giuseppe himself was a gentle old miser, as fond of listening to good stories as he was good at telling them, and endlessly a cause for amusement as he crept softly about cradling his moneybags.

Valmiki and Annabel were happier here than they had been before: I think, indeed, idyllically happy. It was all, of course, very temporary: no one could live like this more than a week or two. But meanwhile the Soho atmosphere was new and exciting, a change from stuffy old Belgravia; the cooking and attention were rather nice; and after all it was fun discovering what slumming meant, that odd phrase one had heard one's parents use.

Valmiki's assessment was more realistic.

"Annabel thinks it's a few days," he said. "I wonder. There's nowhere without money, is there? I'm cleaned out."

"Financially?"

"And as far as work goes. Can you imagine trying to set up an easel in that room? I mind for myself, but I mind ten times as much for Annabel. I would have liked to give her so many things . . . all I've done is make her live in this hovel."

But his wretchedness vanished, his worries seemed to melt— I really think they did—the minute Annabel came in. She was carrying a tray of steaming food, sent in from the Giuseppe kitchen, and looked the cheerful housewife in a blue frilly apron. Her soft face was pink and flushed. She was gay, rather pretty. Valmiki could not take his eyes away from her. Throughout the evening their glances met and clung, fell away only to meet and cling again. Throughout the meal, and despite it, their hands felt for each other—quick blind little movements like the nuzzling of a newly born kitten seeking warmth and reassurance; and when they found it they smiled, the slow secretive half-smile of lovers.

From down below came the sudden rolling thud as Giuseppe hauled down the heavy wooden shutters. We could hear him clanking about—the cash register was chained to the counter, the rusty links had to be de-kinked before the register could be released and lifted into the safe. At length the little shutters banged, and after a while we could hear the old man's footsteps in the corridor. They stopped outside the door, there was a pause, and presently with elephantine tact (Giuseppe must have forgotten, as he often did, having let me in) an envelope was pushed under the door, stuck in the slit, was pushed through again. The footsteps retreated. Annabel looked at it and began to giggle. Valmiki looked at her and they began to rock together.

"It's from Caroline," said Valmiki, picking up the letter at last; and they both stopped laughing. There was an uncomfortable pause, the kind of guilt that afflicts people of ordinary propensities over a severed relationship. Valmiki simply sat there turning the envelope over and over in his hand until Annabel reached for it; then he opened it.

"It just says come round for drinks," he said with relief.

"A *rapprochement*," said Annabel, not greatly interested in Caroline's proposal, but her spirits reviving with Valmiki's. They were intertwined closely enough already to act and react upon one another, even to minuscule changes of mood.

When I got to my flat I found a similar invitation awaiting me. I don't know why Caroline wanted me, unless it was to lend my weight to her evidence. But of course I could not guess this, and so in the morning I rang to thank her and say I'd come.

33

FROM the beginning, that evening of Annabel's *rapprochement*, there was a sense of strain. It was perhaps naïve to imagine there would not be, or to believe that civilization at whatever efficient peak could withstand the severe sexual stresses of a discarded mistress meeting the reigning one. Yet such was my faith in Caroline, her superb powers of surmounting the most glacial and chilling of obstacles, that I really did believe it would be a calm, if delicately poised, occasion.

Indeed Caroline at the start could not be faulted. It was Valmiki who seemed on edge, making no effort at conversation, withdrawn from Caroline, withdrawn even from Annabel, his curiously colored gray eyes blank and unfocused as if his mind was on something else. Why, I thought with some irritation, had he agreed to come at all if he had never had any intention of easing a meeting which he knew would have its difficulties? I wondered, with a lessening of regard for him, if the motive had been a mercenary one under social guise, aimed at taking possession of those paintings of Ellie which nothing so far had induced him to sell. But he had not attempted to remove them when he had left Caroline, nor did he try to steer the conversation around to them now. He simply sat with his eyes gone mad, the vacant look that I remembered from long ago, the years of his childhood, like an animal left too long in a trap.

"Darling, you are distrait tonight." Caroline rose, coolly solicitous. "More brandy?"

"If you like."

"I think you ought. Annabel, what have you been doing to this man of yours to kindle such dolors?"

Annabel flushed. She had come lightheartedly, her trim satisfied body and her small limited head humming sweetly with the knowledge of having dispossessed a rival. The triumph was being poisoned, and she was not practiced enough to counter it. She turned to Valmiki: after all, they were lovers, she could with reason expect him to support her. But tonight he was gripped by demons, he sat hunched in his chair, not so much withholding his help as in a kind of inanition. Annabel's face fell, you could see the marks of this sudden undermining showing clear and defenselessly on it.

"Moods have always been part of Valmiki's armory," I said, out of pity for her. "I hardly think Annabel can be blamed, considering this is the first time—isn't it, Annabel?—he's been in one since he left, and remembering their frequency before."

Annabel recovered herself swiftly in the breathing space afforded by this intervention.

"It's sort of *de rigueur*, isn't it?" she said suavely. "I mean artists are expected to be moody. It's been terribly disappointing for me the way Val hasn't run true to type until tonight."

Caroline ignored her. She said, to me, with her deliberate insolent rudeness, "Suya, your opinions are no doubt invaluable, although I cannot recall having asked for them. Can it be that the old Oriental itch to finger every pie is getting the better of you?"

She was really angry, a controlled anger that scarcely flawed the magnolia skin, but anger all the same. I suppose it could not have been easy, finding herself alone despite all her power.

"Well, you know me," I said, "years in England, I still revert sometimes"; and the moment passed.

Valmiki was emerging now, partially, with a kind of residual stiffness, from whatever region he had been in.

"Awfully sorry," he muttered. "I believe I've been half asleep. Most remiss of me . . . it's that damn noise all night long, one never gets any proper sleep."

Caroline's eyebrows rose in delicate arcs. "Darling, I should have thought if there was one time one would simply drop off, noise or no . . . I mean one does, doesn't one? Or perhaps I ought to say one *should*."

Annabel went pale. She could have shrugged off, from her own closed knowledge of their exultant union, the implication of her sexual insufficiency; but I think she was now really beginning to get Caroline's measure, and it frightened her. Nevertheless she said, attempting good humor, "Of course we do, until the quarreling begins, usually after midnight. My dear, you'd scarcely believe the number of quarrels that are sorted out underneath our window, it's quite alarming. No wonder old Giuseppe's as deaf as an adder: it's the only defense."

"Dears, you must move," cried Caroline in anguish for them. "At once! I'll ring my agent . . . miracle man, he'll fix you up in no time."

"We can't afford to move," said Annabel in the tone of the

newly poor relishing poverty. "We simply haven't the money. Not a sou."

"Then Val must sell," said Caroline decisively.

"I've sold as much as I want to," said Valmiki distinctly.

"There's nothing left," said Annabel.

"But Val, that's hoarding," said Caroline.

"Hoarding? Hoarding what?"

"Those paintings. My dear, he *hasn't* been holding out on you? I can see he has. Really, Val, it's too bad of you . . . oh yes, there must be dozens of pictures up in her room, all of the same girl—no, *not* a model, a rather dreary little thing—a Jewish waif—that used to work for me, not that she was ever any good. You remember her, Suya? The one who got pregnant and left?"

"Yes," I said, and waited, and got the feeling that we were all waiting, each in his private little cell of fear, for the screw to turn and show us what lay behind the door.

"Now what was her name?" said Caroline. "Lise—Elsie—no, Ellie, that was it. Quite an obsession of yours, wasn't she, Val darling? It was nothing but Ellie for a long long time. Right up to the time she went away."

"I was sorry for her," said Valmiki stiffly.

"Yes, it was all very sad. Poor Ellie," said Caroline, "she killed herself."

"*It's not true.*"

We spoke together; even Annabel, who had never known Ellie.

"My dears, you are not calling me a liar?" Caroline's voice had a hard edge to it. She rose and went to a bureau, picked out the clipping placed ready to her hand.

There it was: the brief, endlessly familiar little paragraph of a suicide. So brief and dull that few other papers had printed the item, otherwise I might have seen it: four lines of small print about a pregnant woman, an unemployed domestic, reaching the end of her tether.

"But Val—this girl, you didn't, it wasn't—" Annabel, frightened, confused, was groping for the terrible truth, the unfinished truth that Caroline had hung in the air. But Valmiki was frozen, numb with horror, he did not answer and probably had not heard her.

"Of course it was," said Caroline, coolly incredulous of naïveté. "Val's child. You don't *blame* him for not wanting it?"

"To leave her like that." Annabel's voice was a whisper. "It can't be true—say it isn't true, Val. Or is it? Is it the truth, Suya?"

I could not bring out the answer, and she turned again to Valmiki, crying, pleading, "Val, please, please—I don't want to know anything more, only that . . . she *killed* herself for that. Val, please . . ."

"The child was mine," Valmiki spoke thickly, "but she never said—I didn't know she would—was going to kill herself."

"Emotional," Caroline murmured. "Unstable. Foreigners are. Dear Annabel, you must realize they aren't like us . . . you would never be able to rely on one of them."

"You let her go," said Annabel. Her eyes were wide, tearless, fixed in a rabid contemplation of Valmiki. "Your child, and you simply let her go, you—"

"You mustn't blame Val," interrupted Caroline. "I'm sure he did everything he could. Ask Suya—he was staying with her when it happened, she'll be able to tell you he did all he could."

It had been worked out with a cool mathematical skill. If

Valmiki had not been there I would have lied to convince Annabel that this was so; or if I had not been there Valmiki, just conceivably, would have reassured her. But in each other's presence we could not live out the lie. Valmiki broke the silence:

"I did not do everything I could," he said huskily, but with a terrible clarity as if to be done with sham once and for all whatever the consequences. "I meant to go after Ellie and see that she was all right. I meant to, I talked about it a lot and I worried endlessly but in fact I did nothing because it was easier not to. Can you understand that? It's the easiest thing in the world to let that happen, it only becomes impossible *after-wards*, afterwards it is the unforgivable. How could you? How could *I?* Well, I did because I wanted the whole thing to end without blooding me. I knew that was impossible, I had been told it was impossible but I tried. Hundreds of poor sods do. Like me. I didn't want to think what sort of an end it would be for her. I didn't want to think at all. I didn't want to know."

"You ran away." Annabel's face was dry and tight, the skin stretched taut like the membrane of a drum and underneath the color was blotched and uneven. She looked unbearably ugly.

"You ran away," she said again with a kind of cold vengeance. "You got her into trouble and you got out quick before the whiff of suicide could offend your nostrils and curl up those holy Eastern sentiments of yours about the sanctity of life. Well, so much for them. So much for decency. More bloody fool I to have thought you had any because how could you, you aren't like us, you wouldn't even know what decency means. I'm only glad I'm getting out before my stink sends you scuttling as hers did, poor little shrimp—getting out now while I still can."

It was all so callow and distorted, yet there was a swingeing savagery in it; and somewhere in all the misery and hate the seeds of truth were embedded. Because of it there could be no answer, and Valmiki, stricken, hopeless, under the limed net whose preparation had begun so many years before, did not even attempt one.

You can't even walk out on a situation in England. Annabel could not find her coat and was no impetuous Val to rush out into a March night without it. Peabody, who had cached our things on arrival, was no longer available to say where she had put the second of a pair of gloves. This ludicrous miscellany restored a kind of normality by which, avoiding one another's eyes, we could move and speak.

Annabel was even able to say good-bye.

"Good-bye, Val." She said it neutrally, all emotions back in a well-stoppered bottle.

Valmiki had no such capability: after all, he was as she had said an Oriental. He could not command the ritual answer, but some of his conditioning began to act, sluggishly, and he held the door open for her. He even made to step forward, but she stopped at once, in a harsh prohibition that he could not ignore. Then she went down the steps and walked away, her well-shod feet clicking neatly on the empty ringing pavement.

34

VALMIKI packed his things, watched by the sad-faced little monkey Minou and by the equally sad-looking Giuseppe and Emilia.

"You pay when you are millionaire, very soon, ha-ha," said the old miser dismally. "We wait."

"No," said Valmiki patiently, as he had done several times already. "I wouldn't even if I could but, don't you see, I can't."

"There is of her nothing left," said Emilia, practically. "The window is open—pouf, she is gone. You throw away the old cage, you get for yourself another bird, soon everything is fine, yes?"

"No," said Valmiki, packing steadily, putting away the press-clipping books, the feverishly full scrapbooks of his first successes, the peacock finery which Caroline had rigged him out in and on which Annabel had doted: then sitting on the bulging lid to explain that it was not simple.

"Ah, simple!" said Emilia. "Love is not simple, who is so big a fool to think it? You stay." She patted the faded cover of the bed-settee. "I will make different, you feel fine."

But Valmiki was adamant: not in foolhardy fashion, or with the reckless impetuosity he had often displayed, but in a calm and even gentle way, as if older influences swayed him.

Both Giuseppe and his wife came to the street and stood in

front of their shop to see us off—and not even a taxi to get the thing over and done with quickly. Valmiki humped his suit-case in one hand, held Minou against him with the other. We moved off. A hundred yards on and there was a great rumbling crash. Giuseppe had brought down his shutters—while it was still daylight, and the street thronged with potential customers. Valmiki put down his case and waved, and they waved back energetically. Giuseppe had his arm about his wife. The old couple, childless, were leaning toward each other—a kind of loving that recalled their own youth, revived by memories of Valmiki and Annabel in love.

Further on— "We must get a cab," I said.

"I've told you, I'm skint," said Valmiki.

"I've told you I'll pay," I said, and bore him down so that we drove to my flat. But it was only for him to leave his case there, and of course the monkey, while he looked for a room.

At the moment of separation Minou, her eyes liquid and piteous, began to whimper—a thin hiccuping cry like an aban-doned baby. Valmiki turned at the door, came back and picked her up to nurse. In the weeks since Annabel's going he had turned to Minou for comfort, clinging to her in this bad patch of his life as he had fitfully done over the years and as she had never failed to do. Poor faithful little Minou, so con-temptuously bought, who had not varied her attitude an iota over those years, content to forget his fits and starts and finales of affection—or unaware of them in the capacity to live in the happy present, twined lovingly close to him so that when I unwound her arms she cried like a baby.

Eventually, by late evening, he found himself a room. It was a cubicle in a basement off a crumbling backyard, damp, stuffy, smelling of cats' urine and rotting mushrooms and cost-ing thirty-five shillings a week with four weeks' rent in advance. Valmiki had already paid it, amounting to nearly the whole of his resources.

"For God's sake, you can't stay here," I said as soon as I saw it.

He sat down dispiritedly on the trundle bed. "It's not too bad . . . there are much worse, higher rents. I can't really afford even this."

I sat down beside him on the creaking bed. I did not know what to do. There was my flat, but it hadn't a backyard, not so much as the square foot of earth that Minou needed; and Valmiki refused to be parted from her.

"I'm not rich but I'm not poor," I began. He laughed.

"Dear Suya. You're going to offer to give me some money to tide me over and call it a loan. No. This time my problem is mine. Besides, why should I live any better than this? Hundreds of people don't."

The landlady was hovering, armed one could see with a devious and disapproving explanation of our relationship. Minou sat quietly, subdued by her, by the atmosphere. She was no longer young—would she be middle-aged, old, by monkey standards?—certainly not the skittish creature that had rioted through parties, scarlet jacket flying.

I went back to my flat, vaguely troubled as one is by its comfort in contrast with Valmiki's quarters. Of course he had been born to neither luxury nor comfort, but there was a quality of drab, rather shady squalor here, epitomized for me in the rapacious slattern of a landlady, that had been absent in the pared poverty of his village. Or perhaps time blunted memory.

My session in London had worked to a close, I knew that. The ache to be back had begun, and but for Valmiki I would probably have left weeks ago. But here he was unsettled, which as far as I could see would be his state for some time to come. I had been—however slightly—responsible for his coming to England; I could not leave to go my own way now. I let a few days pass, then suggested he should return with me. He would not: there was the fare to find.

"Why can't I lend you the money and you pay me back when you can?" I asked exasperated. He could chain me to London when I wanted to be in India, but he could not touch my money.

"Because I don't know when that will be," he answered, not without reason. "Who will buy my work in India, *or* pay me what they do here? If I work."

"You will never work here," I said bluntly. "No space, no light, no freedom—nothing."

"Nothing," he repeated. "That is the truth, Suya. If you could look inside me you would find nothing but deadwood."

A memory stirred. Someone else had said those words—similar ones—long ago. Deadwood, ashes. The memory came alive, Ellie's voice said clearly, "Inside I am burnt out . . . it is not easy for me to feel because I am burnt out."

Their lives which had run parallel now touched, although she was in her grave.

On my next visit I suggested, with an odd feeling of shame in doing so, that he should claim his Ellie pictures from Caroline and sell them.

He was not, after all, completely dead inside.

"I loved her," he said, and he began to tremble, the light continuous tremor of an old man. "She knew it before I told her. I think she loved me in her way, she did everything she could to make things easier for me, right up to the end. What did I do, I gave her up, because she was not quite—simply not quite. She couldn't dress and she couldn't talk—well, they don't teach you that kind of thing in a concentration camp; and what did it matter? It didn't matter to me, but when there were other people I did not see with my eyes, I saw with theirs, I had no heart, there was no *me*, then it became very important. Two lives snuffed out. Hers. My child's. You knew about my child?"

"From the beginning," I said.

"No bigger than my hand," he said. "Small. Helpless. Blind —they have no eyes then, have they? But living, it was living. When the mother dies it doesn't die at once, if they're quick they cut it out alive. My child, living, fighting to live while her blood ran cold. I let it happen. Annabel was right, I cared nothing for the sanctity of life—I, a Hindu, wearing the mantle of a Brahmin and it was a sham, a hypocritical mockery, otherwise would I have let my child die slowly?—and for what? For what?"

It was too much, this suffering: this cancerous proliferation that came out of one injury: the suffering too much for the sin until one remembered that other calvary, the lonely crucifixion, the stifled cries, neatly packaged into one printed paragraph. Did it make sense, even then? Expiation of sin, so little understood. Expiation and the easy Christian peace. Or simply expiation, prolonged and absorbed into the consciousness so that one never looked at the world in the same way again.

"It showed," he said. "It was so small but you know, it showed in every part of her body. So miraculous—all that preparation going on in every part of her. It fascinated me, I had to work on it: every single painting came out of that. Well, I betrayed her for other things, there's no reason why I shouldn't do it for money too. One more betrayal to complete the picture."

Minou came and clung to him, chittering softly. He stroked her absently, murmuring endearments in Tamil. My eyes: as dear to me as my eyes. I had not heard him speak Tamil for a long time—not for years.

"The picture is not complete," I said at last. "There's Caroline—always Caroline. She fits into it, she is responsible for some of it. She was born and bred to power, nothing has ever curbed it."

"People do not have power unless you allow them to have it," he answered.

I went back to my flat, alone, to sit and think, and all the time those four little figures jigged in my head: Caroline, and the three puppets whose strings she held and pulled and jerked, so that I was never alone. And there was a fifth that Valmiki had evoked, the unborn child that was blind, with helpless buds for limbs.

I must get him away, I thought: take him away before he is engulfed by the images of his guilt. Haunted creature, haunted imaginings, haunted images. But how, but how? The blank wall undulated before my gaze, a sly shimmy to question the acceptance of its substantiality. I had been, I realized, gazing at it for a mesmeric length of time. I focused again, made my eyes work, made them see, and on the wall was the square, darker than its surround, where a picture had once hung.

Caroline had never returned that portrait in oils of me.

35

THE portrait was Valmiki's early work but it was good, Caroline had always said so. It would sell, would probably raise more than he needed for the fare. Whether it belonged to him or to me could be debated after it was sold.

I rang Caroline. She was away for a fortnight. At the end of a fortnight I telephoned again.

Her assured voice said, "Which picture?"

"The one of me that you borrowed."

"*Whose* did you say?"

"Mine."

She rang off.

I was furious. I determined to go around at once and have it out with her, but when I got to the house she was out.

Mrs. Peabody opened the door, her face a nice amalgam of disappointment at seeing me unaccompanied by Valmiki, and pleasure at having anyone on whom to inflict her perpetual tea. I declined her offer at once, before the possibilities of the situation had dawned on me, but she had already annexed me for company, the door was shut.

"I know you've had words with her ladyship," she said hoarsely. "You mustn't take no notice, miss. She hasn't been herself like not since the young gentleman went and left her. Real upset she's been, banging about but quiet, not a word, not so much as a good morning to me sometimes, I can tell you it gets on my nerves. Still there's nothing, is there, miss, like a nice cup of tea to cheer you up?"

The large brown pot was on the kitchen table, muffled to its eyes in a knitted cozy. Mrs. Peabody was mother and poured.

"Here you are, dear. Lovely cup, though I say it myself as shouldn't." One would have thought she had blended the tea leaves herself, not to mention having grown them from seed.

"You do make nice tea," I said.

"That's what he always said," she sighed. "Poor young gentleman, always a kind word for me, it's never been the same since he went with the young lady—not but what I didn't see it coming, I mean it wasn't natural him living with her ladyship her being old enough to be—older than him, though you wouldn't think it to look at her, now would you, miss? Youth calls for youth," she said surprisingly, and then, lowering her voice, hoarsely, "It's not for me to say, miss, her ladyship's been very good to me and I can't say different, I wouldn't speak a word against her, but it's my opinion he's well out of it and all, and good luck to him!"

It was then that I thought of getting her to help. If I simply went upstairs and took the picture from Valmiki's studio, I knew she would send for the police. But if I asked her for it? The balance was delicate: between her strangely rooted liking for Valmiki and an interest in his welfare, and her reverence for Caroline, for the capital *L* in her name with which went the cavalier manner on which she thrived as well as the self-interested charity which she interpreted as bounty.

"He's broke," I said bluntly. "He wants to sell one of his paintings but Lady Caroline won't give it to him. That's what I came here for really."

"The cheek." She bristled. "Holding him up like that, it's not right. Just you tell me which one it is, miss, I'll fetch it down for you. It ain't"—a peculiar expression came over her face, a cross between prim disapproval and a leer—"one of them nudes?"

"It's a picture of me. I think it's in Valmiki's room."

"Get it for you in a sec, miss. After all," she said virtuously, "if the young gentleman called for his property it wasn't for me to stop him, was it, I mean I wasn't to know no different, nobody told *me* nothink."

She sipped her tea while I chafed, though there was time enough, for Caroline was having her hair done. Presently she had finished and shuffled upstairs, her heels jacking up from the furry carpet slippers at every shuffle.

Ten minutes went by. She staggered down, arms wrapped round a large framed portrait of Ellie.

"Does that look in any way like me?" I asked sarcastically.

She bridled; I had overlooked her marked skill at repartee.

"How should I know? If you ask me, none of these here paintings looks like what they're supposed to be."

"The one of me looks like me," I said mildly, conciliating her.

Another absence.

"Here you are, dear." At last, there it was. "Must say, miss, it do make you look a proper Turk."

I hugged her silently. I took the framed canvas from her and walked away in triumph with it tucked under my arm.

Then, I found I could not let it go. Valmiki had given it to me, long ago at the very beginning; it was his very first present to me, I found I did not want to part with it. I tried to think of the issues involved, but all that came was the low wail of a tenacious possessiveness. Possession, I thought, appalled:

attenuated form of the powerful craving to have, to hold, which was so dominating and menacing a part of Caroline: which left a gray and ugly trail of human misery such as, horribly swollen but not unrecognizable, one saw stumbling in the wake of power-societies and empires.

But for that I would have kept the picture: stored it somewhere, pretended to Valmiki that it was sold and given him the money, somehow getting over the difficulties involved in such a course. As it was I took it around to Léon, Caroline's influential art-man who had arranged the Boston exhibition and the only art name I could summon.

Léon turned out to be Leonard, very mild and English, with the endearing vagueness of a man who has never troubled to run in the rat race, whose reputation of influence in art circles I found difficult to marry to the considerate, kindly actuality.

I explained the situation to him, as much of it as I deemed necessary. There must have been undertones, which he picked up at once.

"Bad policy, selling halfheartedly." He spoke without emphasis, but with the solid assurance of a leading stockbroker. "Call it a loan, for a fee naturally. You can have it back when you like."

He wrote out the check and that was all. When I attempted to thank him, he began to talk with gentle enthusiasm about roses.

That solved, of course, a good many difficulties. Valmiki could receive the money and keep his conscience, there need be no recriminations about a deal so revocable in its nature. There were the other difficulties; the formalities of departure, the uncertainties of his arrival in India; but I was happy enough as I walked to the flat, taking the check to flourish at him, for Valmiki knew all about checks although he could neither read nor write.

But before I could begin he had started to speak, rapidly and jerkily as if he had already worked everything out and wanted nothing more said.

"I'm going back to Caroline." He wouldn't even meet my eyes. "I know what you're going to say but I must, I can't stand living like this, I can't stand watching Minou die in this damp hole. She will unless I get her out. I've done a lot of damage, haven't I, but I'm not going to do any more, I'm finished, this time I know how it's going to end and I won't let it happen. Look at her. She's been shivering like that all day and I can't make her warm, I can't keep her warm—I can't even do that."

He bent and picked up the small shivering creature, and at once, a little feebly, she climbed onto his lap, clinging to him and hunching herself against his body.

"Bought for show." He rocked gently to and fro, to and fro on his heels. "Used for show, by me. Animals aren't created *for* men, are they? You do not subscribe to that belief, Suya, do you?"

"I do not," I said, "but a lot of people do: the whole of Christendom."

"Animals are created in their own right." He spoke gently. "I do not know when I stopped believing that, but I must have, mustn't I, to do what I did? Bought her in a shop, took possession like a god, for ends of my own."

"If you hadn't, someone else would," I said—stupidly, for his conscience would never now allow him such easy relief.

"But *I* did," he said.

"Caroline—" I began.

"*I* did," he repeated. "The suggestion was Caroline's, the act was mine. *I* bought her, *I* made room for another creature like her to be brought here, exiled from its climate for life . . . in the end it is *my* responsibility. You only see that when you think things out to the end, but one must, mustn't one, not run away from it. Run away, look for escape—you begin and you find you are never done with running. That's right, isn't it, Suya? Tired! You're so tired you'd give anything to be able to stand still and see what's coming but you can't, you've lost the habit. In the finish it catches up with you."

"You're upset," I said. "You've nothing to feel guilty about. Minou has always had the best of everything. More than your brothers and sisters ever did."

"I know," he said wretchedly. "On Caroline's money. Look at her *now*. Look what I've done for her."

He turned her toward me—with difficulty, for Minou cowered and tried to hide her face against him, frightened as animals are of the evil of malfunctioning, of disease. She was, I realized, seriously ill, not merely cold and miserable from the uprooting as I had imagined. Poor Minou, used to brandies and warmth, the glowing fires in every room on which Caroline turned her naked back; fed on plums and peaches and hothouse grapes that Caroline provided with careless lavishness, succumbing now to the gray cold of this cramped bed-sitter.

One fire burned in the room: a chaplet of five gas jets behind glass colored amber to provide a fraudulent glow; with, on top, a metal chimney with vents in it to conduct the fumes upward together with a sparse tremulous heat. A more frugal heater could scarcely have been perfected. Valmiki huddled next to it, the monkey in his arms. His face looked tired and gray from the meager lighting in the room or perhaps, I thought, it was hunger. There was little food that I could see: on the table, on a plate, some apples, a few overripe blackening bananas. Next to it part of a loaf of bread, butter, half a bottle of milk, a tin with a little jam in it. There was no other food. Valmiki, living prodigally on Caroline's "Darling, what *is* money between us? I've got enough for both," had reached a level of reckoning for which, physically, he was little better equipped than Minou. Both had grown unfit for poverty.

"We'll take her back to India," I said. "We'll all go. There's no need for you to live here like this any more. There's no need for you to go back to Caroline either." I produced the check and explained about Léon. I was half afraid he would still refuse the money, but by then he was beaten.

"When Minou is better," he agreed.

Due to Minou, there could be no firm date. Nevertheless I made whatever provisional arrangements I could, hampered by the impatience of travel agents who wanted everything sealed and delivered—as indeed I did too.

There was no difficulty about my flat—the lease had nearly expired, the few remaining weeks would see me out nicely. I wrote to Caroline, unable somehow to bring myself to face her, telling her Valmiki and I would soon be leaving for India.

DEAR SUYA (she wrote in answer)
Do you want me to be terribly British and congratulate the winner? I can't, because it wasn't all your doing whatever you may think, I handed you quite as much as you took. But the game was worth the playing.

CAROLINE

I wrote to Jumbo as well, jogging his memory of promises given in London, and enclosing a note for the Swami in the faint hope that he might be back in the country.

Then there was nothing to do but wait.

Minou had double pneumonia. The vet, whom Léon's check was paying for, wanted her put down, but met by Valmiki's anguished refusal set about trying to save her life with as much efficiency as, no doubt, he would have brought to her destruction. There was penicillin and oxygen, eggnogs, brandy and whey and home nursing, if one could call it that in a basement room, for Minou was too weak to be moved.

I walked the streets, waiting. Everything seemed to me to have a calm luminous quality, especially in the cold deserted nights. I knew I was realizing again my love for London as I always did on the eve of departure. Would it be the same, I wondered, for Valmiki? Had this beautiful alien city, cold and warm in turn like its people, the same kind of hold on him as it had on me so that going away always became a kind of small death?

Whenever I went back, it was always to find Valmiki sitting patiently beside Minou, sometimes in the same position as when I had left him an hour or two before.

"Do you think she looks better today?"

Minou was asleep, huddled under shawls that the vet had provided—lightweight covers that would help her to breathe more easily, but her breath seemed to come torn out of her, the room was filled with the laboring sound. I looked down at the sleeping face and her eyes opened. Dazed brown eyes, burning with fever—or was it drugs?—but the effort was too great, the hand fell back, the fingers plucking at the covers but so lightly as hardly to disarrange them.

"She's very weak," I managed to say.

Valmiki knelt, offering his hand, and at once the plucking fingers curled around his thumb and quieted.

"But her grip," he said, "isn't it marvelous? I can hardly make her let go, it's so strong."

The next day she was markedly weaker. Her fingers still

curled around his, but even a pretense of strength in that tenuous hold on life became impossible.

Valmiki was silent, watching her go. Toward the end, interpreting the weak movement under the covers, he picked her up.

"Monkey on my shoulder," he said, smiling grotesquely. "Am I worth an extra sixpence for the monkey on my shoulder?"

He laid her down a long time after that, after she had died and become meaningless, a huddle of bones and stiff grayish fur that we wrapped and buried in the courtyard.

36

WE went by sea and during the twenty days of the voyage I watched Valmiki walk like a gentle dreamer among the other passengers—permanent outsider, as dreamers often are. In a way, I thought, Caroline had come nearest to speaking his language—from the very first, when the usual communication by language was absent. Now that she was lost was there, I wondered, a part of him gouged out—empty, or slowly filling with hopelessness, as he wandered among this motley crowd of tourists and stipendiary altruists? For all his dreaming, I could see no sign of vacancy, even if there were no longer those charged outbursts, the impassioned outpourings of an overburdened conscience; but their absence might equally have betokened a sheer exhaustion of mind and spirit as an accession to inner calm.

Jumbo, in spruce white duck, came to meet the boat. There were also friends and relations for me. No one came for Valmiki. From inside my welcoming circle I tried to force Jumbo to Valmiki's side, but he was too old a hand to do anything he didn't want to, and he never wanted to leave a crowd. I prayed for a diversion and to confound me there was one, in the shape of a telegram for Valmiki.

He took it uncertainly, turned it over and his face changed color. So far he had held back, I suppose from fear of intruding; now he came up to me without hesitation, holding the envelope aloft.

"What does it say, Suya?"

It had been a long night, I thought, since I had heard him speak like that: since there had been undercurrents of an old eagerness and purpose.

"It's from the Swami," I said. "He just says he is waiting for you."

So in the event, none of those anxious if none too hopeful plans for Valmiki's rehabilitation proved necessary. Jumbo, lighthearted from relief, was spared a sponsorship liberally endowed with delicate situations. Not one of Valmiki's relations put in an appearance. There were no receptions and no recognition. In fact everything was much as Valmiki wanted it, and although I would have liked some awareness of him and his work, I was grateful enough for the peace such neglect afforded.

When Valmiki had gone I moved into the small house I owned near the Fort, kept vacant on my instructions. Starting without charms, it had been battered by tenants, so that a

good deal had to be done to make it livable. I was settling re-
pair bills with the local handyman when the bearer announced
there was a lady to see me—a European lady. He did not give
a name, and I walked unsuspecting into the room to which he
had shown her.

It was Caroline.

Three months to the day since she had wiped Annabel off
the map, she had come after Valmiki to India.

I think I actually recoiled: away from it the restraints of
gentler English living were soon extinguished, I suppose as a
matter of climate.

"Well, Suya. Is the surprise so total?" Caroline missed nothing, particularly in the field of social mores.

"I certainly didn't expect you to come," I said.

"Odd thing, nor did I," she said, "it was a completely im-
pulsive act: spur of the moment, I assure you."

"Times have certainly changed," I said.

She considered me with that curious oblique stare of hers
that summed you up, gauging your resistance to what she was
going to say, to how much she felt you might take from her
without gagging.

"Well, perhaps some planning went into it." She dropped
her gaze. "Scheming if you prefer. But you know, Suya, getting Val out of the wilderness *was* on impulse, I didn't give it
a second thought, I wouldn't have given way if I had, I mean
all those early frightful difficulties . . . but the early days
were fun, I don't think anyone could say they weren't worth-
while, could they?"

There were times with Caroline—briefly illuminating the
ease with which over the years she had got her way—when
you would have spread your possessions before her, begging
her to take her pick.

"He could have done so much," she said with faint regret. "Realized all his ambitions and all mine for him. It's what I wanted for him of course. That little bitch Ellie—she destroyed so much and she didn't even have the brain to realize what she was doing."

"For God's sake," I said, revolted. "Didn't she pay dearly enough for whatever it was she did?"

"You are a sentimental fool," said Caroline.

In the next breath she said, "I'm here because I want your help."

"What do you want me to do?" Sheer curiosity made me ask.

"I know Val's back in his wilderness," she said carefully. "I can't get to him. Physically. There are two warders, on the hill—I expect you know about them?

"Yes."

"Two old fools. One mad, the other a disgusting cripple," she said somberly. "The Swami knew what he was doing, didn't he? Always has done. Fool's game, believing anything else."

"Yes."

"They wouldn't let me pass," she said briskly. "But you speak their primitive language: you could get me through."

"So could the local police chief," I said. "He'll fall over himself to provide a suitable escort for Lady Caroline Bell."

"I'm serious," said Caroline. And she was, she really did think that I, who had taken so much trouble to get Valmiki away from her, could now be brought to lead her back to him.

I simply shook my head, beyond words.

She sighed and sat back in her chair, crossing her silken legs. She was wearing a fine straw cartwheel which she took off and placed on the table, craning her neck exaggeratedly to look at the broken punkah an ex-tenant, some poor broiled clerk, had rigged up in the hope of cool air.

"Weird place you've got," she said.

"It does." I said. "At one time, I seem to remember, it did quite well for you too."

"When the adventure was just beginning," she said.

"Does it strike you as singularly appropriate that I should be here again when it has just ended? If it has. If there isn't after all to be a new beginning. From where we left off."

"It's over," I said bluntly.

"Is it?" Again the long cool measuring look. "You know, Suya, you're not exactly the best of all possible judges. *You* are back in your own society, in the nice little niche that's been kept warm for you. What about Val? What's *his* niche—being a cave dweller for the rest of his life? Is that what he wants? He's been at it for a month now: have you troubled to go to ask if it is?"

"I've left him in peace," I said. "As he wanted to be left. That's something you will never understand."

"*Whose* peace?" she said with cold scorn. "His? Or yours?"

Caroline could, as she always had been able, position a splinter even between a man and the conscience with which he had lately been at peace. Divide and rule. It was a formidable inherited skill.

"All right. I'll go with you," I said wearily.

37

WHEN we were safely past the hill guards Caroline said, "You've come so far, you may as well stay to the end."

"Yes," I said. "Not that it will make any difference."

"No. You're nothing any more. I don't mean to be offensive."

"I'm not offended."

We climbed steadily, despite the heat. Loose shingle, dislodged, clattered down the hillside, a constant cannonade to our progress. Presently we came to the Swami's lean-to—flimsy and weatherbeaten but standing. Presumably there had been rain, for gunnysacking was stretched across the entrance. Caroline drew it aside. "Empty," she said, half smiling. "He's chosen his own territory."

We began the final ascent, the last hundred feet of steep incline that led to the caves. At the top Valmiki and the Swami were waiting, darkly silhouetted against the sun.

"We expected you to come," the Swami said, simply.

"I had to," Caroline answered, equally simply.

She looked for a boulder and sat down. There was a sweat on her forehead, tiny glistening drops at the roots of her pale gold hair. Valmiki brought water in a mud pot, tilting the heavy elongated earthenware neck while he poured her a cup. She put her hand over his to steady him while the water gushed, and he allowed it to rest there, his own unfaltering, until the cup filled and then he withdrew. Caroline's hand remained, pale, fallen, drops of water sparkling like crystal on the smooth white skin.

"Val," she said. "You know why I'm here, don't you?"

He looked at her a long time, and then he shook his head. "No," he said quietly.

"Because I couldn't run away from it any more," she said, and she was very quiet too. "I had to come and see for myself, I had to find out what I had driven you to. It wasn't easy."

"It's the most difficult thing in the world," he said, and both of them were silent, the hidden river of all that had happened flowing slowly past them.

"My dear," he said at last, "you must believe me—you have driven me to nothing—"

"Except back to this wilderness."

"I am no stranger to it."

"But you are, Val," she said. "You are a stranger here. I have made you one. I don't regret that, I never shall, the crime doesn't lie there at all, it's *here*, sending you back to this. *This* is the crime, *my* crime."

Her voice was bruised; her hand lay near his, limp wet flower, but he made no move to take it.

"No crime," he said gently. "The wilderness is mine: it is no longer terrible as it used to be: it is nothing."

"Nothing," she said. "Exactly nothing. A wilderness. A waste. All of it, waste."

There was a quality of loss in her words, contradicted by the long, tranquil silence that fell: a silence that ushered her out, kept her at bay while it considered her charges and without undue insistence or interest in her reaction rejected them, dropping them slowly into pools of stillness.

Until at last the Swami said, "Even this wasteland may have something to show, other than what you have seen."

And instantly Caroline was transformed, as animated as if she was once more on the verge of adventure, and as blithe as if this fresh start automatically assumed the innocence, wiped out the evil, of previous pioneer trails.

"I can never see enough," she said, and her voice and manner had returned to their norm, light and brisk and concentrate upon garnering pleasure from the exquisite surfaces of life like some inverted Western version of geisha—a role which no doubt suited her better than the inturned contemplation she had wrapped about her like a penitent's cloak so short a time ago.

We all rose, Caroline dusting herself down carefully. She had linked her arm to Valmiki's, so casually that I did not notice it until I heard his sudden sharp breath, her drawling, biting, "Can't you take it, darling? It's only flesh, you know, not a branding iron."

Only a few minutes ago, I thought, his hand had not faltered under hers—what had she done between then and now to evoke this quivering response? I waited, not turning, feeling the loud hammering of my heart, and at last he said, gently, "My dear, I can take it. But can you? And if you can't—do you think I can bear to watch?"

When I turned again he had disengaged himself, but she was walking close, very close. She had not yet accepted his withdrawal, final as it would have seemed to anyone else; and his compassion had made her purposive, as if it might be interpreted between weakness and emotion both of which could usefully be made to work for her. But I think she was wrong; and, also, I knew something of the strength in the thin lonely figure leading the way to the caves, from which Valmiki drew his own.

And so we came to the third and probably last cave, according to Caroline ground of the Swami's choosing.

We had never been allowed to enter it before, Caroline and I: had only glimpsed it, looming beyond the first two chambers. It was larger than either, more symmetrical, of loftier proportions, but unlike the others still rough-hewn, with projecting eaves and ledges that had yet to feel the chisel. One of these did duty as a shelf, and on it I noticed, placed impersonally side by side without precedence, a ruby ring, a tiny golden column of sovereigns, and a pile of uncashed checks under a stone weight. Promissory symbols all: from the magnificent ring that had never been asked to redeem good-mannered pledges that were empty when Jumbo had given them, to the hoarded coins Valmiki's distraught mother had pathetically imagined would build some improbable bulwark for her son, to Caroline's checks—new ones all that she must have sent in frantic chase of him one after the other out of her loneliness: symbols all of power and influence promising the kind of strength that Valmiki no longer needed, emasculated, meaningless now, and arranged here in dumb show.

Any other woman would have invoked blindness, gone by in silence. But Caroline had never been afraid to attack, had never been afraid.

"Val, you bad boy," she cried, "you've been living on nothing! You haven't cashed any of the checks I sent, not a single one."

"No," said Valmiki, and smiled, the slow smile of unwilling admiration Caroline drew from the most diverse of her protagonists. "But they make, don't you agree, excellent exhibits?"

"Exhibits," said Caroline, and her eyes narrowed. "Darling, what do they exhibit: my greed? meanness? avarice? cruelty? Which of the great iniquities would you lay at my door?"

"My dear—" Valmiki's voice had lost its earlier mocking level. "My dear," he said again, wrung. "None of those things. Only one, that you wanted to own me, and it is not an uncommon iniquity."

He took her hands in his and kissed them—the wrists, the open palms; and then he turned and left her.

There was iron and steel in Caroline, and superbly crafted façades. She was pale, but no paler than at the end of a tiring evening: and now she began, as composed and elegant as if she were at a preview in which she had an interest, a detailed inspection of Valmiki's work.

Valmiki heretofore had always worked abundantly, or not at all. Now he seemed to have achieved a middle stage of serenity, avoiding both the frenzied labor that had eaten up canvas as well as the long fallow terms when he had been incapable even of looking at his paints without hatred. There was, too, a change in his work, so subtle it might easily have been a flight of fancy: but to me there seemed to be a moving, extraordinary yearning in the human countenances he had depicted upturned, groping toward the light, a quality of compassion and profundity in his divine images, that had never been apparent before.

Caroline moved slowly around the chamber, attentive, rapt, followed by the Swami, equally absorbed and, because he was what he was, soon lost in a contemplation which at first her words did not pierce.

"A waste," said Caroline again, with cold bitterness. "All of it. Wasted beauty, wasted work, a wasted man."

He could not take it in at once: then his face grew strangely blotched and ugly as if he were under deep strain, the face of a man who feels insult not so much to himself as to what is most precious to him. "Waste," he said thickly, and his voice was edged with anger. "Do not speak of it, it is blasphemy. . . . Where is waste, in the work a man does to glorify his God, it is blasphemy to say it."

The outburst had astonished Caroline, had overwhelmed the Swami in a humiliating self-realization: but his disciplines were greater even than hers, he had recovered himself before she could draw her triumph from it.

"Forgive me," he said, calmly now, "but passions are difficult to control, do you not find it so?"

Caroline nodded, half smiling, acknowledging a shared and onerous self-training which neither of them shirked.

"There are temples," the Swami went on, "churches, cathedrals . . . men have put all they possessed into their building and adornment but the names of the creators are lost—yet even you, Lady Caroline, would not look on it as squandered labor?"

"They are seen," said Caroline. "They are not buried in a hole in a hill in a country which has forgotten the meaning of art. Here Valmiki creates and there is only you to glory in it. That is not enough—except for you."

"Not only me, I am the least: there is also a divine spirit," said the Swami gently, and the chasm between them widened, carrying them to different continents. "He works for that, and therein is the glory . . . it gives men a satisfaction so rich they cannot explain it, and mostly they do not even wish to."

The Swami's calm tone, his absolute assurance, must have lacerated Caroline. "Do you think," she said furiously, "you can keep him here with your cant forever? Hold him, keep him, exploit him like this?"

"Not forever," he answered. "It is a lesson we all in time have to learn. But now he is at peace, and satisfied."

"Now is not forever," said Caroline. "He has tasted other satisfactions—satisfactions that I have given and which he knows I can give. One day he will crave them again and then—"

"—then he will be free to go," said the Swami, "but he will never stay until he has an equal freedom to return."

Caroline knew, as the Swami knew, that so radical a change of her imperious nature could only mean death to her: but the sophistry pleased her, dissolved her anger.

"There is still one thing," she said at length, equably, "to be taken into account: Valmiki is yours now, but he has been mine. One day he will want to be mine again, I shall take care to make him want me again: and on that day I shall be back to claim him."

The Swami's eyes were troubled. "If that day comes," he said.

Caroline came of a breed that never admitted defeat.

"Of course it will come," she said with a faint contempt.